A Ta

CW00862912

A Story from t

By Damien Tiller

Publishing

A Black Flag Publication
A Tailor's Son
A Story from the Oakenfall Chronicles
by Damien Tiller

ISBN: 9798667257455

Neeska in the year 87AB as depicted by Aaron Fenton Blake

Prologue: Dear Diary

Neeska was a continent at the heart of a world of heroes, magic-wielding mages, demonic dark lords, brave knights, and brutal barbarians. In its vast history, there had been many great wars fought and won, dragons banished, kingdoms felled, and legends made, but behind the heralds and trumpets, it is important not to forget the everyday people on the streets.

People like the bakers that wake up long before dawn to tend the ovens and make the bread that feeds armies. Or candlestick makers covered in wax so the city can see in the twilight, allowing clandestine deals to be made in darkened alleyways. And the tailor, yes, the humble tailor – master of stitch and twine. In the many tomes written in the Oakenfall Chronicles, one would never expect the humblest of tailors to change history, but the hand of fate is fickle, and its gaze lands in the most unexpected places.

The years had moved on since the Dragon Lords return to Neeska, The Dragon's Blight had ended, the lineage of the Hanson family was snubbed out, and the death of Harvey led to the rise of William's government.

Oakenfall that had been a sleeping beast for generations now moved with a new purpose. Fuelled by the fear of the demons released at the end of the last Blight, combined with ingenuity leaked from the dwarven halls, industry had progressed in leaps, and a new chapter dawned for Oakenfall.

This new chapter was one of steam-driven machines, belts and cogs. With the hard iron of decades laid down, the mighty arm of the Poles resting, and just a busy twenty-eight years later, during Wastelar, the first month of winter in the year 128 AB, our story starts in a gloomy room.

Sitting alone in the dark barely lit by the small flickering candle, was a frightened Harold. He was hunched over a woodworm-ridden desk, franticly writing upon a darkened parchment as if possessed. The moon outside the window was hidden behind the smog and clouds.

It was cold, dark, and damp. If he was asked, Harold could not have been so precise as to tell the time for he did not know it; at best, he could guess that it was late.

The last bells that he had heard from the tower of the newly constructed cathedral had sounded midnight before a storm brought with it such harsh rain that it drowned out the vibrations.

Night-time in Oakenfall was the time of muggers, pinch-pricks, and even constables. The force was introduced when Lord William had taken the throne at the end of the Second Coming of the Dragons.

The constables had been introduced to help calm the relationships between the Iron Giants, the Northmen, and Oakenfall citizens that now shared the same city. They had been charged with protecting the people, but as with most things given time in the danker parts of the city, they became corrupt too.

Harold had never had much need to fear them before, but times and fate can change as quickly as a snuffed match.

As Harold wrote, he shivered, and the weather did little to help settle his skin from its vibrations. His flesh seemed to be attempting to crawl away from his body with outstretched hairs and goosebumps.

Harold wrote so fiercely as he did not know how long he had. The fear in his belly was so powerful that his heart raced like the hooves of a post master's horse at full gallop.

His candle flickered, and its small plume of smoke drifted on a breeze out the window to join the putrid cloud that covered the night sky, a small curse that the end of the war with the Poles had brought.

The golden age that descended onto the city with the war won, and the old trade routes reopened had brought with it industrial growth that spread with the speed of a forest fire, and with fire came smoke.

The choking clouds poured from the newly built factories by the harbor and flowed inland on the strong westerly wind that blew from the sea. This almost nightly occurrence often caused the moon to be hidden behind a deep blanket of smog. The only light outside was from the recently installed Dwarfen gas lamps, but on that night, even they struggled to stay alight in the downpour the gods had seen fit to tarnish the sky with.

The rain clouds swirled across the stars that barely broke through with a wind that was vicious; its disdain was almost palpable in its breath. It pushed the rain hard and bullied it into falling ever harder on Harold's shutters.

With each creak and slam of the aged windows, Harold's heart missed a beat. He couldn't help but wonder what would happen if the creature came looking for him. Even with the strong oak pressed tightly in the doorframe, a draft was creeping in. The oak had been brought in from the forest that the Elves had taken to growing at the edges of the Scorched Lands.

The breeze crept in under the frame and rattled around the room making Harold's fire dance and flicker. The shadows it cast across all four walls seemed intent on taunting him by adding to his panic-ridden state. The flickering shadows turned a hat rack into a shadowy assassin and back again with each pass of light. With each gust of air under the door, Harold was forced to stop breathing and listen to make sure that he couldn't hear footsteps outside.

He worried that the "thing" would come for him, so much so that even the lack of footsteps troubled him. He thought to himself, *What if someone is making no noise outside the door?* The paranoia drove him mad. He had unwillingly become the protagonist in a grim fairy-tale, one that as a new day "dawned," he could not seem to escape.

Harold was the only surviving son of James Spinks, a tailor of East Street.

East Street nestled close to the canals north of the markets in the mid-section of the city of Oakenfall. Harold was of little importance to the history of Neeska for the most part, and few people would recognize him as they passed him in the street. That was because he worked in the backroom of the tailors most of the time doing repairs on the richer folks' clothing, and – if he was honest with himself – he liked it that way.

Harold was a loner of sorts. His job meant he had to occasionally interact with people, but he did his best to keep his contacts with others at a minimum. He enjoyed a quiet life in solitude, avoiding the bustle of the city.

He had worked for his father all his life with few stories to tell that didn't involve a pricked thumb or a missed stitch until that accursed night.

That was the night it all started. His eyes were so sore and bloodshot that he could see how reddened they were even in the deep blue reflection of the ink well he dabbed his quill into before returning it to the parchment.

Harold was no hero from a story; he was not a brave warrior or bard that filled the tales of the many libraries in Neeska – he was the definition of a normal man.

As the moon began its descent toward the horizon, the writing was the only thing keeping him sane. He felt terrified and alone; he knew that it might be his last night on Neeska, but what choice did he have, but to continue?

If his plan was to fail, Harold suspected his notes might be the one thing to save the city.

To understand, they would have read back to the night that it all started, to the last time Harold was just a tailor's son.

Chapter 1: The Queens Tavern

The night that would change Harold's life forever started normally. It was a fortnight before that wintery night he spent in the darkness writing his notes. The date was Nymon the 16th of Thresh, the end of a harsh autumn and one that hinted at an even crueler winter just around the corner. The day had brought with it an icy breeze that kept the rats off the streets and sent them scurrying into people's homes and cellars.

The fall had been the worst anyone had seen since the poor harvests of 100 AB. That combined with the ban on imported food from Gologan due to the damnable potato famine, meant that everyone was feeling the pinch.

Which much of the farmlands still recovering from the war with the dragons, food prices were the highest they had been in centuries. Most people took on a second job just to make ends meet. Starvation had begun to claim the lives of the poorest in the city, and Harold was as much at risk as anyone.

Although his family did have some inheritance and had been comfortable enough during the Dragon's Blight, funds were not limitless. They were far from nobles. They were not as poverty-stricken as most but would still be classed as some of the poor souls the city came to know as "the unfortunates."

His family were positioned as upper working-class traders, not as desperate as those worse-off that worked the streets and docks around him, but only barely. His family managed to scratch together enough to buy clothes and eat while the nobles continued to live off the rich pickings from their broken backs.

The promises made by Lord William at the end of the war had started with potential. It seemed like times could be changing, and innovation came quickly, but men's greed had not taken long to manipulate his intentions and corrupt his government. The nobles that had become rich under the monarchy soon found footholds in political positions.

This had turned William's promise into dismay for many, but Harold's father was very tight with the purse-strings, As he had lived through the war that almost brought Oakenfall to its knees during the first century. He had learned not to spend a single copper where it was not needed, a trait that had been passed on to his thrifty son and allowed them to keep their tailor shop open where many would have folded.

Harold had just finished working at the little shop on East Street to make more coins that would doubtless hibernate in his father's moth-filled wallet.

His father had taken on an order from one of the local factories, two hundred aprons by the end of the next month. Harold had argued with his father that they could not finish the order in time. He was more realistic and accepted that one of the sweatshops with clanking machines the Dwarfs had traded would have been more suited to handling it. However, his father ignored his concerns, as always, and took the work.

Harold was not sure if he did it for the money, or if he feared giving work to the machines that drove the industrial revolution forward would speed up the inevitable end of their little family business. They had gone from a time when black iron and the might of a smith was at the forefront of technology to strange steam-driven machines in barely a generation – coal had become the new black magic.

Whatever his reasons, in his blind hope, Harold's father saw the massive order as a challenge and, as usual, wanted to face it head-on. He knew Harold would do everything he could to make sure they succeeded.

Harold should have left the shop a few hours earlier, but they had already been running behind on the day's work, when his father had rushed home sick with the flu.

Harold had to admit that he was worried about his father's health. He was in his fifties, and his age had begun to weaken him. The flu was a known killer, and over the past year, Harold had seen the huge mountain-like man of his father shrink.

Harold did not have time to linger on his worries for not long after the last stitch had been pulled tight, he left the shop for the night.

With the shop locked up, Harold was off to the Queens for his second job. The Queens was a little smuggler-run tavern down by the docks. Harold had started working there once or twice a week in the evenings to help meet the cost of the family estate and make up for the shortfall in earnings coming from the tailor shop.

That particular night Harold was running late, but he knew that no one would notice. They never did so long as Harold was there before the kegs ran dry. The money was good for the hours Harold worked and for the menial tasks he was required to do, like lugging empties from the cellar onto a cart or unloading full ones that just arrived and tapping them ready to keep the foul-smelling grog flowing.

The money was much more than the work was worth, but the reason it paid so well was that it was hush money to avert his eyes from things going on there.

The smugglers and criminals of the city had always had strong ties to the White Flag pirates, and the Queens was a real den of iniquity. Gambling, fights, prostitution, and other unmentionable acts that should never be carried out by decent Oakenfallian men and women were stock and trade for the little back alley boozer.

The tavern was favored by the worst Oakenfall had to offer. Still, Harold was left to do his job, and he was the kind of person to go unnoticed, so he did not let himself worry about what went on inside its walls. His only worry was the amount of liquor that used to go in and out.

Harold was a tailor, so he was not used to heavy lifting, but thankfully, he did take on a little of his father's shape and was bulky. Not overly muscular like some of the brawlers that he saw fall in and out of the Queens of an evening, but he was not a reed pole.

All the same, the full kegs almost tore his arms from his body and with the number they had going in and out of the place, it was not unreasonable to think half the harbor had gills.

Harold walked the quiet streets alone on his way to the tavern, not eager for the weight of the kegs awaiting him. His body had begun to yearn for sleep, although the sun was only just setting.

He had walked this same path many times before and knew each loose cobble, rise, fall, and slope that beset his path. For just that moment, Harold could relax.

He did not need to think as he passed the high buildings all around him that helped to block out the sound of hustle and bustle.

As usual, as Harold walked along the canals, he was daydreaming. It was a good pastime for him, which he had used most of his life. The trait had started back at school when Harold was just a boy and had caused a fair few chalk rubs to be thrown at him by his teacher, old Macgregor, not to mention the cane once or twice.

Harold had hated Macgregor. He was from the Western Reaches somewhere and seemed to detest all children. He was the headmaster of the school, and ran the place more like a prison, often taking some of the more poorly behaved children and locking them away in his room for hours at a time. Those he took would always come out crying, followed by a red-faced Macgregor.

Harold had been lucky enough never to enter his room. Macgregor was a Pole, not an Iron Giant as they were known in times of peace, but a cold-blooded warrior, a giant-like barbarian, and there were rumors that he had slaughtered children during the war. Harold never found out whether that was true or not, and he did not wish to know. Harold was a coward at heart and just did his best to block out the memories of his school days.

Continuing to walk deep in thought, Harold stepped around a flock of moulted pigeons. He was contemplating how, although his family lived on the edges of the more common parts of the city, he had been sheltered from the worst it had to offer for the most part – that was until he started working for the smuggler family known as the O'Briens. Harold had then started to see a lot he never wanted to.

His thoughts faded from logic to dreams as he walked down Harbor Path. It was the same dream he'd had many times before, ever since he was a child – normally centered around the coast.

His mother and father had taken Harold to Port Lust when he was young, and the sights and smells of the sea stayed with him all his life.

Harold remembered staying in his grandmother's little cottage and he remembered the gulls that flew overhead. They were a beautiful white, not the dirty black-gray of the pigeons that painted the rooftops around Oakenfall.

Harold swore to himself that one day he would go back there but the house was in ruins; it had decayed with years of isolation. His father had always been too busy to travel down and maintain it, and his mother was unable to manage the Oakenfall home let alone a faraway holiday cottage that was rarely visited.

The painted walls of the seaside retreat began to flake, and the once pure green grass of the expansive lawn was now little more than a jungle of weeds.

However, in his daydream, it was still as perfect as when Harold was a boy. Small and full of character, it had some small birds nesting in the thatch roof – swallows, Harold remembered. They used to dart back and forth through the air as he sat on the cliff top.

Every morning Harold used to travel down the stairs that lead from the garden straight down to the shore and spent the day at the beach pestering the crabs that called the rock pools home, and chasing clouds. Then at night they slept with the sound of the ocean as it brushed the rocks, stealing pebbles as it went.

The little windows had wrought iron bars in the shape of perfect crosses. The shutters themselves were engraved with flowers. Harold felt happy and safe there, both as a child and now in his dreams as an adult.

Harold remembered finding a fossil of some long dead creature at the base of those pure white cliffs and still had it to this day, sitting above the fireplace. For him, it was a last memento of his childhood, a memory of innocence that seemed so rare in a city full of beggars and thieves.

Still daydreaming Harold came down from the bridge that crossed one of the waterways on Harbor Path. The sound of the waves in his dream married well with the very real sound of ships' bells that rang out from within the haze of smog. The changes to the harbor had brought in a lot of work and made money for those that already had it, but those that did not were suffering even worse than they had before the century celebrations. They now worked longer hours in hot, smoke-filled, and cramped factories that were run by oppressive managers who had little care for them and worked them to death.

The end of the Dragon Blight had opened trade with the dwarves for the first time in many years and below ground they had built things centuries ahead of the humans.

The trade catapulted industry forward but at a price. The clouds they produced seemed to mix like an unhealthy stew with the smell of the canals. The thick clouds seemed to grow denser with each passing year and now covered most of the city.

On some days, the cloud was so thick that it seemed almost pliable and the buildings around that area of Oakenfall had already begun to take on some of its blackness and were quickly losing what little charm they used to have.

The city had become overcrowded with multiple families being squeezed into each hovel like wharf rats. With the promise of yet more money to be pulled out from the secrets the Dwarfs were finally sharing from behind their huge stone doors in the Kingdom of Goldhorn, there would be need for more people to come to the city – and the overcrowding only promised to get worse.

The sun was falling over the horizon as Harold's daydream was broken by a husky and desperate voice close to his left ear.

"Looking for a good time? You look clean enough, so I'll do it for a halfpence. What do you say?" the young woman leaning against a nearby wall asked him, as she staggered out of the shadows looking like a scarecrow.

She instantly made Harold feel ill at ease. She sported two blackened eyes, no doubt from an unhappy client the night before or from her pimp or, worse, her husband. Her ginger-red hair was pulled tightly into a ponytail and was thick with grease. The few hairs that escaped the grasp of the ribbon clung to her forehead as if glued in place.

She gave Harold a smile full of remorse and the smell of cheap bourbon hit him. Harold watched, unsure whether he should risk aiding the poor girl as she almost lost her grip on the wall she had taken to holding. She had been drinking. Harold suspected it was to keep out the cold or to block the thoughts of what she would have to do for her meal that night. Harold could not say for sure which.

It was a world he didn't understand. He skimmed along its edges and in his naivety, he even went as far as blaming the poor girl for letting her life end up that way. He did understand that having to work the streets could not be an easy task, but didn't understand that for some single women it was the only life they had ever known.

Taking a closer look at her, Harold noticed that she was young and not one of the leathery-skinned old hags he normally saw at that time of day. It was a horrible thought, but Harold knew that some of the girls working the streets were as young as twelve or thirteen years of age. It sickened him to his core to think that this poor girl might be that young.

Harold could tell she was nervous. She clasped her hands together, all the while fiddling with the pocket of her blouse which hung loosely from her young body. She did not seem to carry the same hard-edged attitude as other bangtails that Harold had seen throughout this area of the city, but being young, she had not long been on the streets. That made the whole situation worse for him.

Harold had no love for whores or their trade. He didn't understand why they didn't leave the city and go tend to the farms or head off to one of the southern cities away from the reach of the Poles or criminal families and start again.

Harold thought for a moment about what would make such a young girl turn to a craft like this and his disdain for his employer at the Queens flashed through his mind once more. Whatever the young girl's story, O'Brien would have had a part in it. Harold's anger was due to the fact that O'Brien was no doubt her pimp. Harold was prone to flights of imagination, and in the moment, he imagined her life story.

He dreamt up the story that her mother died in labor – as was common – and her father – a drunkard like most men from the wooden built part of the city – had abused her. She had finally collected enough courage and run away, just for O'Brien to find her begging on the street somewhere, no doubt asking for nothing more than a scrap of bread.

O'Brien would have spoken to her in his charming accent and offered her to come back to the Queens for a meal. He would have given her a bed for the night, no doubt treated her well, all the while getting her drunk on free ale.

Then, like a spider trapping the fly, he would change, demanding payment for the ale, threatening her, and finally when she couldn't pay, putting her out to work, the bastard. The workhouse would have been better for the poor girl, although Harold did admit, only barely.

O'Brien put her out to work but she was not bringing in enough money, so he taught her what happens to those that did not deliver what O'Brien wanted. He beat her, not enough that she would be permanently useless to him, but no one cared if a prostitute had a few bruises and before the blood on her nose had even had time to dry, he'd sent her back out on the streets to stand in front of Harold.

His heart sank at the thought and as if she sensed the sorrow in his eyes the girl looked away. She brushed her front down, loosening the rags to reveal more of her young bosom. Small freckles dotted her chest that mirrored those around her nose and cheeks. Harold could imagine from her small trim jaw that she would have been attractive but for the swelling on her face. One eye was almost closed and yellowing from the bruising.

It was then Harold noticed the filth on her, so much dirt on her clothes that calling them clothes was too much of an honor. They were more like rags that had once been a cheap cotton dress, but all shape had fallen from it so that it hung loosely over her small shoulders.

One sleeve of her blouse was torn, and Harold wondered if that had been an overzealous customer. Harold looked at the unfortunate girl in such sadness. She approached him with the same statement as before in her brittle tone as his glance met hers.

"Halfpence, what do you say?"

Listening past the cold she carried and the slur from the alcohol, Harold could hear in her voice that although young was likely to be a little older than he'd first thought. It was hard to tell under all the dirt.

No matter her age, she was desperate and that was for sure. If Harold had thought of it at the time, he would have wondered why she hadn't moved toward the ships with the rest of the whores who wanted easy coin, but Harold guessed she had some reason to avoid sailors.

It saddened him that there were so many nightwalkers along the docks. The place was littered with them, all hoping to make an easy penny from the sailors coming in from their long voyages. There were plenty of nameless young women or old hags for them to satisfy their urges while they visited the shore. Most of the poor women received a black eye or a bloodied nose from their swift visit lovers.

As much as Harold hated the sensual crafts, as he called them, he hated the men that abused such desperate women even more and it pleased him that fate would have the last laugh as the cowardly bastards had no idea what they would carry back with them onto their ships. They would have a rash, and a vile one at that, but it served them right, no doubt, as the scurvy took them and sent them mad.

Harold stood there awkwardly deep in his own thoughts unaware of the moments passing. He did not want the services the young woman offered but he felt obligated to do something to ease her pain or be as bad as those that caused it.

"How much do you need to earn for a room tonight?" Harold asked, feeling around for the loose change in his pocket. He didn't have much to give as most of what they earned went straight to his father. The little he had, he had reasons for not wanting to carry on him after sunset in that part of town.

"I only need a halfpenny more. I will do whatever you want and I'm clean too. No warts or anything," she replied trying to sound provocative but was clueless about achieving it in her drunken state.

That might have been enough for some of the potbellied pond-scum that had somehow managed to get a handful of coins to bed her, but Harold had no interest in anything other than getting her off the street. Whatever he planned to do, it would need to be quick as he had to be at the Queens before the kegs ran dry and O'Brien turned his anger toward him.

"Anything I want? You promise that?" Harold asked, her as he pulled the lint out of the handful of small coins he'd found at the bottom of his pocket. It was his whole earnings for the day, but Harold knew he would still have food waiting for him when he got home, more than could be said for the redhead.

"Yes, for sure, mister no matter how weird, less it's magic. No magic," the young girl said, eagerly snatching the small handful of coins from him. "Cor-blimey, there's got to be almost two pence here. What weird stuff you after?" she asked, and suddenly her face changed.

It seemed darkness had seeped into some people's hearts ever since the demon Rinwid had broken through the Spirit Realm into the waking world and there had been talk of working girls going missing. It was clear she was worried just what Harold would expect for such a pay-out.

"I want you to get home, get off the street. A young girl like you shouldn't be working like this," Harold said with a smile.

Suddenly his attention was diverted as a coach rattled by passing between him and what he would loosely call a woman, and almost knocked them both over.

Harold took his chance to trot on quickly leaving her behind. The near collision had startled him, and it took him a few minutes to notice a leaf that had entangled itself in his cropped brown hair. As Harold removed it, he began to daydream again.

He had needed the money really, but not as much as the girl did, and it was worth it for the thought that for just one night she could sleep peacefully, just as peacefully as Harold had in the bed at his grandmother's cottage.

The Queens was already in full cheer when Harold arrived. The proprietor, O'Brien, could be heard singing some old folksong, the patrons inside clapping and jeering him on. There was no doubt in Harold's mind that O'Brien was half-cut already – he usually finished off a whole bottle of whisky before the sun fell behind the horizon.

Harold wondered if it was from the money of poor innocents like the little girl he had passed. It angered him that such joy could be made on the backs of the tortured souls he had built his criminal empire on.

Harold looked straight up at the towering buildings and into the sky. As much as he hated what had been happening to Oakenfall in the last few years, he did have to give the city its due. The sleeping beast that was Oakenfall with its disgusting polluted breath had created such a spectacle.

The last golden rays as they fought their way through the thick smog above the city was a secret beauty only known to those the nation classed as unfortunates – providing they didn't breathe too deeply. The nobles locked themselves away safely in their homes while the poor still worked or begged for coins from those barely any better off. It was as if the gods made the little beauty just for them, a silver line to an otherwise blackened cloud. It was a shame that the sound of a drunkard vomiting in the street spoiled the sunset for Harold that night.

Harold's eyes grew accustomed to the coming darkness as he drew his gaze back down to the streets. He didn't know why, but his gaze fell on the buildings as if it was the first time he'd seen them. They were not huge stone towers like those estates at the noble end of town. No, these were not the rich four or five stories high masses of brickwork. They did not overhang with polished windows and sculptures that had been painted in the dried excrement of the flying rats that littered the skies.

Instead they were a mix of wood and clay, simple hovels made for purpose over beauty. The buildings were all so square and unwelcoming, coated in blackened ash and moss from the ever-wet air. They still managed to both impress and impose on Harold even after all these years. Most of the city was built in the same style, crushed together with no space between the buildings. The overhanging balconies blocking out what little of the sky could be seen above the smoke.

The city was growing so quickly that there was no space for houses, and it would not be many more years before stone giants took their place instead, if construction kept going at the pace it had since the war ended. With the prosperity that the golden age had brought, people came from miles around to work in the factories that were sprouting up like weeds.

The city hummed with the sound of machines and the hammers of stonemasons building places for the cheap labor to live. It made each street feel like a secluded island and there were only one or two spots within the city where people could see the sky clearly – and that was why with the light bouncing off the clouds and the moon starting to climb ever higher in the sky, Harold savored the moment.

The Queens' Tavern was a real contrast to the buildings around it and was one of the last of its kind. Harold did not know its history fully, but it was one of the oldest buildings in the city and had survived the fire that had swept through the harbor when the Poles first invaded. It was one of the last reminders of the days before the city was occupied by the Iron Giants.

At one time, not so many years ago, the stone buildings ended at Market Crescent – aside from the statues at Celebration square – but now they pushed further north and only the most common parts of the city were still made in the old way, with clay and beam. It had been both a blessing and a curse for Lord William Boatswain when he opened trade with the Dwarfs of the Goldhorn Mountains. The city prospered and grew, giving birth to and helping fund the Brilanka Monks' march into Neeska.

They had been called in to aid in the battle against the Shadow Demons of Briers Hill that had been summoned forth by the mage that ended the last Dragon's Blight. Their first Cathedral had started being constructed with this newly found wealth just south of Celebration Square. Close by, a massive wall that stood five men high was built running around the natural Oakenfall ridge from the west and south of the city to save it from ever falling to barbarians again. The city folk felt safe and blessed but not everything had been so wonderful.

With so much money flowing into the city and so quickly, and the sudden boom of new technologies released from within the secretive Dwarfen halls, trouble was guaranteed. The machines themselves rivalled even the magic of mages and led to corruption the likes of which Oakenfall had never seen.

It was not only pirating now that threatened the harbors. With their wealth from bringing in these Dwarfen masterpieces, the Brilanka Monks funded a crusade that saw mages outlawed and in 118 AB Lord William, one of the saviours from the return of the Dragons at the turn of the century, was voted out of office and replace by the current lord, Malcolm

Benedict. Malcolm Benedict was a mad man, obsessed with stamping his religion across the city and getting more and more Dwarfen machines.

How the Queens' Tavern had survived all that and not been forcibly torn down in the developments was a mystery. On the other hand, with hindsight, it was not. It had been in the O'Brien family for seven generations. The upper classes of the city were so corrupt that the O'Briens, no doubt, held a lot of sway with them and that had kept the place as it was. There were even rumors of their coercive reach stretching as far back as the monarchy of the dethroned Hansons.

The Queens was a small thatched building, not as pretty as Harold's beachside home, but it did have its own charm – if you looked beneath the blackening of age through the thick clouds of smog.

The side street was emptying and only a few people were headed along it making their way home. Harold watched them from the shadows wondering what stories their tired and worn-out faces hid. As always, they seemed oblivious to his presence as they busily scuttled home like disturbed woodlice from under a dampened log.

While Harold untied the barrels from the horse and cart, and prepared to move them into the tavern, the drunkard who had ruined the sky painting earlier, staggered off out of sight. Harold was alone once again. It was strange how it always happened. The city had a twilight period where the beggars vanished to go off to sleep wherever it was that they went, the shops all closed, and the streets emptied.

Given another half an hour the streets would be bustling again with a different type of Oakenfallian, but for now those families that could afford food ate, and those that could not, still sat around their dinner tables. Once the meals were finished, the tidal pulse of Oakenfall would change; the street gangs would come out, the prostitutes would move away from the docks and into the markets; the children would vanish; and the lantern man would light the city up which signaled the awakening of the seedy underbelly of Oakenfall.

The cart of ale was waiting unattended by the opened cellar hatch. Very few places could afford to leave things unattended nowadays, but no one in this part of the city would steal from the O'Briens. Half the whores in the district worked for them, and most of the men they called friends were more than a little disreputable. The few constables that had been issued to this area of the city got more of their pay from O'Brien than they did from anywhere else.

When William had first brought back a City Guard. He made the city safer than it had ever been, but after he left the castle, the budget for the safety of the common man was sent upstream and didn't make it past the last noble brick. If you wanted anything, O'Brien could get it for you and if you wanted anyone disposed of then he could do that as well – and the guards knew that. For the small pittance they were paid they turned a blind eye to anyone whose allegiance lay with the O'Brien family. It was rumored O'Brien had connections to the pirates on White Isle, and even as far as Portsea.

The smell of spirits almost choked him as Harold approached the trapdoor leading into the tavern's cellar. He rolled the first keg in front of him with relative ease making the most of the silence before the city re-awoke. The sun had gone down, and

Harold was tempted to light a match to see if he could shed some light down into the depths.

His hand was already sliding into his white sleeveless jacket for his tin, but common sense took hold just in time. The fumes, that were strong enough above the hatch to get a sailor pissed, would ignite, and Harold did not fancy burning to death that night. He admitted that he could really have used the lie down, but he would rather do it above ground than below, and anyway, Harold had never been a fan of worms.

Pressing his sleeve against his face Harold had to wonder if one of the barrels must have fallen from the racks and smashed. If it had been a full keg, like the smell suggested, then half the rats in the catacombs would be waking up with a hangover if the eye-watering smell was anything to go by.

Harold gazed into the darkness trying to see what had happened down there and reached gingerly for the rope. The last thing he wanted to do was lower down onto broken fragments of keg, so he hesitated. They could not afford two sick people in the family and Harold had his good shoes on. They were red leather and decently made – a favor from a local cobbler in return for a repair to his daughter's wedding dress the previous year.

Harold swung himself back giving up on seeing anything by leaning over the dark hole. Once up onto the cold cobblestones of the street, he laid the keg on the ground. He still used his arm to cover his face as he tried to peer over the edge again. It was no good. He would have to get down there and clear up the debris before being able to drop the keg. Harold couldn't afford to lose any more money after giving everything he had to that working girl. He doubted O'Brien would accept it was a mistake, if he broke the keg by lowering down without clearing the way first.

As Harold had reached for the rope a second time, he thought, just for a moment, that he'd seen something move down there in the darkness. He took it to be nothing more than a large rat, which was another one of the many plagues that littered the docks. It did occur to him that the shadow had seemed too big for a rodent, but then, what else would it have been?

As Harold started to lower himself down, he couldn't help but notice that, although he might not be an expert on spirits, the smell down there was so potent there had to be more than just one split drum. The cellar was dark, and Harold didn't fancy staying in it longer than necessary. He took only a few moments to look around and it was obvious that whatever had broken must have been cleared up. There was no broken debris on the floor at all, only an ankle-deep puddle of liquid.

Harold could not see any splintered wood or signs that one of the kegs, barrels or any other container had leaked. It almost seemed like every keg had been emptied on purpose. Harold thought about mentioning it to O'Brien once he'd loaded the new kegs in. If someone was emptying the kegs into the cellar on purpose, then O'Brien should look into it.

Harold pulled himself back onto the street glad of the fresher air. As he begun to tie the rope around the barrel and slowly ushered it toward the opening, a sudden small flash from below lit a figure in silhouette. Harold could see clearly that it had not been a rat that he'd had heard down below. In fact, it was someone watching him. Harold had barely enough time to realize that whoever it was had just lit a match before a wall of heat forced him to turn his back to the cellar door, barely giving him time to scamper out. Another much brighter flash shot into the air sweeping him clean off his feet as the fumes caught ablaze.

Time froze and for what seemed to him like a lifetime, Harold sailed through the air in the explosion before he came crashing down into the center of the street, barely missing the cart that held the rest of his workload.

The horses fled in fear of the sudden noise, sending loose barrels rolling toward the river's edge. Dazed and confused, his breath stolen from his lungs, all he could do was lie there and watch as the flames danced their very own jig to O'Brien's song.

The fire did not dwindle in the slightest as it spread, the blaze feeding on the fuels inside. The whisky, rum, and ales gave it speed as it riddled the aged woodwork of the walls. Flames leaped out of the small hatch with burning fingers that searched for a way to escape. As one of these long red fingers wrapped around the barrel that Harold had held in his arms only moments before, it shot into the air before exploding and showering down burning timbers that set the roof ablaze.

Within seconds, the song inside the Queens stopped and screams echoed out. Harold could see from his resting place in the now frozen street that the flames had made it to the door before the first person could escape.

Smoke poured out from the doorframe like rivers carving their way through the sky. The inside of the tavern echoed with the explosions as more kegs, barrels and bottles joined the massacre on the ground floor.

The explosions were so loud, they drove Harold's hearing to silence, replacing it with a continuous whistle. Cries faded as smoke pushed its way out of the second story window. The music had gone, the singers were dead, yet the flames danced on.

His head was sore and pounding from his flight and Harold could feel himself begin to lose consciousness. He raised his hand shakily to his bleeding forehead where some debris must have hit him. His body shook and Harold felt cold even through all the heat. Shock filled every pore in his body. There was a coppery taste of blood in his throat, and he was sure he could feel death calling to him.

The horror that was unravelling in front of him became little more than a dream as his eyes lost focus and whitened. The sound of the sea and the sight of brilliant sandy beaches filled his mind.

Falling between the living nightmare and the dream, Harold swore, just before his head fell back against the cobbles, that he had seen a man crawl from the flaming hatch into the street.

His clothing still smouldered, his flesh bright red like a lobster, yet Harold heard no yells of pain. He turned and gazed at Harold. His blistered and raw flesh hung from him like a decaying corpse.

The zombie-like vision, something out of a nightmare, took to running off away from the blaze leaving Harold to his fate.

Interlude 1: Small Eyes Often See More

The flames barely missed Dante as he darted into the hole just below the bucket left for weeks in the cellar corner. The little hairs that had once been on his tail had been singed in the heat and the smell of burned hair followed him down into the cold dampness of the crack that ran between the brickwork to the sewers.

Dante had crawled up through the same crack just a week before hoping to find something tasty to eat and thought he'd struck gold with all the fine meats, bread, and cheeses, left out once the tall ones left the pub at night.

He had got used to the odd interruption as one of the smugglers came down to carry up a keg back into the bar. They didn't notice him as long as he stayed still, and if they did, they just threw something at him, but Dante darted under the shelves and vanished until they were gone.

It was still safer than on the streets with the rat-catchers, and there was no sign of a cat within the Queens. Dante had planned to grow old and fat there. Maybe start his own family. But as the smoke made its way down behind him while he escaped, it was clear that was not going to happen.

Dante was considered a renegade rodent in so much as he had jumped ship and left his flea-ridden relations in search of a better life on dry land.

Life on the boardwalk by the ships hadn't been easy, and the local black rat population had chased him further into the city and the path of the rat-catchers.

It had been that human who had taken away his haven beneath the Queens. Something had smelled different about the one who had set the fire.

All humans smelled dirty, a mix between souring milk and lustful regret, but he smelled like soiled meat. He smelled more like the corpses that some of the less refined rodents chose to feast upon in the harbor's darkest alleyways.

There was the way he moved, too. Dante had seen the bipeds walking strangely, if they smelled of the spirits, but that one didn't smell as if he'd consumed any, and yet he moved as if his actions were labored.

Some of the sailors on the *Cassandra* had moved similarly after consuming a keg of dark black rum brought in from the Green Stone Isles, Dante's homeland. Even when the tall and walking-dead humanoid had almost stood on Dante, he hadn't seemed to notice.

Dante had never known a creature with two legs, not try to kick him or scream when they saw him. It was strange, really, why they seemed so scared of him. He was around the size of their feet and wanted nothing more than a quiet life somewhere warm with enough food to feed his fluff covered belly, but for some reason, all humans hated him.

That was aside from the fire-starter. He was different and so strong too. He hadn't needed a hammer to break the kegs like the rest to drain them. He'd done it with his hands, but he didn't seem to want to drink it and didn't even seem to mind when it began pouring on the floor.

Dante had barely managed to avoid getting wet as he clambered up onto the loose cobblestone slab next to the bucket, near where he'd made his escape. The weird smelling one let the alcohol pour out over the floor while he just stood there motionlessly staring off straight ahead, as if he was entranced.

Dante had seen them do that often with the odd tankard, but that customarily sparked off a brawl. In any case, he couldn't understand what the human was doing down there in his home.

Dante would remember that one's smell. He was more dangerous than the rest. Dante didn't know why, but his nose just told him to steer clear of that one. He would do his best to avoid ever coming across his smell while he made his way back to the harbor, hoping his ship was back and docked with his kin at the wharf.

The pickings aboard the *Cassandra* weren't as nice as they were in the Queens, but at least it was safe. The ship's old tomcat was as likely to catch a rat as he was to take a bath. The fire was the final straw that sent Dante heading home.

Chapter 2: Reverend Paul Augustus

Hindsight is a wonderful thing. Harold, like many others, had passed Saint Anne's Chapel so many times in his life. It was also the place where his parents married shortly after its construction was complete in 112 AB; however, Harold was unaware of the significance the building would play in the following days.

It held some happy memories for his family, but Harold knew little else that had gone on there. Few who were not an inner part of Sacellum did, and his family, although religious, were far from devout. Sacellum was a new religion for Neeska and spread on the fear that persisted after Rinwid and other Shadow Demons had claimed the lives of so many on the battlefield.

William had sent for the Brilanka Monks, experts on the occult, at the end of the war and they brought with them wealth and power. They turned the city's small chapels into great churches, the massive stone and brick constructions sweeping religious fervor across the city.

It seemed they were integral to the Sacellum religion, housed the monks and allowed the priests to spread their beliefs through the city.

In the years after Malcolm Benedict took the seat as governor of the city, the old religions were all but banished. With the old teachings having faded from book burning, Harold's mother and father remarried under the eyes of the Great Creator, the god of the Sacellum religion, in fear that they would not be allowed into the holy city of gold when they died, if they did not.

It was fearmongering like that which allowed the Brilanka Monks to take over every position of power within the city in less than two decades. That gave them access to more of the city's funds than any other guild. With their riches, they built massive structures to impose their beliefs even further. Saint Anne's was by far the biggest and had taken just twenty-one years to complete, on the hard work, blood, and broken bones of hundreds of souls. Some claimed the priests had used banished magic to aid construction; others put it down to the introduction of dwarfen machines. A building that should have taken generations to build sprang up in the blink of an eye, but few dared to openly question how.

It had been built in stages. Firstly, making use of the small stone chapel that had been there, additional wings and floors were added. Then as the flock that congregated grew, it grew, and now, it stood taller than any other building in the city aside from the castle.

It was said that the foundations for Saint Anne's had been dug so deep that they broke into the catacombs and the hidden labyrinth that ran below the city. The plot of earth it sat on was as spacious as Hanson Castle and showed that true power in the city had shifted from the once-powerful royal line of the Hanson's to that of the Brilanka Monks.

Fear of the demons that the battle with the dragons had brought into the world fuelled the religion's growth. This fear and this need for the presence of something greater than the standing army led to the once-humble Saint Anne's being turned into the stone gargantuan it was today.

This fear also pushed many of the priests past the boundaries of normal men. They had begun to be seen as demigods. People began to follow their word as gospel, even though they were merely normal men and women behind the mask of their religion – and some carried just as dark a secret as any dockyard thug. It was one such secret that led to the fire at the Queens that changed Harold's life for good.

It was already dark before Reverend Paul Augustus made it home from Saint Anne's. The walk from Common Road south of Celebration Square was too long for his liking and made all the worse by the chill to the air. The cold got into his bones and set off his damnable arthritis. That, mixed with the fact he had to battle past the masses of people cluttering the streets, put Paul into a foul mood.

His knee ached, but he refused to show his weakness and struggled on without the aid of a cane. They were for old and feeble men, and Paul refused to be either. He thought the leeches he kept at home would help, but he still needed to do more experiments to make them safe first. He was not a man of science but was doing the best he could to learn the secrets they held.

Paul slipped off his collar as he turned the corner from Common Road into Monks Walk. The newly paved and constructed Monks Walk had been built with small basic accommodation to house the rapid influx of monks and priests from the order that Paul was part of. His home marked the very eastern edge of Oakenfall, and few traveled the path that curled back in to join the city again by the canals.

He turned into the last dark alley before he reached his front door. That was where he could finally relax. Although the small white collar had been keeping Paul's neck warm in the cold breeze, he hated people pestering him with "Father" this and

"Father" that. He was always glad when he was home, and he could remove it.

The grace and majesty of the church captivated most, but Paul Augustus had grown bored of its beauty some time ago, and now he found disdain in himself while he wore the marks of his office. If anyone had asked, he could have pinpointed the moment his faith had left him. It was during his trip through the Eastern Empire.

Paul had been a missionary trying to pass the word of the savior to the uneducated of the human provinces, but shortly after arriving in Green Stone Isles, his zeal for God had left him. Memories of the place flooded over Paul engulfing him in a past he wished he could forget. Leaning against the wall of his house, Paul Augustus faltered. He forced his mind to focus and physically shook the graphic memories from his head before continuing onward.

"God damn it!" he muttered under his breath with a wheeze. His stomach churned, almost forcing him to arch forward. Biting down hard, he swallowed the feeling deep within until it fell into the pit of his stomach.

The images faded from his mind, but not wholly – they never left him completely. No man could forget the imagery of the sacrifices. How could the word of Sacellum be true, if man's freedom could lead to such vile and violent acts? The whole teaching of the Brilanka Monks was to prevent the debauchery of the demon world spilling into Neeska; however, if men could do such horrible things without the sway of dark magic, then what meaning had his life had?

Breathing heavily, Paul gazed around the poorly lit alley, hoping no one had heard his outburst. A faint smile slid across his lips when he found he was alone, just how he liked it. Since returning to Oakenfall, a year ago, he had grown to love being alone. With no one around to pester him, he could give up the act, stop playing the part of the priest, and finally relax. His clammy hands still shaking, white at the knuckles, Paul hunted through his black clothing for the familiar coolness of the copper keys that worked the lock.

The house he stood outside was an absolute contrast to the grandeur of Saint Anne's. There was no grand dome above the doorway, no tower reaching to the very heavens. The windows did not show-off the colors so rich and vivid that they never left the mind. There was no idol to his God illuminating the dark alley; instead, it was a simple built multi-story hovel. It was the home supplied by the church for Paul. It was hidden away behind the huge stone giants that blocked out the skyline in an alley littered with filth of every kind.

Paul had chosen the dull scent of the smog, darkness, and cobbles over the solitude of Brilanka Isle because here he could continue his work unquestioned. There might have been dead animals cluttering the gutters, and rats the size of small dogs, scurrying around. Yet, this was his favorite place to be. Paul did not own the whole house but merely one room inside; the others were full of dissidents and drug addicts.

As Oakenfall had grown and prospered, the common man found he had more money to spend, more gold to flash in taverns and spend on herbs imported into the city.

This had started a plague that even the wise Lord William had not been prepared for. Scores of people had started toppling into decay at the wooden edges of the city.

It gave the Brilanka Monks more sway as they, in false modesty, gave homes to those who could not house themselves. Paul's main door opened on rusted hinges. It was made of rotten wood, and the corridor behind it was filled with damp. It was more than a little cold and unwelcoming.

Inside, doors lined every few feet of wall space. It was a hostel for the poor and smelled of old stew. It was not much of an improvement from the smog-filled air outside, but it was what Paul called home. The sound of shouting echoed from some far-off room. *No doubt another couple arguing*, thought Paul.

He heard a thud and then the murmur of a woman crying. It seemed the glory days of Oakenfall were ending. The brutality of the Iron Giants became more prominent as the native Oakenfall's numbers dwindled. Paul sealed the outside world away with the click of the latch and made his way to his room.

Once inside, Reverend Paul Augustus closed and bolted the door. One could never be too careful. He slid the second latch into place.

There was a thud on the wall behind him. The drunken husband stormed out into the corridor before crashing against the wall. Paul sighed as he dropped his keys onto a small and cracked table close to his front door and reached for the matches he always kept there. They had been sold to him by a match-girl from one of the flats upstairs. She was an orphan now. Her father had been one of the unlucky souls, who'd had to guard the crater out by Briers Hill.

His life had been taken in one of the uncommon appearances of the Shadow Demons. Her mother, unable to maintain the rent on the family home, had moved into the building shortly after. The very next winter, she had fallen sick with the flu and succumbed to the bitter cold.

Paul did what he could for the girl, bringing her food from the church donations and buying matches from her whenever he had the coin to spare. Although Paul had seen and done things that would curse a man to an eternity in hell, he was a good man. He had a good heart, before he was changed by the darkness he had been exposed to in the Green Stone Isles – desperation can lead even the most righteous down the wrong paths.

With a sharp flick against the uneven brickwork, the match illuminated the one small room that Paul called home. He savored the warmth the match gave off in his hands before limping forward.

Cupping the small flame as he went, he passed the mess of books and manuscripts that littered the floor. They had cobwebs coating them, and small black pellets that Paul guessed were rat droppings. He had no idea how long ago it was since he had tidied the room, but then that didn't matter as no one came to visit him anymore – he had made sure of that.

Stepping over a torn copy of chorus songs, Paul looked for the darker shadow in the center of the dull room, the one he knew was his table. On it was the remaining stub of a candle. He couldn't be bothered to travel to the market to get a new one, not now, not while he still had work to do. People might find out what he was working on, and he couldn't have that. Paul's weakened mind was riddled with echoes of paranoia.

He skulked across the lonely room and married the match to the wick. The glow from the candle was reborn, pushing back the remaining darkness. His room was pressed so tightly against the surrounding buildings, that it had no windows. All four walls were solid brick. The room was bare apart from a bookshelf against one wall jammed from edge to edge with religious books. It was clear from the cobwebs they had not been moved from their resting places for some time.

Paul knew all the sermons within them off by heart. Such lies and hypocrisy – he now thought – but at one time, he had lived for them.

Alone in his room was not a time to dwell on such things, though, as he still had much work to do. A final glance toward the door and Paul pulled back the only chair and sat at his dining table. The candle in front of him flickered gently in a draft that crept in from under the door. The moving light caught the ridges of grime and showed up the many ring marks in the table's top, each from the hot tea Paul enjoyed so much. It was one of the few pleasures left in his life since the darkness came. The pattern of rings almost made a decorative top on an otherwise plain piece of furniture. Paul had stolen it from the monastery before he moved.

Stretched from one corner of the room until it almost touched the table where Paul sat, was his bed. Unmade from the night before, the blanket huddled in the corner as if scared of intrusion. Paul had made sure it sat close to the fire to keep out the cold and stop his damn knee from locking during the night, although it had been many weeks since he dared light it.

The fire brought back the nightmares. In his dreams, he could hear the screams of the brown-skinned person from the beautiful Green Stone Isles. Paul had seen a child ripped limb from limb in sacrifice when he stayed there. He wiped a bead of sweat from the end of his hooked nose. Those ingrates had such strong magic, but their mystics converted the wisdom into such barbaric acts. None of these acts had made it into the report that he passed to the bishop. As far as the church was concerned, the mission had been a success. The village had renounced their false gods and took on the word of Sacellum.

Without fear of interruption, Paul Augustus pulled open a large leather-bound book that had not moved from the table in some weeks. Inside were the notes on his research and documents from the mission. The pages were yellowed with age, and the ink was smudged from a hand rapidly scribbling words with a blunting quill.

On the first page, a creature taunted him. It was a detailed drawing of a leech. Around it, notes were scribbled with arrows pointed to different parts of the creature's anatomy. The bloodstains on the page were a memento of the dissections Paul had carried out on it during his time in the Green Stone Isles.

Paul hovered above the page for a while, taking in the detailed description of the creature and trying hard to see what he had missed in his research. He had seen many leeches in his time. Having been born in the country and having lived there until his thirtieth birthday how could he not? As a boy, he had found a few stuck to his leg from swimming in the stagnant pool behind his house, and every time he had been to a doctor's, he had seen them in jars around the consulting room.

It seemed leeches were used to cure almost any ailment since magic had been banned. However, it was not until the mission to the seas around the

Tropical Bounding and the Green Stone Isles that Paul saw creatures as large as this.

The "Holy Crusade" of the new century was what the bishop had nicknamed it. A sudden flutter from the candle's flame caused Paul to regain his focus, and he continued scanning through the pages.

The notes there described his time in the Green Stone Isles, the villagers he had stayed with, and their way of life. Paul missed the village so much. If it had not been for the acts he had seen within its temples, he might never have returned to Neeska.

Returning to the city had allowed him to continue his research and it was almost finished. The last test subject had been so close to a success that he could soon return to the village in Chhottaa-Ghar, a settlement on the Green Stone Isles coast.

Paul longed for the solitude and peace of the isle. It was so remote that most of the people who lived there had never before seen a white man; mostly, he longed for the mistresses he had left behind.

When Paul had first arrived in Chhottaa-Ghar, miles of thick jungle surrounded the village so that it felt separate from the rest of the world. The villagers did not fear him as he had expected them to, but, once he had grown to know the secrets they held within the place, Paul found himself accepting of the knowledge that they would fear no man.

He found the village peaceful, and the people, instead of fearing him, treated him with mild neglect – the same way most would treat a stray dog found starving in the street.

A few children came and gave Paul scraps of food, then stood around, staring as he wolfed them down. It took weeks before they started to respond to his so-called teachings, but Paul watched them from his isolated pew, and during this time, began to study them.

When he started to understand their customs, he noticed an air of fear over the whole village, which confused him. It was something he could not see or understand, and although his stay was only supposed to be for a few months, it quickly became a year. This was unauthorized by the church, of course, but he could not leave the people.

He became more and more accepted and soon moved into a hut with a bereaved woman. During his time from talking to the women, Paul learned that they all seemed to be scared of their devil god. They did not share the same beliefs as the rest of the Green Stone Isles. Their teachings mentioned nothing of the Titans but instead fixated on the Changed Ones, which had been shocking to the bishop in Paul's final report.

During the twelve months, Paul had stayed in the village, he had tried hard to learn the secrets of their religion, more obsessed with that than preaching the word of the Brilanka Bible. It was only after his first night lying with his landlady that she told him that the Abrus herb that each villager hung around their necks was used to ward off the effects of their god.

She had also given Paul a small cluster of the herb to keep with him as the villagers believed it protected them or granted them some power over the bestial creature they worshipped.

He withdrew himself from his memories, as the thought of her face was too painful for him to linger on. Paul continued to flick through the book until one word caught his eye. It was a reference to the villagers' idol, the false god he was to rid them of – Rakta Ishvara, as the locals called it.

Paul had learned enough of their language to get by during his time there and had learned that the bestial god's name translated to *Blood God*.

The memories of the day when he finally gained access to the temple flashed through his mind and he dropped the book to the table with a thud. Paul cradled his head in his arms, the sickness returning to his body once more. Paul had seen the bodies that littered the temple and had watched the child torn in two and then fed upon. So scared were the people of this being that they celebrated as it devoured the child, knowing it would bring them another period of peace.

"What have I done?" Paul whispered to the shadows of his cold and tiny room, but the shade did not answer his question. Paul Augustus gave in to his anguish and wept.

Chapter 3: Unknown Questions

Harold awoke to the loud pounding of rain against glass, matched only by the drumming inside his skull. It was another cold and damp Thresh night. He had no idea how many hours he had been out cold. He could remember the fire at the Queens, the heat and whiteness, then the beach.

Amongst the confusion, the memory of the burning man stood out. He had seemed so real, but as horrid as a nightmare at the same time. It took some minutes for Harold's mind to entirely clear and for the random confusion of his thoughts to align with the waking world.

The journey from the explosion to his hospital room was a blank, but even with his sore head, Harold could still remember the image of that man crawling from the flames. Even as the flames engulfed him, Harold felt he recognized the man's face; he was sure he had seen it in an artist's drawings in the *Oakenfall Times*.

Harold tried so hard to remember the article accompanying the sketched face. He had always had a great memory for faces, but could never remember the names that went with them. Harold had cloudy thoughts that the man had been a criminal who had done something horrible.

No, thought Harold, *that was not it*. Suddenly his mind sparked, and it came to him like a racehorse across the line. He was the man found dead in Common Road.

Harold remembered reading the article on how the man had died. It was a mugging and a vicious one at that. There was no way that it could have been him; dead people do not get up and become arsonists – yet Harold was so sure.

He put it down to his concussion and moved on to haze-ridden daydreams while waiting for the rest of his senses to awaken.

Laying there with his thoughts, Harold could hear the rain outside falling heavily. His vision was still impaired, and the darkness did not help matters. He tried to push himself up the hard pillow his head rested on but without luck.

Harold could feel himself being ineffectual in his efforts to sit up. He was unable to gather his bearings with the pain agonizing every part of him. It felt like he had bruised everything from the roots of his hair down to his toes.

With the weight of his own body pushing him back onto the mattress, Harold felt defeated. He slid his hands up his body and reached for his forehead. As his arms slipped out from under the blanket laid over him, the cold instantly bit at his fingers, and goosebumps dotted his arms.

Harold felt fresh blood on his face and wanted to find out how badly he was hurt. His fingers quivered as they found cloth wrapped around his skull. It was a coarse bandage, softened only by his damp blood. Harold tried hard to understand what was going on but needed to stop the beating behind his eyes before he could do that.

He had a worse headache than ever before in his life, and with his trade of long hours sitting in the dark trying to thread needles, he'd had had a few. It made sense that Harold was in a hospital, but the question became which one? He had heard some horrific stories from clients that had lost loved ones to physicians with their butcher-like procedures.

Even before the Dragon's Blight, mages had been pushed from the city, and when they went, their potions vanished from the market stalls, but people still needed healing. So, it fell to butchers, barber-surgeons, and nobles with macabre minds to set up small surgeries.

Most of them had no clue about the biology of the human body, and the healing arts they practiced were little more than experiments. Mistakes in surgery, people catching infections from the filth and open wounds, and the medical practices themselves, killed more than they cured.

Harold knew he was safer battling his wounds at home than letting some knife-happy surgeon at him with rusty implements.

At that moment, Harold wished to the Creator that he had fallen asleep while working on the apron the previous night, so that all this was a bad dream.

This small thought began an avalanche of questions in his mind. Harold had to get some answers, and soon, before his head imploded under the pressure of his thoughts. He had stayed unmoving for long enough. It felt like days, but Harold knew it had only been minutes; the constant thud behind his eyes kept time like a pendulum on a grandfather clock.

Harold pushed himself up onto his elbows, not giving in to the pain this time. He continued until his back rested against the brickwork behind him. Grunting with the effort, he allowed himself an imaginary pat on the back.

The room felt warm to him, but his breath crystallized in the air. Harold knew that the pain was warming his blood from the inside and blocking out the chill. It felt like his insides were an oven, but Harold could feel the cold on his arms.

He was suffering from a sort of fever from the agony and could only pray it wasn't an infection from the dirty sheets. A light shone in the hallway outside, and Harold could just make out the silhouette of another door close by. If that was another ward, this was not some small practice. It could be only one of a few places, one of the governmental institutions.

As the darkness lost its power over his vision, Harold began to see the large room around him in monochrome. He could tell there were other beds in it and along the walls. Harold could just make out an assortment of jars, no doubt containing leeches or body parts in formaldehyde.

On a small table next to his bed, Harold could see a jumble of shiny tools that looked more like things a carpenter would use than a doctor. The sheet that covered him was dirty, so Harold dropped it to the floor, relieved to see he still had all his limbs when it fell from him.

He was surprised that there were no candles or gas lamps in the room. The only logical reason Harold could think of was that he was the only patient in the room, and he had been out cold, so there had been little point in lighting the room for his benefit.

That did make him wonder if the doctors had planned for him to wake up – or had they just left him here until a dead collector came around? Something flickered causing a brief shadow to darken the light outside in the corridor. It cast a deep phantom that engulfed the whole ward in blackness.

His heart leaped to his throat, and Harold hoped that it was just the wind blowing out a candle rather than the surgeon coming to "treat" his wounds. Harold thought of calling out, but his throat was so dry that not even a squeak escaped. He really needed a drink, but the taste of smoke and the awful smell of the spilled spirits still haunted him.

The shadow receded, but Harold could hear footsteps slapping against the flagstones outside in the corridor. The disturbance to the source of light that dimly lit the walls around him had not been the wind, as Harold had hoped. Someone was coming his way. The light grew brighter as the intruder's candle grew ever closer, and Harold got a better look around the shoddy ward.

A wardrobe was open at one end below a barred window, and inside it hung six pure-white nurse's uniforms, including the silly hats worn to keep their hair from falling into open wounds.

The beds around him were empty, and some had the sidebars up, turning them into odd-looking cots. The floor was surprisingly clean and well-partnered to a bucket and mop that looked like it had a lot of use. They hid in the corner next to two peeling, white tables, like the one next to his bed. Being able to see in color in the light was pointless. Other than the whites in the room, the only different color seemed to be gray. The floor was gray, the walls were plastered gray and the only hint of color was a limp plant sitting isolated at the other end of the ward, and the odd stain on another bed that Harold didn't want to think about.

Harold glanced to his right and took a better look into the tools the surgeon had placed next to him. They were not, as Harold first thought, just tossed on the table but were displayed neatly. It was their strange shapes and jagged edges that made them look jumbled in the dark. The tools themselves had delicate ivory handles. The fact that each one seemed to end in a point or a blade, and that a large wooden hammer around the size of his fist was sitting next to them, meant Harold didn't want to stay long enough to see them being used.

His attention left the macabre tools as the footsteps stopped outside the room. The door slid open, and Harold prayed it was someone coming to tell him he was fine and going home soon.

As it opened, a self-assured man strutted in and made straight for Harold's bed. The visitor was full of confidence. The only other people Harold had seen that cocky were the constables. As he got closer, Harold began to make out the blue of his uniform, confirming his suspicions that it was indeed the law, and Harold wondered what a constable would want with him.

His uniform was impressive. It had huge brass buckles all along its front and buttons that, with a little imagination, could have been bronze ashtrays. It was neat, pressed, and still dry. His visitor must have arrived by coach, otherwise, he would be sopping wet from the rain which Harold could still hear clashing against the window. The officer wore a full top-hat that nestled against his huge bushy sideburns. He removed the hat and tucked it under his arm as he drew close to Harold's bed, but not before Harold noticed the bronzed marking embossed in it. It showed him to be a city guard. Harold thought that he could bet his day's takings that the constable was corrupt and no doubt on O'Brien's pay; they all were.

"Good, you're awake. I had half expected to have to sit around and entertain the nurses," the officer jested. "My name is Inspector Francis Fraser. I'd like to ask you a few questions, my lad," he said in a voice that was deep and dry, displaying an accent foreign to the city. There were too many hints of southern Neeska blood chiselled into every syllable for him to be able to hide his lineage, but strangely, he still tried.

As much as the officer attempted to mask his accent, his bright orange hair, which grew down through slug-like sideburns into a full beard, gave away his true heritage.

The inspector was of southern blood, no doubt from Riversdale, and Harold guessed he hid it to allow himself to progress in the force. Most people in the city still held a grudge against the kingdoms of the south as they had not sent aid during the Dragon's Blight – it did not matter to most, that they were being ravaged by a plague that threatened the very existence of the village at the time.

A rounded fat face and a reddened nose showed signs of heavy drinking, and it was not until the officer sat down on the end of his bed that Harold noticed the band around his wrist that marked him as a high-ranking commander.

Francis was stocky, and from the scarred knuckles, Harold knew that he was a man who got the answers he wanted. Harold did wonder if he was the type of man who joined the city guard for the good of the city, or if he was just another crook who had joined to abuse the laws for personal benefit.

The inspector coughed abruptly, and it was only then that Harold realized he had not replied for some time. Harold guessed the concussion made his daydreaming habit even worse. He had been fortunate to have the tendency – had he not been daydreaming at the Queens, he might have been quicker loading that barrel down and might have been in the cellar when it went up in flames.

Harold's heart sank as he realized that O'Brien's boys would also be in to see him. O'Brien, no doubt, had died in the fire and they would be out for the blood of whoever started it. Harold was the only witness still breathing. That must be why the inspector was with him, but once he left the hospital, Harold would be at their mercy. All he could hope was that he was discharged before O'Brien's gang found out where he was being treated.

"Let's get a few things straight, shall we?" the inspector continued, ignoring Harold's lack of reply. "William Boatswain might have let the guards go soft, but he isn't in power anymore. So how about you give me your name, then answer my questions, and you get to leave here with only the bruises you came in with," Francis said, hinting at his allegiance to Malcolm Benedict.

The city had been torn in two ever since William had been superseded in government. Harold truly believed that if the people of Oakenfall did not so strongly fear another long and drawn out war like the one at the turn of the century, then the tension between the religious and the ordinary people would have led to bloodshed. Those loyal to the extremist Sacellumian, Malcolm, and those who – like Harold – wanted William back in power.

"Sorry. My name is Harry Spinks, son of James Spinks, tailor of East Street," Harold replied, having no idea why he automatically introduced his father's name. He guessed it was to show that he came from a good family and was not the type to set fires.

"Not a Pole is you then, boy?" Francis asked unexpectedly. Harold waited for a second to see if it was some inside joke, but the inspector's face remained unchanged behind the walrus mustache.

"No, sir," Harold answered. The question annoyed him. The Poles had been the name given to the Iron Giants' army when they invaded the city.

They only carried that name during times of war. Now they worked hard for what they had, though you could see in Francis's eyes that he did not think they deserved it. Racism was ripe in the city; Harold's annoyance was ignored by the inspector, while he continued to scribble in his notebook as he spoke.

"You saw the fire at the Queens Tavern earlier tonight. In fact, there are reports that you were seen loading things into the tavern where the fire started. Would you like to give me your account of what happened, or shall I just get the cuffs on you now?" Francis spat out in a mouthful, without needing to breathe.

He obviously thought Harold had done it and was praying Harold was of Iron Giant descent as it would be so much easier to blame him without any questions from his superiors if Harold was.

The law was so corrupt that if you were of any race but Brilankan – like the monks and the current ruling leader – decent laws, such a fair trial, did not apply. They could have him in the cells by morning; such was the fear of the Shadow Demons.

"Well, I know you're not deaf and dumb, so answer me, boy," Francis said with spittle forming on his lip.

Harold could see the anger growing inside the inspector. He tried to remember the fire, but the details caused him to shake again. The fear had left his mind for a while – but it had not left his body. His fingers trembled, and Harold could feel his mouth become even drier if that was possible.

"Where am I?" Harold croaked, ignoring the question for now. Harold had a few of his own he needed answering first and felt he could get away with pushing the inspector's temper a little more.

"You're in Saint Bartholomew, the governmental hospital just off Duck Street, if you must know. Though, if you don't give me an answer to my damn question now, you'll be out of here and off to a rat-infested cell before you can call your bloody mother to wipe your snotty nose, lad. Now tell me about the fire," Francis said, and the angrier he got, the more the almost musical tone of his southern voice came through.

"I was loading the kegs into the cellar as always, when I smelled spirits–" Harold replied carefully.

"Well, I should hope you bloody would, or there'd be little point putting the kegs in there!" the inspector interrupted, and Harold supposed he had a point. The kegs did always smell of alcohol, but never as strong as that night.

"Get to the bit where you set the fire," Frances said, already growing bored of listening.

Harold didn't answer straight away because his attention snapped elsewhere. In the distance beyond the ward, he could hear an accent he recognized as one of the O'Brien's.

It was faint but could just be heard over the whistling wind. That was all he needed. Harold had the law trying to slap him in irons and O'Brien's gang on their way to gut him. As much as Harold wanted the inspector gone, he knew he had to keep him there. Inspector Fraser's humor was less painful than what would happen to him if O'Brien's gang even suspected Harold had started the fire.

"Ok, you really want to know what I saw. I'll tell you then," Harold said, still barely able to believe it himself. "The place stunk of spirits, more'n normal. As I was about to lower myself down to check for a broken drum or something, I saw someone inside the cellar light a match," Harold said, trying hard to fight through the fog inside his head and focus on his memories of that night.

It sounded mad to him, even as he said it. Someone had burned themselves for no other reason than to torch the tavern and then crawled out of the fire and ran away. Harold guessed it could have been a mage that had somehow protected himself from the flames, but then why use the match when he could have cast a spell from a safe distance away? It didn't make any sense. Harold doubted anyone else saw the man either, as he had darted off in the panic.

Harold was the obvious suspect, so he had to tell the whole story in the hopes that Francis would believe him.

"I was tossed into the street by the blast. That was when I saw him crawl out from the wreckage. I recognized the person from a newspaper article. The guy was supposed to have been killed about two weeks ago, but it was him," Harold said – and instantly felt stupid.

There was no way it could be him. Harold didn't know much about magic, but even necromancers would have had trouble controlling the dead the way Harold saw the burning man run – but it was definitely the man he had read about. The more Harold thought about it, the more he was sure.

"So, let me get this cock-and-bull right. You want me to believe you did not start the fire. It was started by a dead man? He came back to life somehow and set fire to the pub? Then, and let me be totally sure of this, he crawled out from the burning building in which twenty people died and ran off down the street?" Francis said, and Harold noticed the inspector had stopped taking notes.

"Yes, that's about it," Harold said lamely.

He had seen it happen, and it seemed like madness even to him, so how could he expect anyone else to believe him?

Francis was waiting for more from him, but Harold had nothing to give. The awkward silence went on for what seemed like eternity before the door to the ward opened. It swung on its hinges until it bounced off the wall with a thud that caused one of the nurses' hats to fall to the floor.

In walked two dark-skinned smugglers, both short and in almost matching brown overcoats that reached down to their knees. They wore similar red shoes to Harold's, though not as nicely cut. It was an odd thing to notice, but, even in his weakened state, Harold noticed the single beading stitches which showed their shoes were cheaply made; Harold guessed it was the tailor in him.

Even in the dark, Harold noticed the pair's features. They both had curly dark hair that bounced as they walked, and squashed noses, no doubt from countless drunken brawls.

A glint in their eyes showed they owned the room. The one on the right had a limp, and Harold noticed his hands were shaking slightly, a sign of the scurvy no doubt caught from one of their pinch pricks.

Something told him that as small as these men were, they could handle themselves. Harold knew by their faces that they were O'Brien's boys, in every sense of the word. They were not just a couple of his gang but his two sons. Harold had seen them at the Queens before. They eyed the city guard inspector at the end of his bed and Harold's breath froze as he saw one of them reach into his chest pocket.

"Please, God, not a crossbow," Harold whispered to himself. If they had even the slightest likeness to their father's personality, they were a couple of psychopaths.

Harold was thankful to see that it was not a weapon that came out from the brown-shaggy jacket's recesses. Instead, it was a small wedge of pound notes tied together with string. It was more money than his tailor shop earned in a month. The one holding the money chucked it at Inspector Fraser before speaking.

"There is a mother hen there, copper top. Why don't you go buy yourself a drink or a brass and forget you seen us?" O'Brien's son said, his accent strong even though they had never even seen Lashkar Gah, their homeland.

Inspector Fraser scooped up the money, before turning to Harold. He was on their payroll, that was all Harold needed.

"I'll be back to talk to you later, boy," he said. "Don't hurt him too badly, lads. I need to take him in alive," Francis said, as he pushed his hat back on his head, shooting Harold a smile.

"Slimy bastard," Harold wanted to say, but he was far too scared.

It was no wonder no one had any respect for city guards, so many of them were on the payroll of the criminal families.

The door clicked closed as the inspector left without another word. It was just the two O'Brien boys and Harold. As the two goons took a final glance into the corridor to make sure they would not be interrupted, Harold closed his eyes, asking himself again why he had left the tailor's that night.

Chapter 4: Restless Dreams

His books becoming the playground of spiders, Paul Augustus's dreams were plagued by the secrets he held. He lay in bed with the fireplace out regardless of the cold.

The darkness that hung like a smothering blanket over the room comforted him and helped block everything out. The shadows were more potent than even the cold's waking grasp.

The rain stopped for a short time as the clouds moved on, and with the sky clear, the temperature fell fast. There would be snow by morning, not that Paul could see any of that from his windowless room.

He tossed and turned below the sheepskin blanket. He knew his knee would lock and that he would suffer the agony that came with arthritis if he didn't keep warm, but the shadows were the only thing that kept his dreams at bay – it was worth the pain.

He had to hurry up and finish his tests. The experiments he had been carrying out on prostitutes had been going well. But that was until that bloody smuggler swine, O'Brien, had got involved.

Paul fell asleep thinking about the smuggler's involvement. Exhaustion finally won, but his mind continued its trail of thought back through the last few weeks.

With his eyes shut, the back of his eyelids made the perfect screen for his dreams.

It had all seemed so simple when Paul had set out. The catacombs under Saint Anne's Chapel had been empty for so long; the church used it for storage. The rumors of them being haunted had been spread by Paul himself and meant the altar boys would never go down into the gloom.

Paul rewarded himself in his dreams for the imagination he had. Capturing a pigeon from the street and letting it loose down there, was pure genius; its fluttering and crashing around made sure the rumors had some substance.

Once he was sure that no one would go down there, it became the perfect place for him to work. The damp and cold of the underground tombs kept his failed experiments fresh and stopped them smelling too much of rot. If not a little icy, the conditions were otherwise perfect for the leeches he had brought back from the east.

When the makeshift laboratory was set up, the priest became, by his own admission, a mad scientist. At the start, he had tried using the strange leeches on animals that he gathered from the streets. If anyone had noticed Paul as he walked into the church at night with a stray animal, he would tell them that it was the Creator's work.

He relished the foolishness of the average degenerate on the street. Because they feared the demons coming so much, they could have caught him flogging a child, and if he said it was the Creator's work, they would have joined in.

He had tried attaching the leeches at the neck of the animals as he seen the mystics in The Dark Gulf do, but they drained the animals of blood too quickly. The process had killed them before the parasite could cross into the animal.
Paul was unsure of just what happened to make the changes happen, but whatever it was, it did not have time to take effect on such small creatures. After many failed experiments, Paul found that one corner of the catacombs had turned into a pet cemetery.

If anyone had braved coming down there, it would have led to too many questions. Getting rid of the dead dogs was easy. All he had to do was sneak them outside into the gutter when there was heavy rain. The citizens of Oakenfall were so used to seeing rotting animals in the gutters after an intense downpour that no one questioned a few more. If anything, it brought more prosperity to the area with an increase of rodents for the rat-catchers to claim.

The first tests on humans had proved a little more complicated, though the corpses were harder to get rid of when experiments went wrong.

Things improved when Paul found a loose slab on one of the sarcophagi. A couple of urchins from the street helped him open and clean it in return for a free forgiveness. This made the perfect place to drop the bodies as they would slide into the miles of hidden labyrinth below the city.

Paul could then progress at speed in his research. Frustration at what he had missed had almost driven Paul mad. It had taken five girls' lives before he found the secret in his notes that the herbs hung around the necks of the villagers weakened the transition of the Rakta Ishvara, the Blood God.

These herbs poisoned the leeches and killed them off before they could drain their victim fully. Not, however, before the toxin had entered the body, and the change had started. Paul knew it was a toxin of some kind as only minutes after the leech fell from the neck of his subject, the veins in the area blackened, and, eventually, the blackness seemed to spread to the eyes at which point the subject died.

It was on the night when he had become impatient and taken two girls at once that things started to go wrong. He'd become greedy. The anticipation of mastering his technique forced him to make a mistake. Both girls had come willingly with his pound notes pressed tightly in their blouses, their young skin exposed to the neck. The corsets worked their magic, Basque-styled, they flowed down over the girls' pale bosoms.

Their dresses seemed to be made of cotton and had a decorative frill at the edge. They were from somewhere in Lashkar Gar and chirped back and forth with each other in a language Paul did not understand.

Their hair was messy and hung down in greased mats to their shoulders, but they showed no sign of disease, and that was enough for the experiments. Paul Augustus was no longer a celibate priest – he had forgone that teaching of Sacellum during his time in the Green Stone Isles – and when he entered the catacombs, he was already hard with excitement.

As he led them down into the darkness, his hands caressed the poor girls. He tried to reach into their clothes with his lecherous old and wrinkled hands groping them as they walked. Although used to this sort of sordid ordeal, the two girls were made uncomfortable by the urgency of his need.

They seemed to relax slightly in the dull light; it was cleaner than some of the places, they had been forced to work a man, and at least they could relax in the knowledge that a priest was unlikely to hit them.

Paul was sure they noticed this was not in character for a priest, but they did not seem to care, given for what he paid them. Paul had planned to restrain the girls and attach the leeches, but seeing them in the dim candlelight had made his mind wander from his work.

His God had stopped listening so long ago – who would notice or judge him if he was to sin? Therefore, he did. He bedded both in the dank setting, deep under the streets where the girls were used to working.

They swarmed over him, hoping to earn his favor for future visits for the wealth he offered. They touched him frantically, doing their best to please him. The pleasure was great, but his mind never left the real reason they were there.

As he grew close to climax, the faces of all the girls he had killed flashed across his mind, but they did not halt his violent thrusts and hard grasping, his nails and teeth drawing blood.

His orgasm came quickly, but not quick enough for the girls he soiled. Once it had passed, Paul rolled off the top of the young girl that had become his favorite.

She was still panting below him as she wiped the blood from the teeth marks on her bosom. His breath was short, but he had to move fast before they grew too eager to leave.

The second girl, who had not come off quite as badly, was already getting dressed. Paul knew he would have to get her first. He reached for the tongs on the side table and pulled open the water-filled jar.

He reached down inside it and pulled out the large black mass that shook itself out of its coiled position. The size of the leech still amazed him – a foot long at full length. The dressed prostitute turned to look at Paul and went to scream as she saw him come at her with tongs outstretched.

It was too late as Paul grabbed her around the mouth. He may have been old, but he was not yet wholly feeble. He pushed the leech against her neck, and it attached itself instantly. Her struggling stopped quickly as the pain paralyzed her.

The priest went back to the table and delved into the jar again, clutching another leech in his tongs. As he turned, he saw that the girl on the floor had moved quicker than expected. She had run for the door in tears, leaving her friend behind.

Being nude, as shameful as it was, was not the be-all and end-all for a prostitute. After a life of servicing men, she had grown used to her bareness. Paul took a step toward the door with his anger rising in him, but it was cold down there, and he could not give chase. His arthritis-ridden knee ached, and he knew it would lock if he tried.

As he looked down, he could see the assault on the first woman had left her lying, eyes closed, on the floor. The leech's toxin was already sedating her. Paul reached for the table once more and let a scattering of dry leaves fall onto the girl's body. It would stop her dying, he hoped.

He looked back at the now open doorway into the main church. Paul thought about following the girl but decided that it did not matter that one girl had escaped. His experiments were too valuable, and the city guard would not believe her anyway.

It did mean he would have to work quickly to remove the bodies, however. Such an inconvenience to his work, but that was the benefit of doing his experiments from the chapel, as it allowed plenty of graves he could use.

The images of the bodies in his dream made Paul struggle in bed, battling with the guilt. He wondered for a brief moment of clear-mindedness whether he had lost himself to this shadow, but at that moment, his dream flickered onward.

Hours of real-time passed in moments. It was during morning confession while Paul was alone in the booth that they had come to him. The slut who had escaped had been one of that smuggler mob's whores.

"Morning, Vicar," the seafarer's accent rasped through the carved wooden grill in Paul's dream. Paul went to flee the confessional, realizing his mistake instantly, but a strong arm held the door firm from the outside. It was much stronger than his.

"Please, sit down, Vicar. My friend seems to be blocking the door and will be until we've had a little chat," the same voice said.

Defeated, Paul reluctantly sat down. The shutter slid open, and Paul could see the shadow of a man sitting in the room through the grill. The stranger continued to speak, his accent prominent. "A little birdie tells us that you got a little overexcited with some of our girls last night. Muriel is still stuck at the Queens and O'Brien is not all too happy that she cannot go to work. Ruby-May is still missing. What do you suppose happened to her?" The smuggler asked in a blatantly patronizing voice from inside the dream.

To Paul it felt all too real. He felt like he had slipped back in time and was no longer in his freezing bed but trapped again in fear inside the confessional. *That damnable hussy*, thought Paul, *She should have died too*.

"Also …" the voice continued, "We seem to have misplaced quite a few other girls recently, and we happen to wonder, what that has to do with you, Vicar? … Now, Mr. O'Brien is not too worried about the girls themselves. They are just stock and trade – another boat will be over soon enough, no doubt – and he would not hurt a man of the cloth. It is just the money side of things. You see, we need that back. So, you stay in your little box there and forget we ever came here, and we'll just collect from the church what is owed, right?" the stranger said and anger boiled inside Paul – he would make these pigs pay.

At that moment, Paul started to wake up and faded from the dreamworld to thought. He reached for the parchment from the floor by his bed and, as he had taken to doing, scribbled down the events from his dream. His experiments may have failed, but the body he had used from the morgue seemed to have worked.

The banker had been stabbed in a side alley and left to die. The city guard had put his picture in the papers hoping they could find the killer, but Paul could not care less if they did or did not. The body had taken the toxin perfectly. Everything had been a success.

The man was even controllable for a short time, his own mind as dead as his body. Paul was sure of this at the time, but he would soon see he was wrong. Whatever it was that the leech transferred and used to bring William back from the dead had taken over, and William went rogue.

Paul had sent him to get revenge on the O'Brien's for leaving the church in such a state, and he had burned the Queens down as ordered, but then he had disappeared. His blood-hunger would start growing soon, one of the downsides to the so-called cure that becoming a Rakta Ishvara necessitated.

He knew that the victim would have to start feeding. Paul had to cure the hunger before he used it on himself; he didn't want kill people. *He wasn't a monster,* he thought to himself. It was just that he didn't want to die. He had to find a way to get the leech to attach correctly in the colder climate before he could worry about that anyway.

He wanted the toxin to cure his suffering, stop the pain and weakness his age had begun to bring. He had learned in The Dark Gulf that the temple held the infected one who had lived for millennia.

Paul's experiment, this so-called William the Banker, would be the same. His strength would be unparalleled to anything anyone had seen before in Neeska, and he would be brutal and deranged.

Those turned by the Rakta Ishvara had to feed off fresh blood often to satisfy their cravings. The people of Chhottaa-Ghar had taught Paul that the leeches offered long life and strength for a price, but it was against their laws to use them, and the Rakta would kill anyone who tried.

As they called them, the gods were very territorial and wars had plagued the Green Stone Isles for centauries even as the Titans walked Neeska.

For this reason, the village had hidden in the jungle away from the rest of the world.

A sudden thought crossed his waking mind. The image of the Rakta Ishvara ripping a living child apart burned like a smithy's fire in his frontal lobe. The sound of the Demon God's screams as it fed on the child echoed through Paul's mind. The image was so vivid that it shook him to his core. His pores leaked a cold sweat.

The morning had arrived, and with it, the burden Paul carried.

Chapter 5: Welcome Back William

As Harold lay in the hospital, he knew little of bloodsucking William except seeing him blow up the pub, but their paths would cross more than once in the days to follow.

The second time Harold would come across the recently deceased body of William started the moment the flames claimed their last victim at the Queens.

William had fled the arson scene leaving Harold unconscious on the ground and had headed for the sewers.

The fire had burned away the herbs that Paul had placed around his neck and had allowed the parasite to extend its tendrils into William's brain.

He had been a mindless zombie similar to those raised by necromancers, but with the herb gone, the Rakta Ishvara was free from Paul's control.

It spread quickly, and its first instinct was to flee to safety. William had raised a sewer grate and headed for the cold below to supply the parasite the moisture it needed to survive.

The sound of water running overhead became familiar to William in the days that passed. The darkness of the sewers was no longer a problem for him as it would have been, had he still been alive, as his eyes seemed keener.

Now, much like the priest who brought him back from the grave, the gloom was comforting to him.

The only light source was a series of small dust flecked rays falling in through narrow slits high above in the city street. It was so dark that even a cat with its shining eyes would have had trouble seeing, but William could see every crack in the slime-coated wall of the sewers under Oakenfall.

The sewers were a new construction to the city. Many broke off into people's cellars or led to unfinished tunnels that had been abandoned after the funding was withdrawn from this "frivolous expense," as Malcolm Benedict had called it.

This almost total abandonment of the tunnels had given William the perfect place to hide. In the days following the fire, William rarely left the sewers and spent most of his time in the dark. It had given him time to think and control the urges. He felt strange in his own body, and so much of his mind felt as if it was missing.

Memories and emotions had gone, and in their place was another consciousness, one whose hunger seemed to be getting worse. William had to keep himself here in the filth that the rest of Oakenfall ignored so he could fight what was inside him.

The strength the parasite had given him made it impossible for anyone or anything to stop him – not even the fire in the cellar had killed him. The parasite inside had begun to heal him before the flames had even blistered his skin. By the time he hid away with the rodents, his wounds had vanished.

He had wanted to go to his family to tell them what happened and that he was still alive somehow, wanting more than anything to hold his baby in his arms once more, but he daren't.

William knew he was only a passenger in his body now. Something in him had changed and it was unsafe to go to them. His mind was fighting the creature's control inside him, but he could feel he was losing already.

As they pressed deeper, sinking into its soft and quickly cooling body, William's teeth dripped red with the blood of one of his fellow residents. The rat's head hung limply between his jaws like the prey of a great jungle lion.

In the silence, William watched as a raindrop slid down a stalactite and fell to the floor with a splash. It sickened him that he was feasting on rats, but the hunger in him never ended.

It was worse at night; William sat and dropped the rat's carcass to the floor where it bounced off the stone and fell from the upper steps into the small brown stream below.

It floated along with the putrid waste from the living city, and as it slowly sank into the filth, the rat's struggle for life faded as its corpse disappeared into the darkness toward the canals.

Satisfied for now, William rested back against the wall, but he knew it would not last for long. Many of William's memories had been taken when he passed into the spirit realm, but he could remember his family. He could remember the smell of his newborn's head. He could not forget the fear as the mugger beat him to death.

William hated that he had died and left his family, but he wished he had stayed dead. It had been dark and peaceful and so very restful. Then without welcome or invite, the intruder entered his body. Its soul had come like a blinding light, and the Rakta Ishvara had confused matters by becoming one with him.

It had begun as a faint whisper, the words of a priest strongest in his mind. Something had kept the Rakta Ishvara at bay, its demand little more than a whisper, but eventually, the priest's words had fallen away like a discarded item of clothing. In the void that remained, his mind now echoed with a past that William had never lived.

The being inside his soul seemed to have a voice of its own, but not one that William could understand. It took over at times and then faded again and left William confused and alone in the dank sewers. The smell down there was terrible, choking William's senses. His thoughts flickered back to the world of filth that surrounded him.

He could not risk going to the surface as there were too many people to feed on, and he knew the hunger would return; he could already feel it ebbing just below his consciousness – beneath whatever he was becoming. He was still human, at least for now. Deep inside, he still felt guilt for the fire at the Queens. He had heard the screams and seen the deaths, but he had not been in control of his actions. He was not entirely in control now, either, but Paul had worked him like a puppet.

The thing inside him taking over had a voice and personality of its own, one that seemed pure evil and filled with hatred, but at least he had seemed able to fight it until the sting of the herbs had fallen away.

William's body had changed so much since he had come back from whatever death was. He had been an average-built man before – nothing special – but when he came around as he was wrenched from the spirit realm, he found his body had grown stronger, each muscle pushing hard against the skin, growing with renewed purpose like the barbarian chiefs of old.

His chest heaved and contorted as it forced outwards with the growth of this new parasite, a hardened shell replacing his broken ribs. There had been a change to his throat as well. His tongue had split, his pipes opened and twisted, and his teeth grew and sharpened to look more like a wild cat's mouth than a man's.

With his newfound strength and speed came more than just one burden. The hunger and company within his mind were not the only thing to plague William. He had pains in his chest that came on fast and were suddenly excruciating.

Even though he had never read the research Paul had carried out and couldn't point to where the Green Stone Isles were on a map before his death, William knew where this pain came from. It came from memories of a past he had never lived. It came from the parasite – they were becoming one. The knowledge that had been crammed into his skull like a complete set of encyclopedias explained why his chest hurt so much.

It was from the being inside him, weaving its way into him more each day. His own heart had stopped beating long ago and where it had been something new was living. The pulsating parasite moved stale blood around his body. It lived in a hard shell and ran its tendrils through his body like roots through the soil. It was keeping William alive but at the cost of forsaking others. It needed fresh blood to keep its host body alive.

The memories that appeared in his mind were from the shared hive mind of the parasitic Rakta Ishvara.

Light from a sewer worker came into the tunnel drawing William from his thoughts. William could hear the man's heart beating and the fainter sound of a canary before they even entered the tunnel, he called home.

They had come to fix the bulwark of dead rats that William's hunger must have caused.

The piles of decaying corpses had blocked the tunnel and had forced rainwater and sewage to breach a nobleman's wine cellar.

It did not matter to William why a person had entered his domain – it was time to feed.

Within seconds and without a sound, the sewer worker's lantern fell into the water. There was a spray of feathers and the clanking of the empty cage as the bird escaped in the commotion.

The red color of claret mixed with other red colors floating in a place no one would see.

Interlude 2: A Rat and a Rose

The sweet yet bitter smell of the spilled spirits all but faded from memory, Dante had escaped the tavern and made his way through the maze of cellars below Oakenfall. It hadn't been a total loss since having to flee the Queens, as one or two of the cellars along the journey had contained fine round balls of cheese.

Dante had even managed to find the scent trail of a friend he remembered from the *Cassandra*. Finally, he had found a hole made by his cousins that lead into the underbelly of the sewers. Now all he had to do was follow the scent home.

The sewers were safe, unlike the city streets that were filled with predators. His kind owned the sewers. The bats might think they could claim them, but those flying show-offs daren't creep into the sewers' depths.

That was the domain of the rat. Dante himself was too classy a rodent to feast on the moths and worms that also dwelled in the darkness, as he had grown accustomed to fine cheeses, dried hops, and oats, but he wouldn't look down on his fluffy brethren.

The journey through the sewers below Oakenfall had been uneventful for Dante as he made his way back toward the harbor, where he hoped the *Cassandra* would still be waiting – if it hadn't already set sail. It used to sail a lot more than it did now, but after the monks stopped coming, it seemed to rest against the harbor walls more often that it sailed.

The flagship *Cassandra* had many a tale to tell of its own. It had started life as a cargo ship for the Dean family before it was commandeered by

William as the prize of Oakenfall when he took office at the end of the Pole invasion.

It was aboard this vessel that Dante had been born in a sack of grain a year before. He was midway through his life now and had enjoyed his first few months within the creaking hull. However, he was a rat born for adventure, and his wanderlust had soon driven him down the chain and onto dry land. However, if Dante had known the horrors he would face on dry land, he would never have made the journey. He had to let the others know when he returned.

Dante had left the Queens and made his way through one sludge-lined path after another in the darkness below the city before the smell had hit him like a thrown shoe. It was the stench of death. Hundreds of his kind had come to their ends close by. There was something in the dark feeding on them.

The tiny hairs on Dante's neck stood on end. There was a smell there he remembered too. The one that he had grown to fear more than anything else. It was the human from the Queens. Dante wondered how the beastly human had found his way into Dante's domain; it seemed even the sewers were no longer safe.

The light from a sewer worker's lantern hinted of a way back to the surface, and away from the horror in the dark, so Dante doubled back, headed away from the harbor and started to make his way up to the city streets.

The sound that followed as the worker came to a horrid end chilled Dante to his core. He knew once he was up on the streets, he'd have to avoid stray dogs, cats, and rat-catchers, and just about any human with a shoe or shovel that took a dislike to anything with four legs a tail and a taste for cheese. But something deep inside him suggested it was safer than facing the shadows of the sewers with death waiting just around the corner.

The journey out of the sewers had been quicker than the one into them. Squeezing up between two rotten floorboards, Dante had found himself in a small damp corridor.

Dante froze, hidden in the shadows as his eyes noticed he was not alone. It was there, with his nose just peeking out, that Dante watched and listened.

"So, you just moved in then, lady?" the young match girl, Rose, said to the old woman who had been struggling in with a bag thrown over her hunched shoulders.

"Lady! I'm no lady, my girl. Call me Granny – most people do – but yes, dear, I have moved in," Granny said, as she tried to smile through a mess of gums that lined her thin, wrinkled mouth.

Granny had last been seen in Oakenfall shortly after the end of the Dragon's Blight. She had left on horseback with the demon, Rinwid, but her work had called that she needed to return to the city.

"Be nice to 'ave a Granny. Don't know where mine are. The old priest used to be like a Granddad to me, but he's been weird lately, and he's starting to scare me. Don't seem right no more, that-one," Rose said, with the usual carefree chirp she carried.

She had lost both her parents and lived alone scraping by on what she could get for a few matches peddled to those with the coin to spare, or from the gutters. She was not averse to feasting on half-eaten apples from the edge of the street if it meant filling her belly at night, but she never lost the thin smile that coated her lips.

"There's a lot not right within this city now, young miss," Granny said. *It's been heading that way for a long time now,* she thought to herself.

"You mean like the women that been going missing?" Rose said with a certainty that outshone her years.

"What's a young lass like you know about the missing women, then? – But no, I don't mean that. I mean the priests, Sacellum. I don't think even Rinwid had planned for that," Granny said, drifting off into thought.

"What's a Rinwid?" asked Rose.

"Not so much a 'what,' as a 'who,' but never you mind. Help me up to my room with this bag will you, girl, and we'll see about getting you something to eat in return," Granny said.

It had been a long time since she had looked after children, and she'd never had any of her own. The late Darcy Dean had been the closest she had ever got to having them, and she felt she had failed him.

She'd been the one to pack his bag and send him off after that stupid Dragon's Heart, but how was she to know he'd end up dead and buried in the Scorched Lands?

This young girl was her chance to repent. She could look after her with what little she had managed to hide away before leaving the Dean estate.

Dante watched as the two shuffled up the corridor. Once they were out of sight, he twitched his nose and pulled his backside out from between the wood with a bit of effort; time gorging at the Queens had made him fat.

He'd have to be extra careful not to bump into any flea-ridden cats in the rain-filled streets, or he'd be an extra plump meal for them.

He made for the door with a happy squeak, and was still just slim enough to slide under it – it seemed like his luck was turning.

Chapter 6: Ernest and Neill

Dante continued his journey, Granny made dinner, and William skulked around in the sewers ending the lives of rodents and sludge shufflers alike, but Harold was unaware of these other unfolding tales. He was still counting his breaths at Saint Bartholomew's.

The inspector had gone leaving Harold alone with the O'Briens and thinking that he would not survive the night. These were no gentle rogues that had come to visit him; they had no honor among thieves and even less for those they figured to be marked.

They were not the honor-bound pirates of the White Flag era – they were common thugs. When William Boatswain took control of the city, a lot of the flags settled and became citizens. Still, without his charismatic leadership, it was not long before they gave in to their baser natures.

Harold knew they would shed no remorse for his death. He shut his eyes as soon as the inspector left and sank back down onto the paper-thin mattress.

Through the sound of the wind outside, Harold could hear the mismatched clatter of the bow-legged thug clambering toward him.

Harold could sense the other thug, who had passed Inspector Fraser the money, had not moved. He had stayed back toward the door.

Before Harold could wonder why, a sudden sharp point at his neck caused his eyes to snap open. Harold was staring into the deep green eyes of his attacker.

He felt the chill of metal pressed against his neck, not hard enough to cut his skin but enough that he dared not swallow.

Harold was instantly scared half to death and feared for his life. If he had been a brave man, he could have fought them off, leaped from his hospital bed, and somehow made his way past them. He could have escaped into the cold city streets where he could have stolen a horse and ridden to safety, just like a hero from one of the great stories he'd read during the cold winter evenings in his armchair. But he was only a tailor's son and could barely hold himself up on his elbows after his injuries, let alone take out two of O'Brien's own blood.

If the stories of O'Brien's boys were to be believed – and Harold had no reason not to believe them –they were a pair of right evil bastards. With the city torn in two between the haves and the have-nots more than ever before, criminal numbers had flourished, but sitting at their head was O'Brien. There had to be a reason for it.

"Don't worry. I'm not going to kiss you," the goon closest to him whispered with a laugh.

Harold could smell halitosis on his breath; it was obviously a lifelong friend.

Harold felt a sudden warm sensation drip down onto his bare chest and realized the knife's point had pricked his skin.

It was no more than a scratch, but the blood that trickled from it confirmed Neill's threat. With the slightest wrong move on Harold's part – or at the will of this man – Harold would become another dissection dummy for the surgeons to play with.

Harold bit down hard and clenched his teeth together. The urge to swallow grew, as did the pain, but he dared not risk it.

"So, Harry, is it not?" the thug by the door asked. "… it would seem you were at the Queens when it went up. We have a few questions for you about that. The relic that was our old man died in the fire but I'm guessing you realize that, or there would be no need for my brother there to be getting so close to you," Ernest said, nodding toward his brother with an almost worried smile. "Now you're lucky in some ways. My old man was past it, and it's about time that I got to take over the running of the business. Still, someone's got to bleed for his death. What kind of son would I be if I let it go without retaliation? So, you might want to answer quickly if I was you. My brother can get a little excited." The words confirmed Harold's suspicion that even Ernest was unsure of his brother's sanity. "How is it that your scrawny little self managed to climb out of there alive when my kin went up in smoke?"

The room fell silent as the question hung like a death in the air. Harold could not answer with all the pressure on his neck.

The slightest movement would sink the cold edge of the blade deeper into his flesh. He had a sickening feeling that they were going to kill him.

A sudden flicker of shadow passed before Harold's eyes, and the heavy had pulled the weapon away from his throat.

Harold waited for a second or two to see if he was cut and bleeding out. When there was no new sharp pain across his throat, he realized he had not been sliced open and remained in the living hell surrounding him.

The knife's new resting place did not look any the better for him. Neill's face was so close to Harold's cheek that he could feel every foul breath that Neill took.

Harold would have turned his face away from him if the knife was not now touching his upper eyelid. With the shakes Neill had from the scurvy, Harold could see the point wobble back and forth like the pendulum of a grandfather clock.

"Now, you will be telling me what you saw, or you won't be seeing much of anything … you get my meaning? Pops always brought us up to believe an eye for an eye," Neill joked.

The knife slid back with a sway of his hand, and Harold took his chance to blink. His eyes refocused and settled on Neill's companion, Ernest, who was pacing back and forth by the door like one of the governor's guards outside Hanson Castle.

As if he knew that Harold's gaze had fallen on him, Ernest stopped and looked toward Harold.

Harold could see he was uncomfortable, and it surprised him to realize that he did not like what Neill was doing any more than Harold did.

He guessed that is why Ernest had not taken over from his father before now – he lacked the killer spirit. A stupid man may have thought this meant he was safe, but Harold knew he was not. Just because Ernest did not want him dead did not mean the short goblin of a man next to him would not as soon kill him as waste his time with questions.

It was then that Harold felt the expectancy of Neill by his side and mustered up an answer.

"William!" Harold damn near shouted the name, his voice trembling with a mix of fear, anger, and plain fatigue.

The random outburst confused matters, but what else could he say? He dared not say William's last name. As scared and confused as Harold was, he was clever enough to realize that telling the over-eager Neill that a dead man had killed his father was suicide.

Harold thanked the gods for the moment of genius that struck him. "Some drunk in the street called out his name just as the cellar went up–" Harold lied. The lie slid out easily, and Harold just hoped they would not notice.

"–I don't know any more than that honestly. Your father paid me well, and I needed the work. I would not have had anything to do with this." Harold added, hoping his time serving the family would give him the benefit of the doubt at the very least.

"Sounds like old Cavanaugh to me. The swine's sobering up back at Brandies," Ernest called out from his doorway patrol.

"Don't be going too far, though, Harry. I wouldn't want to have to go visit your father if you've been telling us porkpies. Say, he still owns that place on East Street?" Neill asked, sounding disappointed that no one had been killed.

The question was followed by another stench-ridden and deep-throated snigger. Anger peaked in Harold, and he wanted to attack the swine, to stop him before he got to his family.

Harold had never really had a fight before, but he couldn't just stand there, or lie there, while the brute threatened his sick father.

Harold started to slide up on his elbows, ready to, well – do something. He wasn't really sure what he had planned, but Neill's fist came down fast, striking the side of his face with a blow like thunder before he could do anything. Harold felt the world shake as he sunk back into the sheets.

"You leave them alone," Harold weakly demanded, but he knew his warning was worthless, and so did Neill. He let out another chuckle from between his toothless grin.

"You got spirit, and that's for sure. No wonder the old man gave you the job as a barrel slugger. You'd better hope you got sense not to have lied to us," Neill said to Harold, whose stomach churned like so many sour curds.

Neill turned to address his companion and joked. "Let's leave her ladyship here alone. She could most definitely use her beauty sleep," he said and paused. "He's still a damn sight better looking than your ma," Neill added with a belly laugh.

"That's your mother too. You're such a bloody halfwit," Ernest said with a sigh.

It was clear who the brain in their partnership was.

Neill slid the knife into his jacket as if nothing had happened and made for the door.

Harold could hear the two of them playfully bickering as they left the ward.

Harold had been lucky for now, but he had to get to his father and warn him. The blow to his head had left him shaking, and darkness soon swept over him once more.

It seemed his body was not ready to deal with the stress it had been put through. In his dreams, the cottage called to him once more.

Chapter 7: Father

While Harold's concussed brain went on another a trip down memory lane that would last all of three days, in the darkness below the unknowing city streets, William's bloody feast continued in his underground home.

Unlike the dwarves of the Goldhorn Mountains, humans were not especially adept at mining. Working within the sewers was a perilous job that few wanted. It was not unusual for gas to silently take a worker's life, for masonry to crack and fall under the weight of the earth, or for tunnels to be dug too deep and flood with water from some hidden underground reservoir.

However, it was not for any of these reasons that four new postings would be nailed onto the recruitment board outside of the Mason's Guild, by the end of the week.

The first unfortunate victim had awoken something sinister in William, and the taste of rat would no longer sedate his hunger. In the following days, he had killed four sewer workers, and before the last corpse had even cooled, William decided to seek out Paul Augustus and find a cure for his craving.

He was still conscious of what he had done, even with the evil growing inside him. Unlike the demons rumored to be stalking the night since the gateway to the Spirit Realm had been weakened at the end of the Blight, William was still human enough to feel guilt for what the presence inside him made him do.

On the evening of the 17th of Thresh, William left his sewer home and headed for a confrontation with the Reverend Paul Augustus.

William never knew, but it would be the last time he was truly himself before the Rakta Ishvara devoured the last of his humanity.

William listened under the roadway grate while he waited for the crowds to pass by. It was still raining heavily, which meant the streets would soon be empty, as even pinch pricks did not stay out in weather this bad.

A whistle in the distance and the clatter of horseshoes marked the departure of the city guard officer William had seen entering the hospital earlier that very evening and more than once in the last few days.

He'd overheard the officer's name, Francis Fraser, called out by the driver of the black guard cart. Fate and hindsight often find humor in the chronicles of man, but luckily for Harold, William had no idea that the only other living witness to his existence slept just a few yards away.

"He's still out cold; get me back to the yard," the officer had said, and it did not take more than a moment for the horse to pull the last remaining occupant of the street toward the horizon.

If William had known that the man who had seen him escape the fire still lived, he would have killed him. The Rakta Ishvara would have made sure of it. It could not risk anyone knowing it was within the city before it was strong enough to rule it.

The Rakta Ishvara, the creature embedded within William, was one of a few such creatures within the world. They saw themselves as beings above mere mortals, superior to their host species. They were driven, strong, and cruel by nature, but William was yet to understand this fully. Even the

Reverend Paul had not fully understood what he had allowed to take a foothold in the city.

A final glance through the slits into Duck Street and William pushed the grate open. Its rusted hinges creaked with the effort. The grate had only been down a few years, but the small budget put into manning the sewers had made for shoddy craft, and the poorly set iron had rusted almost solid in the wet winter.

William felt the new strength inside him grow further as his arms strained under the resistance of the reluctant grate. The creature within William's chest beat and squirmed, sending a pulse of stale blackened blood into William's muscles, and with a sudden snap, the aged metal broke free, landing some yards away from its housing.

William climbed up into the rain-sodden air enjoying the fresh, if not fierce wind. It was only a short walk to Common Road, and the streets were empty apart from an old tomcat chasing down its dinner, but the fat rat, Dante, gave it the slip by sliding under a crack in the nearby masonry.

It was a distraction William didn't need, and he found it strange that he had to fight the urge to join the hunt. The sensation drew him like a drug, but he had more important things to do than feed – for now.

It would be at Saint Anne's Chapel that William would wait for the priest. He remembered it from his rebirth. William's legs began to move with a vigor he had never had while alive. Having spent most hours sitting behind a desk, he'd grown feeble and sluggish while alive, but now, he ran faster than an athlete in one of the tournaments.

The rainwater splashed up from the puddles and pounded against his face. He ran faster than any horse he had ever seen, and, at that moment, William felt alive.

William made it to Saint Anne's Chapel unhindered. He knew that the Reverend would not come to the chapel until the morning, and he would have to wait. He didn't mind though; Saint Anne's was far more comfortable than the sewers he had been calling home, but the air was too dry even in all the rain for the Rakta Ishvara sitting on his chest like a giant callus.

So, William made his way down into the basement below. It was the first place he remembered after the mugging that had killed him. The world had gone dark. There were faint thoughts, dreams of the Spirit Realm, but William never really knew if he had believed in it or not, but then there had been a presence – there had been something calling him back. He now knew it was the creature living within his shell.

When he had been dragged back from the Life Stream, as a visitor in his own body, William had awoken in the catacombs. He remembered being contained within his body, but not of it. He had been a guest, a puppet, with Paul pulling his strings. The priest would pay for the things he had made William do.

Standing back in that place made William feel nothing. His logical brain told him he should feel something, anger, sadness, fear – but he was calm, waiting, skulking in the obscurity, unmoving. He was like a spider waiting for a fly.

One of the strangest attributes of his new state was not needing sleep. At night, when most people would tire, William felt more energized. The creature inside him despised sunlight, but in the darkness, it could grow. The Blood God, the Rakta Ishvara, grew in strength as the sun hid from the night.

Its barb-like tendrils pressed deeper into William's body each night, piercing his organs and turning them black as it slowly took over his soul night by night.

William was becoming more powerful than a giant, and swifter than the fiercest of wild cats, but the price to pay was the total absorption of everything that made him. This strength would weaken come morning, but it would still leave him with attributes most could only dream off without magic.

Eventually, the sun rose outside the chapel to a perfect and calm day, bitterly cold but beautiful. The door above him opened, and Paul shuffled in, making his way down the stairs.

William waited until the grumbling had passed him by, the soreness in Paul's knee, obviously causing him discomfort in the bitter cold.

In the flick of an eye, the shadow skulking in the corner had moved, and William was now crouched at the foot of the stairs. Even with the true strength of the Rakta fading, William moved with lightning speed. Before the dust he unsettled had landed, he had blocked Paul's escape.

Paul turned slowly, his eyes wide with fright. He saw William standing behind him. In a moment of fear, and as a kneejerk reaction, Paul reached for the table, trying desperately to grab the tongs he had left there.

They were not sharp, and Paul would have preferred the point of a blade between him and his experiment, but beggars, or, in this case, priests cannot be choosers.

Paul barely blinked, but he did not see William's lunge. A sudden and firm grasp upon his collar lifted Paul clean off his feet and sent him sailing against the cold stone floor with a painful thud.

He lay there, helplessly. Like so many of his victims, Paul ached and feared for his life. Even riddled with fright, it was funny to Paul to think that he would come to an end at the hand of the Rakta Ishvara at the very place he had created it.

"William, wait!" Paul begged, hoping the controls he had put in place would still work. It was old magic, a controlling spell of sorts that occurred naturally within the plants brought back from the islands. It was a type of druidism that even those without access to the Spirit Realm could use.

The herbal leaves that the villagers had given Paul should have worked. It was the only reason the Rakta Ishvara from the Green Stone Isles had not left its temple. It was how they kept their god contained. It should have been able to resist herbal leaves, but they soaked into the body and dulled the brain.

But as William bore down on Paul, he could see through the rags of scorched clothing that hung from William's muscular form that any trace of the leaf had gone. It dawned on him – as hindsight had its fun – the fire, he thought It must have been the fire that destroyed them.

Paul felt foolish and old. It was an oversight he should have thought of. The dry leaves would have turned to dust and ash in the inferno's heat at the Queens. That was why William had never returned as he should have.

"So, you learned my name before you did this to me," William said through a snarl.

Inside the hunger was demanding that he kill the wretch in front of him and feed. Old blood was still blood to the parasite, but William fought against the urge. He had too many questions to ask first.

"What is happening to me?" he asked.

"You are alive. I saved you …" Paul said, his fear subsiding somewhat, "Surely you are thankful for that?" he added, glad that his test subject was still human inside and that the Rakta Ishvara had not fully taken over.

William was not yet like the beast Paul had seen rip the child apart back in The Dark Gulf. No, he still had humanity, and people were weak. Paul hoped he could talk his way out of danger and convince William to put the herbs back around his neck and enslave him again.

"Alive? You call this existence being alive? Do you know what I've done?" William asked, showing his blood-stained body as an example.

His clothes had burned to a crisp during the fire. Some fibers remained attached to his fully healed skin, much like that of long-dead mummified corpses. Instead of having blistered and rotting skin, William looked refreshed, almost sculpted, with renewed muscle mass.

Paul shook his head to buy himself time to admire his creation. The burns had cleared up completely and Paul could see the solid, rock-like structure attached to William's ribcage.

It moved and pulsated like the heart of a normal man, but looked more like a crustacean clinging onto William's chest. It had grown to the point that it had erupted out of the skin. It looked crablike in structure but with the ends of the legs still buried deep within the flesh.

Paul knew from his experiments that once the parasite had taken such a strong hold onto a host body, it was almost impossible to kill. If the host body was mutilated, then as long as the Rakta could feed on fresh blood, the parts would re-grow.

The only way to finish it off was to insert something hard and sharp into the ribcage structure. If the Rakta Ishvara was punctured that way, it could safely be removed. Paul remembered for a moment the enormous golden spikes that had lined the temple in The Dark Gulf. Their devil god was so sure of its strength that it taunted the villagers to kill it. Shaking the memories from his mind, Paul flashed back to the urgency of his situation.

"You mean the fire? They had to pay. They were going to stop what I have achieved here. I am so close to perfecting you," Paul said, obviously proud of his work.

He tried to push himself up. His fear, almost gone, was being replaced by anger at his creation's stupidity. That was until William grew infuriated at the sniveling old man in front of him and sent his foot crashing into Paul's chest with the strength of a blacksmith's hammer.

He pressed Paul back onto the bitterly cold floor and then Paul's fear returned, as did his silence.

William told Paul in gory detail the entirety of what he had done. How he had escaped into the putrid sewers, how he had fed on mice and rats, how his hunger had grown, how and he had lost control, killing no less than four people.

"Stop! Just stop, please! You don't understand what I'm trying to do," Paul begged like many of his victims before him.

He felt a mix of trepidation and self-loathing as he begged for his life. Paul could tell by the blackening of William's eyes that he did not have long before the beast needed to feed again. If he really was going to talk his way out of this, he had to do it now.

"The Rakta Ishvara – I mean you – it will save us all, it's the cure to so many things. It can stop even death, just as soon as I cure the bloodlust, and I am so close, so very close."

Paul said, offering up the cure like a carrot to a donkey.

He didn't know much about the man he had chosen to raise from the grave, but he did know he had a family. Paul hedged his bets that William would want to see them again and the curing of his bloodlust would let him do that.

"I don't care what you're trying to do. I want to know how to stop this thing inside me," William snarled.

His hands shook as they clenched the priest's collar. The hunger inside his mind urged him to sink his teeth into the priest's wrinkled neck and taste the sweet, bitter nectar within.

"I don't know how to yet, but–" Paul began to grovel as he saw the blackness growing over William's eyes.

"When?" William interrupted the urge inside, screaming louder than a flock of gulls.

If he didn't leave the priest soon and get back to the sewers, he would kill him.

"Soon, I will. I just need to do more tests, and it will be perfected," Paul hazarded a smile, as he tried to play to William's sensitive side – if he still had one.

Paul had seen the newspaper article. He knew William was a family man. He had been a good man before he was killed, and if enough of that remained, then Paul just might get to see another dawn.

"More tests? Is that what I am to you, just a failed experiment?" William was losing control, and his words became guttural and animal-like. He needed answers but would not be able to hold on long enough to get them.

A huge grin filled Paul's face, and William knew that the man he held in a vice-like grip had long since lost any hold on sanity.

"No, my son. You were my first success. From you, I may find the cure. You will be the one to give me life, just as I did you," Paul Augustus said in a revelation that William would never understand.

Paul was sick – no, more than sick. He was dying; he had lung cancer. It had spread through his body and would soon kill him. There would be nothing that the doctors could do to cure his pox, as they called it, and the magic which may once have saved him was now outlawed.

Paul had resigned himself to death before he found out about the Rakta Ishvara. This parasitic vampire could cure him if only he could stop the beast from taking over. It would repair the damage done and kill the disease. It would make Paul all but immortal.

"If you allow me to use your blood in my tests, then we may be able to perfect you."

"We?! … When was it that we became a team? I never asked for this," William said, backing away from Paul.

The urge to feed was sounding like cannon fire inside his skull. William had to silence it. He dropped his head heavily onto the ornate stone sarcophagus close by, sending a chip of stone across the catacombs. The hunger was almost blinding now.

"True, but then most do not ask for the blessings they are given. I brought the creature that shares your body with you back from The Dark Gulf. That is why you still breathe. Do you still think about your family that lost you when you were murdered? If we stop your hunger, then they can have you back," Paul bargained.

He knew it was risky keeping William close by, but the opportunity was too great to miss. William was the first successful application of a Rakta Ishvara leech.

William suddenly withdrew his face from the stonework and staggered back toward the stairs, something changing within him. The blackness filled his eyes completely as the Rakta Ishvara pumped dead and congealing blood through his pupils.

"No! I will not help you. I've done too much for you already; I've killed for you, Priest! The Creator will judge you for your sins," William spat as he ran up the stairs and through the door of Saint Anne's.

He had wanted to kill the priest but knew if there was any hope of ending the nightmare he was now living in, it would rely on what Paul knew.

"It is a shame that he will have to be culled. The toxin has gone too far. Damn it!" Paul cursed to the darkness as he pulled himself onto his aching knee.

He breathed a sigh of relief at his solitude and relative safety. He knew he was too weak to kill the Rakta Ishvara in its final metamorphosis, but then an idea came to him.

The fire did not finish them all off, so O'Brien's sons may yet prove useful. He could direct them against William and remove himself from suspicion at the same time.

Chapter 8: Arms of a Woman

If Harold had looked back over the times to come, he would have been both thankful and remorseful that William did not kill the priest, Paul, on that visit.

If he had, the way this story plays out would have been quite different, and Harold would be rotting away in jail blamed for the fire at the Queens.

It was a strange thing to wish for, but, at least, Harold would have been safe in jail. If William had spent just a few more minutes in the cold catacombs feeding on the priest, then Harold may never have crossed paths with him again, and the Rakta Ishvara would never have got to see Harold's face.

As fate would have it, Francis Fraser, the inspector, had finished spending his bribe money and had come back for Harold on the 18th accompanied by two officers from the special unit.

He stood by the door reading Harold his rights while the two other baboons forced Harold to his feet, dressed, and then cuffed him.

They dressed him in the same smoke-stained and scorched clothes that he had been brought into the hospital in. The off-white woolen trousers felt like ice as they were brutally pulled up and buckled around his waist.

Before the sleep left Harold's eyes, they led him out of the hospital, pushing him ahead of them, his arms pulled behind his back in restraint.

The two officers loaded him in the back of a closed black cart. The chairs inside resembled two large wooden boxes, one fixed to either side with a small gap between. The two specials sat upfront on the riding bench while Inspector Francis Fraser was inside the booth with Harold.

They both sat gazing out of the barred windows at Oakenfall as it rattled past. Harold had barely been awake a matter of hours before Frances came to collect him, and his mind was still fuzzy from the time that he had lost.

The opening of the market stalls ensured Harold had plenty of witnesses for his lowest moment. Harold assumed he was their prime suspect for the fire, as it was blatantly obvious that his story of a dead man burning the pub was not believed. Inspector Fraser's eyes turned on him in the back of the cart, as if he was trying to assess him.

"Something's bugging me, lad. Why did you do it?" Fraser asked, trying to drop the formal edge he carried the first time they met.

"Look, I didn't do it," Harold replied, frustrated.

In the silence that followed, Harold watched an old woman intently staring at a young girl peddling matches to some noble in a suede black top hat.

"Right. Yes, I forgot."

Fraser looked at a grubby old notepad that he had filled with illiterate scribbling about the case before finally settling on his notes from their first meeting and continuing.

"It was William Bailey that started the fire. You do know they found him dead over a week ago and buried him at Saint Paul's?"

"I even watched his funeral procession myself. Now tell me, before you went to work the night in question, had you been chased by the dragon, perhaps?" Frances asked flatly.

To start with, Harold did not realize what the inspector meant, and it took some moments of silence before Harold remembered reading about a new fad in the city. Called "being chased by the dragon," it was a form of opium abuse that had arrived with the influx of smugglers since the war's end. It was some bard's humor hinting that this drug was a new blight on the city.

"I have never used opium," Harold replied to deaf ears.

It was true. Harold wasn't even that hard a drinker and stuck only to ale to avoid the foul-tasting water drawn up from the well close to his father's home. It was becoming common to try the fancy spirits being shipped in from across the sea that had the power to blister wood and bleach clothing, but Harold rarely touched the stuff.

"Then how else do you explain a dead man walking into a bar? It sounds like the setup to a bad joke."

"I–"

"Then you claim he set fire to it and walked away down the street. Now, I've been in this job for twenty-five years, and this is the best story I've ever heard," Francis interrupted, as he sat looking at Harold expectantly.

Harold knew what he had seen, even if it did not make sense. He was sure he was right, and the more Harold thought of it, the more convinced he was that it had been William Bailey.

It was not unheard of for mages to dabble in necromancy. It was banned even by the Tower itself. and no one would dare openly use magic in the city anymore, but that did not mean there were not little pockets of resistance to the imposed laws.

"I don't know. Perhaps he had a brother. If it wasn't him – but it looked like him – maybe it was a renegade mage," Harold argued, trying to convince himself as much as the inspector.

"Now, that could be the case, but–" The inspector was interrupted as the cart hit something in the road, jolting it forward.

Harold smashed his already sore head against the painted black pine interior and the force of the impact sent Francis flying to his side of the carriage. He bounced from the wall and knocked hard against the floor with a crunching sound that could only be breaking bone.

"What the hell's going on out there?!" the Inspector bellowed from his slumped position on the floor. His voice sounded forced, and his nose was bloodied.

"Someone jumped out in front of the horses. We hit the curb trying to dodge the imbecile," a muffled voice called back.

Suddenly, Harold could hear screaming and the sound of running footsteps receding into the distance. Shortly after, there followed a second smaller judder to the cart and a commotion which sounded like the two specials grappling with someone outside.

Frances, who had pulled himself up from the floor and was watching through the hatch, suddenly bent double. His face paled as he covered his mouth.

The vomit escaped from around the edges of his fingers as he slammed the door open and fell out into the street.

Staring in amazement at the scene before his eyes, Harold saw William ram Frances against the coach's side. The attack came so swiftly, Frances had no time to call out.

William bit down hard into the inspector's neck and as he came up, his face was coated in blood. William looked straight at Harold. *What madness would drive a man to do such a thing?*

Harold did not have time to consider before he was out of the coach and running.

Harold had not gone far before he wanted to look back to see if he was being chased but was too scared of what he might see.

His fear kept him going despite his aches and pains. His vision was blurry from his head wound, so he didn't see the girl standing by the side alley. She grabbed him, almost spinning him off his feet, as Harold passed her.

He froze in front of her but could see she shared his fear. She beckoned him to follow her, and they ran together down another side street.

Pale brown walls overhung above their heads. The street had a gully running down its center, and debris cluttered every inch of the road.

Washing lines ran between the buildings, the hanging gray linen slapping at them as they ran past.

They fled down side streets, followed by side roads, darting over main roads, dodging past market stalls and barely missed a child playing with his hoop. Kicking the wooden ring from his legs, they finally darted into another alley. Harold's lungs felt like they would give out at any moment. Suddenly the girl stopped to fumble with some keys.

Spinning around, Harold gazed up the alleyway back onto the main street where there was still no sign of William. He thanked the Creator.

Feeling a tug on his arm, Harold followed the girl into the house. She quickly slammed the door shut and bolted it behind him. Harold slid down the wall until he sat on the floor, panting.

"Thank you." Harold said instinctively as the girl had helped him, a convict, to escape.

After a moment of catching his breath, Harold asked, "Why did you help me?" He sounded ungrateful, but he was more in shock as to why she had risked her life after what William had done, not questioning its ethics.

"You don't recognize me, do you?" she asked. "The other night, not far from the docks, you gave me money and told me to head home," she said, without the slur of alcohol he had heard the previous time.

She was the prostitute Harold had seen before, in what felt like another lifetime. With her bruising faded, Harold realized she was much older than he'd first thought. She had aged well for a working girl and Harold wondered what her story was, not for the first time. She had to be closer to his age, but she had kept a youthful gleam to her skin that was not common for the local tarts.

"I do, but that doesn't explain why you waited for me," Harold said in a half-truth.

He felt a slight pang of guilt, as Harold knew if the tables had been reversed, he would not have waited for her. After he had given her the money, Harold had not even spared a second thought for the young girl – or young woman, as she had turned out to be.

Without the bruising, she looked almost sweet and innocent, and Harold found himself intrigued by her, almost forgetting the horrors he had just witnessed. He did not believe in love at first sight, but he could not deny his heart fluttered and not only from the exhaustion of the escape.

He brushed the feeling off under the pretense that she had just saved his life, but that did not mean that his heart slowed any as they rested from the run back to her home on the Knoll.

"I saw you that night and could tell you didn't have bad in those eyes. Whatever the guard had you for was wrong. Anyway, I couldn't just let that mad man get you. I have seen a few things in my time, but never anyone that bloody barking. Let's leave it to the city guards now, eh?" she said, showing a strength of character Harold had never imagined her tiny frame could hold. "I meant to ask you, but you ran off so quickly. Why did you give me that money the other night? That was a lot a coin to cough up without turning a trick for you."

"If I am truly honest with you, I thought you were little more than a child." Harold answered, too tired to think of an excuse, rather than the truth. His mind was spinning with what had just happened.

"Ah, so you just wanted to get a youngling off the street for a night. Well, bless your cottons. Aye, I do look young. Plenty a man pays more for me for just that reason. They like the little ones you see. Sick bastards, the lot of them! But it puts food on my table and shoes on my feet," she replied, impressed at Harold's generosity.

"Thank you for saving me," Harold offered by way of changing the subject. He paused before asking. "What is your name?" Right there and then, she was the only person who did not think Harold was a murderer or want to kill him. Harold needed someone to console himself with, and whoever this girl was, she had a strength that drew Harold in like a moth to a flame.

"Muriel Smith, if you must know, but to most people I will be whoever they pay me to be – that is, if they even bother to want a name. Some men prefer not to even think of us working girls as people, and like stray dogs, don't give us names. You are an odd one. What do I call you then, odd one? What's your name and why were you arrested?" she asked with a smile.

"I'm not that odd, and my name is Harold Spinks. The reason I was arrested is that they blamed me for the fire at the Queens last night. No … it may have even been the night before," Harold said, realizing he had no idea how long he had been in the hospital.

"Try four nights back, and you might be closer. So, you do it?" she asked so bluntly, it forced Harold to smile.

"No." That was all that Harold could answer, not wanting to go into the details again. She was one person who did not want him locked up and Harold wanted to keep it that way.

"Didn't think so; you don't seem the type. It was that other guy, right? The one that attacked you? Makes sense that no one goes after the specials like that without reason. I saw it all. There was something not right about him. The cart hit him square on – should have damn near killed him – but he just got up and attacked those city guards. You were lucky, you know that?" the dry huskiness had fallen from her voice without the drink in her belly.

Harold knew he was lucky all right. He was getting used to nearly dying and longed for his boring life back, where the worst he faced was a pricked thumb, bad back, or the odd headache.

"Yeah, lucky, I guess," Harold replied.

"Let's get you cleaned up a bit, shall we? Make yourself at home while I get a brew on. A nip of tea, and then you can wash some of that blood off before you ruin my rug," Muriel said before slipping off into the kitchen.

Harold shook his head in disbelief. This girl had just watched three men being killed, and it did not seem to have traumatized her in the slightest. It would sink in later, but for now, she seemed unaffected by it all.

Harold slowly pulled himself up from the bottom of the door. If William was coming this way, he would have been here by now.

It was a strange feeling to be in her home, modest as it was. There was nothing but a few scattered and worn rugs on the otherwise bare floor. A table in its middle with a bedsheet over its top served, Harold suspected, more than one purpose.

A small set of shoddily-crafted wooden stairs led up from beside the kitchen door, and Harold wondered if her bedroom up there was a place of comfort and security, or if she worked there too.

His mind lingered on the thought of her bedroom longer than was proper, confusing even himself. His feelings toward unfortunates had always been the same; one of pity and disgust, but now Harold started to wonder if his opinions were wrong. This girl had saved his life.

Chapter 9: A Late Order

Thankful as Harold was that William did not follow him, he was still too scared to leave Muriel's, and she seemed more than content to let him stay.

They spent most of the day talking about what had happened. Harold felt he might have been too open with Muriel, but even then, in the first few moments of being with her, Harold knew there was something about her that just made him feel at ease.

He told her everything he knew about what was going on. It was as if he was unable to hold anything back. He wasn't sure if it was because he was so tired that his mouth was running away with him, or because Muriel was pleasing to the eye.

Her red hair washed since the first time Harold saw her, now flowed loosely down over her shoulders. She was petite and slender, and for a woman of her trade moved very elegantly.

It hinted that Harold's suspicions of a hidden past were more plausible than he had first believed. It was the escape from custody, or William, or the horrors he had seen, but Harold felt close to Muriel. He wasn't the type who usually made swift bonds of friendship, though some meet someone for the first time and swear to be friends forever. Harold couldn't think of anyone he called a friend, but for some reason, he could see potential in Muriel that should have taken weeks or even months to develop.

A shiver fluttered from his chest and ran through his spine every time she spoke. Each time he caught her gaze, he turned away, worried she would see his intentions hidden behind his eyes.

Even after the many long hours that passed, and being as open as he had been, Harold had still not told Muriel that a dead man was responsible for the fire.

He'd been so open with everything even telling her about his job at the tailors and the Queens, but couldn't find a way to tell her it was the deceased William who had attacked the carriage. It seemed like madness to him, but any doubt he'd had when he first saw William at the Queens had faded during the attack on the guard cart. The man at the scene of his escape was without any doubt the banker Harold had seen in the paper.

His wounds had all but gone, leaving no question in Harold's mind that he must have used magic. He must have some tie to the Tower. Necromancy, or some other spell to bring him back from the dead – whatever it was – he was dangerous and a stone-cold killer.

Once Muriel changed Harold's bandages with some rags from her sheets – with expertise that Harold found surprising – he said his goodbyes. He was scared of William or the guard finding him, but he needed to check on his father to warn him before O'Brien's thugs got to him.

There was an uncomfortable moment as Harold left with Muriel standing just inches from him. Harold guessed because of the way she earned her living she had no fear of closeness, but the feel of the warmth emanating from her stirred something in Harold he wasn't sure how to deal with.

Harold looked down to say goodbye and felt his lip trembling for the touch of hers. He did not give in as he was not sure if she felt the same. He didn't know how she could. As they had only met a few hours before, he felt stupid for feeling the way he did. He questioned his subconscious – what if her kindness was just a ploy to score more money?

Harold hoped not, but it would still have been improper to kiss her, as they had only just met, and Harold was suffering from shock.

As Harold left Muriel's home, the fresh air outside, bitterly cold as it was, faded the image of her soft lips from his mind and helped him make sense of everything that had happened and allowed him to prioritize.

The walk to his father's was difficult. His nerves were on edge as he watched every shadow on the way, worried that it would be either a constable ready to arrest him or William come to kill him. Harold didn't know why – it was some kind of intuition – but he was sure after escaping William's path of destruction for a second time, he would see him again.

If Harold avoided either of those fates, there was still the chance that the O'Briens would come to kill him. The odds of him making it home safely were not in his favor, as Harold ducked into an alley between Homefield Avenue and East Street.

Harold watched hidden as two officers chased down an orphan who had pick-pocketed some well-dressed man who was still shouting from the other end of the avenue. It was a welcome distraction from his own mind. For someone who had always loved daydreaming, Harold wanted to keep his mind occupied with anything but his thoughts at that moment.

Other than watching the orphan give the guard the slip, it was an uneventful journey as Harold passed the many shades of white and brown that made up the northern end of Oakenfall's buildings.

It was not until Harold stood outside his father's house, with his hand quaking above the knocker, that he could relax even slightly.

Harold knew his parents would either be worried sick about his disappearance or maddened by the unattended shop. Harold presumed he was trying to find some light heartedness in all the darkness in a twisted way, but it now seemed amusing to him that a few nights ago getting that order ready, had seemed so important. Now, Harold could not care less about making clothes.

He dropped the fish-shaped knocker with a gentle clap and waited for an answer. When none came, Harold felt the panic rise inside him. What if the O'Briens had arrived before him? His parents may lie dead inside his father's home. Thinking of his parents' death sent a sudden image of the city guard inspector at the roadside flashing across his mind. It was followed by a cold numbness that stole his breath – it left him feeling faint.

It was the first time Harold had seen someone die. In only a few days, Harold had been present while everyone in the Queens had burned to death, and then he had seen the chunk ripped out of an inspector's neck while two, already dead, specials slumped against the reins.

Harold froze outside the door with his stomach churning over as his mind raced. With everything happening so fast, Harold had barely had time to think on it – even while talking to Muriel, it seemed like a nightmare. All the while he was telling her his story, he had hoped he would wake up and find himself slumped in the chair with a reel of thread in his lap and a sore thumb from the long hours of darning that had sent him to sleep.

It had taken the cold and returning home to make it real. Once Harold was able to think clearly, he realized it was unlikely that the O'Briens had paid a visit. The door was locked shut, and it was late, very late.

In fact, it was well after two in the morning, and his father would be asleep. His mother would have gone up to bed, leaving him sitting by the fire in his slippers. His pipe would have smoked itself out on the arm of the chair and whatever book he had been reading would have fallen to the floor, stalling time in that fantasy world.

Harold knocked again, a little louder this time, and heard movement from inside.

His father came to the door, the sleep still evident in his eyes, confirming Harold's suspicions. His father was wearing his red smoking jacket and his thinning hair on his wrinkled head fluffed at one side, showing that he had been asleep for at least a few hours.

The dents in his face matched the embroidery of the chair his father always sat in. He looked sicker than when Harold had last seen him; the flu was obviously taking a lot out of him.

"Harry, where have you been?" James asked, his voice weak and labored.

His breathing worried Harold terribly. It was so harsh, like air escaping from one of those new-fangled Dwarfen steam engines, but before Harold had time to answer, his father looked around the darkened Greenway area around them and stepped aside.

"Come in, come in, you'll catch your death of cold out there," he said, as he turned and shuffled down the hallway, and Harold noticed how much older he looked.

It seemed like old age had caught up with him in only a few days. Harold followed closely behind his father and he could hear the rattle in his father's chest even over the sound of their footsteps.

As Harold followed his father, he noted that nothing in his father's home had changed. It had after all been only a few nights since Harold was last there, but to him, it felt so much longer.

The aged, thin, golden, and red carpet with its decorative ivy still ran the length of the hallway. It had been handmade in one of the cottage industries faltering in the wake of the toxin-spewing machines that could produce hundreds of rugs in a third of the time.

The wallpaper, a pattern of little flowers in baskets, shone in blues and pinks across the walls, stained yellow from tobacco smoke. Some of its sheets had begun to peel from their top-most corners. His father was too old, and Harold too busy to replace them.

Entering the sitting room, his father headed straight for his chair. Similar in design to the wallpaper, it was now yellowed and threadbare. The arms and legs were dark mahogany and matched the rest of the furniture in the room. There were two large bookcases filled to the brim, and a table between made from wood that had been cut from sacred oak and stained before the Dragons had been vanquished for the first time 128 years prior.

It showed that their family had been prosperous once with ties to Northholm. Harold did not know to which side of the battle his linage belonged. He suspected purely by their stature and strength that they had been in the invading Iron Giant army that had settled in the city, but his family never spoke of it, and Harold was born after the war had ended.

It had been commonplace for some of the Poles to take a second name to try and integrate with Oakenfallians.

It was then that Harold noticed it. The vase on the reading table was empty. To most people, that would not have been something of note, but his father had kept it filled with fresh flowers every day since he and his mother had married.

If it was allowed to sit empty, then his father was in much worse health than Harold thought.

Harold walked across the sitting room to his chair, a lesser-used copy of his father's. It sat opposite by the fireplace, which itself echoed the riches that once filled this home.

Although the house was close to the Execution Fields memorial, the place the late barbarian king Ingaild first displayed his might in executing many of Oakenfall's heroes, it was within the poor parts of the city. Thus it was built of wood and clay. It was not a shabby house and stood as a marking of a new class of men, not nobles and not poor but working men – men of industry – a class between the two. A middle class and as such, it showed both sides of life, luxury, and necessity, without the aid of servants.

"So, where have you been, Harry? Your mother's been worried sick," James asked while he fumbled, trying to load his pipe with fresh tobacco.

The doctors said the stuff was good for you, but Harold was sure they were wrong. Harold could not see how breathing in a weed was good for the body, but his father smoked it regardless of his protests.

"Dad, please believe me–" Harold said, before explaining anything.

Harold really needed someone to believe him and, although he had told Muriel about the fire, the visit from O'Brien's hitmen and the city guard, Harold had left out the fact that it was a dead man who was responsible. Harold needed someone to know, someone who would believe him.

"Believe what?" James replied, his voice muffled by the long shaft of the ivory head that hung from his lips. It was shaped to resemble a lion and had been in the family for years. Harold had no idea where it came from and only knew what a lion was by its carvings. A trade ship or explorer must have brought it back to Oakenfall at some time in the past.

"Friday night, when I left the shop, I went to the Queens as normal. It was burned down–" Harold said, starting with just the basics.

"I know. It was in the papers. Your mother has already got you burned to a crisp and buried in an unmarked grave. You know what she's like. You should have got word to us."

His father always had a habit of interrupting Harold, and it drove him mad at the best of times, let alone now, but Harold hid his frustration as he continued trying to tell him what had happened.

"I was taken to hospital–" Harold continued before he was interrupted again. He didn't get far before a plume of smoke was sent his way as his father carried on talking.

"I guessed that, boy. The bandages give it away. Such terrible stitch-craft on them though. I wonder if we could offer to do them better," he said, and it made Harold smile a little inside. Even as sick as his father was, he was still looking to increase trade to their family shop.

"Father, if you let me finish without butting in, you wouldn't need to ask so many questions. Please, just let me finish," Harold said, a little out of turn.

His father nodded, but Harold could see the scowl even through his reddened cheeks. James did not like the fact Harold had become a man and his equal, not just the boy he could take his belt to if Harold spoke out. He had not been an abusive parent, far from it. It is just that he held discipline and respect at the head of all he did and had brought Harold up to do the same.

"The city guard came to the hospital. They blame me for the fire," Harold said.

"Preposterous!" James exclaimed. "Harry, I won't have it!" he yelled, and Harold knew he was serious, as he put the pipe down.

"It wasn't just the city guard, Father. The smugglers from the docks, the O'Briens, threatened to come here, Father," Harold explained, ignoring his outburst.

Harold hoped his father would take his mother and leave. Oakenfall suddenly started to feel very small and unsafe, but Harold should have known how stubborn the old fool would be, and it took less than a second for him to show it.

"Let them come, there is still life in this old dog yet," Harold's father said, before choking heavily and ramming his sleeve against his mouth.

His body convulsed with the effort, and when he came back up to look at Harold, his eyes were glazed and watery.

"The guard arrested me, father. I was being taken to the courthouse. Before we got there, the horse and cart were attacked by the same person who set fire to the Queens. He killed the three guard officers escorting me and would have killed me, too, if I had stayed, but I ran," Harold said.

He hoped he sounded innocent because, despite being in his twenties, Harold still feared his father's wrath, even though he could barely lift his weight now. His bushy gray and white eyebrows wrinkled. Harold was not sure if it was from confusion, frustration, or just plain surprise. What stunned Harold more was that he didn't reply, he just sat there looking at Harold.

"A woman called Muriel helped me escape," Harold explained.

"Who's Muriel?" James said, his breath still short from the coughing fit.

"She's a working girl from the harbor area, father. She saw the fire at the dock and was there when William attacked the guard officers. She grabbed me and helped me escape."

"Sounds like she has something to do with it all. You can't trust those pinch pricks. I take it she was the one to bandage your head, again? That explains the cheap work. We best get them off soon, lad. God only knows what diseases she has. You checked your purse since you left there?" he said with an air of discrimination only afforded to those with means.

The question annoyed Harold, but his hand slipped down to his trouser pocket, feeling for his wallet, which was still there. Only a couple of days before, Harold would have shared his father's opinion, but the girl had risked her life to save his.

"She's not a thief," Harold said, thankful that it was true. "Anyway, I'm sure she's nothing to do with it. I saw who it did. I even recognized the man."

114

"Then why didn't you tell the guard?" his father asked.

James was unaware of how corrupt the city had become. He thought it was as prosperous as when William Boatswain was governor after the war. He still thought the city guard did what was just and right. In other words, Harold's father was a man who refused to see the downfall of the city he had fought to join.

"I did. They didn't believe me. The man is dead, Father," Harold said bluntly, wishing he had found a better way of saying it, but how many different ways are there of saying you saw a dead man running around as if he were still alive?

"What the hell do you mean – the man is dead? You said you escaped. Did you see him die? Someone shot him with a bow; serve him bloody right. Bet he was one of those immigrants. You mark my words; all those elves from the Alienage are trouble," James grumbled.

Harold thought to himself that his father's racism was as bad as the inspector's had been before Harold had watched him die.

"No, Father. I mean, he was found dead last week." Harold said, knowing it sounded insane.

If Harold had been his father, he would have put it down to the head wound. James's gaze froze, and Harold could see he was investigating him, studying his face for any sign of madness, but he knew Harold had never been one to believe in fairy tales. Hell, as a child, Harold did not even believe in monsters under the bed.

"Are you sure, son?" James asked his tone quiet.

The last and only time Harold had seen his father like this was when their dog had died, and

James had to tell him when Harold was about five or six.

"Yes, I am, but then I also know it is not possible." That was his honest answer.

"Sounds like total codswallop, lad, but I believe you. There is more to life than man knows, Harry. When I was a boy, I swear I saw a woman walking down our lawn, all dressed in white she was. She got as far as the stream that used to run toward the cliff and then just vanished. I got one hell of a hiding from my old man when I told him. I promised myself then that if anyone ever came to me with a story too unbelievable to be true, I would give them the benefit of the doubt." James had never told Harold that before.

When he was younger, Harold's father was a strong man – in every sense of the word – and Harold guessed sharing ghost stories did not fit in with who he was.

Harold's father flicked the last of his pipe into the fire before laying it on the armchair's side.

"It's late," he said, as the sounds of Saint Anne's bell tower echoed across the city. After counting the chimes, he continued.

"Rather, it's early – three already. We'd better be heading to bed. Take my advice, Harry, and steer clear of the devil's work. I don't want any son of mine getting involved with walking corpses, thank you very much, and I'll have no more talk about it. Once my chest has cleared up a bit, Harold, I will help sort things out with the city guard. Until then, just stay home. I'll get your mother to get Janet's boy to mind the shop for us until this is over," he said, before struggling to his feet once more and walking out of the room.

Harold sat there for a while longer watching the fire flicker, but he was tired and went up to bed shortly afterward.

Harold had not slept well for days and expected to collapse as soon as he crawled into bed. He did not, however. He lay there thinking about never having had the courage to make the final move out of his childhood home.

Harold knew his father wanted him married, but housing was expensive, and Harold could not afford it alone. The fact was that Harold had never found the right girl. They were either too self-centered, or too typically middle class, or below his standing, and Harold knew his father would never allow that.

Now with his father sick, Harold could not see himself leaving any time soon. As if to reinforce the point, James exploded into another choking fit down the hall.

He would have to convince him to send for the doctor in the morning, Harold thought to himself as he drifted off to sleep.

Chapter 10: Daybreak

If Harold had hoped for a return to normality the following day, he was to be disappointed. As he sat down for a breakfast of salted oats in water, he took the opportunity to review the papers gathered on the table in the days he had been otherwise engaged.

The broadsheets lived up to their name of Penny Dreadfuls and were filled edge-to-edge with news of the dead. There were rumors of a mage uprising after a missive had been captured coming from the Mages Tower, but this didn't hold Harold's interest for long.

There was an expertly drawn recreation of a shop Harold recognized. The picture was of one Mildred Köln, left brutally murdered during the early hours.

Mildred was a young girl whose mutilated body had been found outside the butcher's shop where she had been visiting to collect scraps. Harold continued perusing the papers, looking for any more references or sightings of William since the fire at the Queens.

It did not take Harold long to see the theme and realize that Mildred was not the only prostitute found dead in the last week. They numbered more than he could count on his fingers. Paper after paper described the bodies being found, disfigured like leaves in the fall.

Harold's fingers found the new paper, one that had only been hammered by the brass font at the printing press a few hours before he returned home. *The Times* had received a new story of more bodies found. Harold soon found out why William had not followed him to Muriel's the night before.

A whole brothel – clients included – was added to the list of those found dead. The broadsheet described how someone had managed to subdue all the occupants and feed on them in a cannibalistic way.

The reports included the information that the vicious murders had all taken place after an attack on a guard transit cart transporting a known arsonist who had subsequently escaped.

The guards were asking any witnesses to come forward, and Harold knew then that the whole city thought that it was him who was responsible for these horrible and most heinous of crimes.

Not knowing of his fame in the papers, William was losing who he was. After he had heard Paul talk of his family, it had sent him into a rage, and he had wanted to rip the little balding man limb from limb, but he knew that Paul was his only hope of finding a cure.

He had skulked out into the street in a rage, and the darkness had taken him. The hunger finally won, and William did not awake inside his own body again until after the incident with the guard cart.

William crept around the city streets, searching for somewhere to hide and fight the hunger, again filled with remorse.

Everything was becoming blurry for him, and he knew that somewhere before he made it back to his hideaway in the sewers, he must have crossed paths with Mildred Köln who had made the mistake of trying to arouse him, in the hope of making a last bit of money before heading home to bed. Instead, she ended up satisfying his hunger.

William had waited by her cooling body, distraught at what he had done. He was not pure evil

– not yet anyway – and he wept for the young girl, knowing he had taken his youngest victim yet.

Her body lay in the gutter, with what little blood William had not fed on, trickling away. William had been there when the match girl and old woman had found the corpse.

He prowled toward the girl, wanting to feed again. He moved slowly so as not to startle his prey and could hear the girl's heart beating. The sensation excited the beast within his chest, but, before William managed to grab his new victim, a crowd had started to gather on the empty street. The girl's scream must have roused those from the houses close by.

William waited while watching the sketch artist from *The Times* setting up for the moment to be captured. The child, promising such a sweet feast, was worth waiting for, but William was left disappointed. The girl was taken inside the butchers by the city guard who wanted to talk to her, and William could not wait any longer.

Escaping the scene before the hunger drove him to make a mistake in front of so many people, he ran into the other prostitutes on their way home. As daylight approached, his strength was weakening, and he persuaded them into the side alley with the promise of money.

They died easily, and something was satisfying about feeding on their blood. Unlike the sewer workers or the damnable rodents, William felt passion inside, a sexual excitement at their weakening murmurs.

This drive, combined with the thrill and peak of energy inside, led William to the brothel.

After crawling out of whatever sewer grate he had hidden in during the day, William waited in the streets opposite the brothel, his back resting against the wall. He remembered it from his old life, having visited once before he married.

He waited in the growing shadows, patiently biding his time until the sun's last rays fell out of view. He knew he had to be fast, strong too. There would be men inside who would try to fight back, and William was sure the women would not give in to his hunger willingly.

He had learned already that the beast inside was so much stronger once the light had faded. The time outside gave him a chance to think about what Paul had said. He even spared a fleeting thought for those he'd killed, but he mostly thought of his family.

Why was it that he could not even picture what they looked like anymore? It seemed to him that they were shadows, or hidden behind water, their images distorted. Every time his mind tried to focus on them, the image warped and flickered away. William had forgotten how long it had been since he had last seen them. He gave up on this trail of thought, the darkness swept over him like a drug, and William made for the door.

The longer the Rakta Ishvara lived inside him, the more like a wild beast William became. He shared more traits with the lion Harold's father's ivory pipe represented than the man he once was.

Chapter 11: S.W.A.L.K.

Unsurprisingly, the disorganized and less than motivated city guard had not come knocking on Harold's door. More shockingly, the O'Briens hadn't either – and neither had William.

This brief respite was welcomed by Harold and even with the horrors he read each morning in the papers, his mind allowed him to slip into the lie that life could return to normal.

It was not as cold as it had been in the last couple of days, and firewood was not cheap. However, Harold could not sit in darkness, and the ashes from the fire the night before were barely smoldering. As Harold stood to take a log from the brass bin at the side of the hearth, there was a knock at the door.

For a second, Harold suspected it was the city guard and prepared to run, but there was only one way in and out of the family home, and that was the front door. He lowered the log back into the bin, – not before the thought of using it as a weapon crossed his mind – but he was not a skilled fighter and didn't want to incriminate himself any more than fate already had.

The knock came again, and Harold had no choice but to make his way to the front door and open it, or else his mother or father would.

Relief flooded over him like the ocean flooding a beach on a stormy night when Harold saw the uniform of a postal worker. He got just one letter, written in a hand Harold did not recognize at the time but since grew to know well.

As Harold closed the door, he knew that he had to leave the house soon. The next time a knock came rapping against the woodwork, he might not be so lucky. Today it had been the post horse's hooves that had stopped their clatter outside the Spinks's household; next time, it could be the prison cart.

Shutting the door, his hands reached for the letter-opener and prized the wax seal off the brown paper. Harold looked at the crumpled letter. It was from an unexpected woman, someone Harold had never met, and who in the normal turn of events would not even know of his existence – William's widow.

Harold wanted to throw it into the fire, but he did not have the heart. Her hardship only added to his heartache. Nightmares of William had replaced his daydreams of the cottage – fate seemed intent not to let their entangled stories separate.

Harold had no idea how William's wife had found his address, and his only guess was that she somehow had access to city guard reports.

He came to this conclusion as the letter explained that she had read about Harold's testimony claiming that William had set the fire. Harold stopped and folded the letter up before reading it to its end. He began to panic.

Harold had been planning to wait for his father to approach the city guard, hoping his father's standing and the honors he had received fighting the dragons would still hold enough weight for Harold to get a fair trial.

However, Harold's father was weakening by the day, and without aid from the mages, there was a real possibility that the flu might take him.

The letter was the final straw that bore down like the weight of many full kegs. Taking the day's paper under his arm, Harold made his way to his father's bedside to read him the day's news.

His father had become far too weak to manage the stairs or the cold of the dawn, so Harold sat at the end of the bed with the curtains pulled closed and read to him, the letter burning away like hot coals in his breast pocket.

Finishing the paper, and with his father falling back to sleep, Harold left him and made his way back to sit alone in the lounge. There he started to stoke a fresh fire from within the ashes of the previous night.

If even William's widow was now on Harold's heels, he had to leave the family home, but he had few choices for where to hide.

The shop or the family cottage in Port Lust? But it was Muriel that Harold wanted to go and stay with. He had to see her again, and anyway, Harold had promised that he would go back to see her.

Alone, after taking the letter from his pocket, Harold started to re-read it.

It was a long letter, and Harold could see from the smudged ink that the paper had been moistened by tears as it was written.

Harold read the letter over and over, his tired eyes making sense of it a little at a time. One line stood out – it said that she had seen William and she knew that he was alive.

She had seen William in a newspaper drawing of the crowd outside the butcher's shop. Harold was relieved that someone else believed him and could confirm what Harold already suspected.

Harold dropped the letter and scrambled for the paper on his father's armchair and flicked through the pages until he found the picture.

True enough, William was there. His cold eyes seemed to stare right through the page into

Harold's own. The artist's charcoal strokes had them recreated perfectly.

Harold dropped the newspaper, feeling an uncomfortable dry uneasiness and slumped into the chair.

He closed his eyes. Someone else knew William was back from the dead. Her letter begged Harold to explain what was happening; she wanted answers for her children.

It was hard for Harold to remember William had been human and had children, as he now seemed nothing but a monster.

Harold could not imagine what could be going through the minds of William's children, but he prayed William's wife kept them protected from the truth.

Her words hurt him so much that Harold wanted to hurl the letter into the fire there and then, but he could not. Instead, he folded it and put it in his inside pocket again, planning to reply one day and explain as much as possible.

The letter mentioned that William's body should have been resting in the catacombs of Saint Anne's, but that bypassed him – as it had when the inspector had mentioned it before.

Harold already had too much on his mind, and although educated he was far from detective-bright. He was, after all is said and done, a tailor's son.

Chapter 12: All Moved Out

Harold knew the city guard would be looking for him, and the letter from William's wife made him realize people knew where to find him.

It surprised him that he had managed to spend a few days at home without the guard battering down the door, but it should not have shocked him too much if he spared any thought to the matter. After everything was said and done, the city guards were little more than rogues with badges. Apart from a few rare and fame-seeking heroes behind a badge, they would not risk their lives for a pound a week. As they blamed Harold for so many bloody and brutal murders, it would be sometime before they darkened his doorstep.

Harold took advantage of his reprieve by thinking about his next move in the twisted game of chess he had been dragged into unwillingly by William.

The board was set against him and all the pieces were black. Harold could feel himself getting trapped in a corner.

It fell on him to prove his innocence, and the only way Harold could think to do that was to find William. If Harold could somehow get William to admit to his crimes, then he could go back to his ordinary life.

His first task was to get out of his father's home, but it would be difficult to say his goodbyes with James's poor health.

Harold may seem cold and unsympathetic, but he loved his family, and he knew the words he said could be his last chance to say goodbye.

Harold told his mother where he was going and made her promise not to tell anyone. She agreed without question.

Harold looked into her face, and he could see the beauty she'd once had masked behind cold eyes. Unmoving and showing no real emotion, her face reminded Harold of the porcelain masks theatre actors wore on stage. Harold heard a snivel from her as she turned away from him, and her shoulders sagged, but Harold knew she was a strong woman. Her mask was there for a reason – his mother would not let him or James find out how shattered she was at the prospect of losing her loved ones.

Harold thought about going to her and holding her but if he did her resolve might fail and she would fall into a sobbing mess in his arms. As much as he wanted to comfort her, Harold knew that he had to go now, or never be able to.

After leaving his father's room, Harold made the short journey into his room, all the while fighting the tears trying to build up in his own eyes. He tossed his travel bag onto the bed, and suddenly found himself filled with renewed urgency and began gathering what few clothes he could carry.

Harold placed in it two pairs of tan trousers, a couple of clean shirts – one white, one off-gray – his spare tanned tunic and his top hat made from the softest of rabbit fur.

It lay uneasily on the top of the pile. Harold was almost ready to leave when he remembered that he had less than a farthing in his coin purse.

Harold pulled the travel bag shut and dropped it to the floor with a thud that shook the old floorboards, and for a moment, Harold half expected it to go crashing down into the lounge below.

Once he realized this was not going to happen, he slid the mattress aside, revealing a small fluff covered satchel. Harold was relieved that his savings were still there. For the last year and a half, he had been putting aside a little money each week. Even throughout the hard times, he kept quiet about his nest-egg and had managed to set aside thirty pounds.

Harold needed the money if he ever planned to leave home, but now, he doubted he would still be free to walk the streets, let alone buy land of his own. Reluctantly, and with more than a pang of guilt he took the satchel from its resting place, and ended his daydream of leaving the nest.

Harold sat and counted out half of the money; he gave it to his mother before he left. The money, Harold explained to his mother, who had at first refused to take it, was to maintain the house while the shop was shut. Harold knew she needed it and was relieved when she finally accepted it.

He hid the rest of the savings under his hat and went out into the busy morning. Harold decided to stick to the main roads as he figured that fighting his way through the crowds was his best way to remain hidden.

It sounded a flawed plan, but it was often harder to see something in plain view than something hidden.

It was out of his way, but Harold stopped by the shop. It looked so empty, so void of life, even the mice seemed to have deserted it. Since Harold locked its door on the night of the fire, the only sign of movement inside a building usually bustling with life was a spider's web.

Harold found himself impressed by the speed of the little creature as the web already stretched from one of the mannequins in the center of the display to the other side of the window. The fine threads and almost perfect lacing were of far better quality than he or his father could ever hope to create. Harold wondered if they could hire the little fella. It made him smile, if only for a second. Darting inside the shop, Harold wrote out a small card which stated, "Closed due to sickness in the family." He left it in the shop window, being careful not to damage the spider's hard work.

The card was an explanation for their sudden disappearance. Part of him still hoped that things would return to normal one day and that they could keep on the right side of their clients.

Janet's boy would not be there for a few days and Harold hoped that the little message scribbled in his hand would be enough to give him something to return to when all this was over.

That done and the store locked up, Harold left it in charge of his new eight-legged friend and made for Muriel's house, hoping that she would be home.

The journey was sparingly uneventful and gave Harold time to rest his exhausted mind.

He spent most of the journey dreaming about a little charcoal-colored rat he had seen giving a rat-catcher the slip as it darted under one of the many bridges crossing the canals on Trade Road.

The daydream over, Harold stood on Muriel's doorstep with a lump in his throat. Harold prayed that she would welcome him to stay. If she did not, he had no idea where he would go.

The image of the summer house flashed across his mind. Port Lust was not all that far – Harold could escape there and start a new life by the sea. It was not the first time Harold had thought of fleeing the city since all this had started. He was trying to be a hero, and it really didn't suit him. *He should just go*, he thought to himself as he stood with his hand hovering above the knocker.

Harold made up his mind he would leave the city and flee. After all, if he could not even bring himself to knock on Muriel's door, how could he save the city?

Port Lust it was to be.

He turned his back to make his way out of town when the door opened behind him.

Muriel stood in its opening with her bright red hair caught in the wind rattling down the alleyway. She wore the same dress as before.

It was definitely a summer dress, and not designed for the cold of Thresh, the cut was short around her bosom, and a narrow belt was pulled tight around her slim waist. It was plain, a dull off-white, and showed signs of age. Its woolen outline had begun to bubble around the edges, and the once tight-knit pattern looked weathered and loose. The small lace leaves on the trims had stretched and looked more like misshaped palm trees.

Harold felt his nerves tingle and run rampant within his stomach as his eyes traced her outline. These observations all happened in a moment and Harold prayed she had not noticed his scrutiny. His eyes ran back over her curves and toward her eyes, but not before her skin had puckered into goosebumps in the passing seconds. She smiled and greeted him.

"Harold. I'm sorry, I didn't hear you knocking. You're lucky, I happened to be passing the door and saw your shadow in the glass." She shot him a warming smile, and Harold was glad that she seemed happy to see him again.

"I didn't knock," Harold replied, cursing himself as soon as the words left his lips.

The moment felt too awkward and Harold was not thinking straight. He was confused and focused on why it felt cumbersome. The last time Harold had felt like this was for Massey Jane when he was still in school shorts.

"Oh, good. Then you've not been there long," Muriel said with a playful twang to her words.

She smiled again and Harold noticed for the first time she wore makeup on her lips, something most prostitutes could not afford, and if they did, Harold could not think of a time they would need to use it.

It looked freshly put on, and Harold briefly wondered if she had put it on just for him. Her tone of voice told him that she knew Harold had stood outside for a long time.

It had been at least ten minutes or so as Harold tried to pluck up the courage to knock at the door. Muriel giggled at the silence, and his heart fluttered, missing a beat. The noise was so young and fresh.

"Can I come in? It's cold out here," Harold asked through quickly reddening cheeks. He felt as flustered as a child.

"Yes, of course, sorry," Muriel replied, flashing him another of her sweet little smiles.

She stepped aside, though not far enough to allow him clear access to her home, and Harold had to brush past her to squeeze through the door.

She was teasing him, clearly able to see Harold was uncomfortable. Harold guessed it came

131

from her line of work that she could see if a man liked her. It was part of her stock and trade.

Walking in front of Muriel, Harold made his way to her lounge and took a seat by the table. Harold should have waited for her to offer him a seat, but he felt so at home there. A quick glance toward the fireplace confirmed his first impression. The room was as cold as ice, and the fire was still bare from his last visit.

"So, you kept your word and came back. I was not sure if I would get to see you again. Glad I have. What's new?" Muriel asked, glancing at the bag as Harold slid it under his feet.

"Have you seen the papers?" Harold asked, taking her attention away from his belongings for the moment.

He wanted to wait for the right time to ask if he could stay for a few nights.

"I've not left the house," Muriel replied, and Harold knew it was because she was too scared after what she had seen.

She was a brave woman, but Harold should have known the sight of three guard officers being ripped apart would have done more damage than it had appeared to.

"What about money, surely you need to work?" Harold asked, realizing it was rude but needing to know.

Muriel had been so desperate for money the first time he had met her, and god only knows what would happen if she did not meet the street charge imposed on her by the O'Briens. The confident smile fell from Muriel's lips, and her gaze fell to her feet.

"It's not safe for a working girl with that thing out there," she said, confirming his hunch that she was as scared as he was.

"I'll get him, I promise," Harold told her, meaning it with all his heart.

Harold had started to develop feelings for Muriel in the few days he had known her and was already willing to throw himself at William just to make her feel safe. That, combined with his overwhelming urge not to rot to death in a prison meant, he'd have to find him anyway.

"How do you plan to do that? You have seen what he can do. Sacellum alive, he would lay a gentleman like you on his arse in seconds," Muriel's reply came quickly, and Harold could see the concern in her eyes.

It was true. Harold was not scrawny because of his job loading barrels, but he had never been a fighter. It left him with no answer to give. Harold had no idea how he would stop William.

"I'll think of something, I promise. I want him gone as much as you do," Harold said, half just to convince himself. "I have a favor to ask of you, though – a big one. The guards are still looking for me. My home is unsafe, and I do not have anyone I can trust but you. I know we have only just met–" Harold did not know how to finish the sentence but thankfully, Muriel interrupted him.

"I saw the bag as you came in. I know what you want. You can stay here, but I have only one room. You can bunk with me upstairs, or you can sleep down here. I have some spare bedding, but it's deathly cold down here at night," Muriel said, showing little preference for either option.

For a moment, Harold saw a sparkle flash across her face again. Harold was not sure if she had really meant for him to sleep upstairs, or if it was a joke. He knew she would be forward if she had really wanted him to bed with her; being shy and a working girl did not go together. However, as much as the thought of sharing a bed with Muriel pleased him, it was not proper and most definitely not appropriate. Harold could not afford to lose himself in the madness that swirled around him.

"I'll stay down here. I have some money for the rent, and you won't have to work until this is over. I will give you sixpence for some firewood too," Harold said trying to sound sincere, but it was for his benefit. The house was freezing, and he could already feel his skin turning purple.

"You don't have to pay," she said, and Harold knew she would have let him stay for free.

That said a lot without the need for words. The girl was an unfortunate, as the city called them. She was a working girl, and for her to allow him to stay for nothing, she must have seen him as a friend at the very least. Putting aside his confusing feelings, Harold was happy that her friendship would be enough for now. At that moment, he needed a friend he could rely on.

"I know, but I want to pay my way," Harold replied, and so it was that he moved into Muriel's house.

The place warmed up quickly with the fire roaring. Even with the price of coal being so high, his sixpence had brought a lot of fuel, and Muriel had taken the initiative to use some of the money to buy some food as well.

Harold sat alone in the lounge, waiting for her to prepare it. If it wasn't for everything going on, Harold thought, he could feel comfortable there.

The smell from the kitchen wafted through, and Harold waited eagerly for the lovely mutton stew, turnips, and fresh bread still warm from the baker's oven.

Harold sat listening to the clattering from the other room. It gave him plenty of time to think. He decided that he would have to find out what brought William back.

Harold had to know what he was before he could stop him. After seeing Muriel risk starvation rather than working the streets for fear of William, Harold knew now that stopping him was more important than proving his innocence.

With the strength William had demonstrated, he would take weeks if not months to catch, and, in that time, he would claim hundreds of victims if Harold didn't do something about him.

Harold could think of only a few places to look for information about what William might be. The occult was not commonly available reading in the city, as most references to magic had been removed in one of the many book burnings instigated by Malcolm Benedict.

Harold personally knew nothing of it. The Devil's Club rumor that the upper classes could pay to join went through his mind. They were a cult that believed they could join the demon that threatened Neeska and had dealings in some horrid acts hidden behind closed doors, but Harold doubted this was anything to do with William.

It was a drinking club and gave bored, rich people something else to waste money on. His only other lead would be the papers; they would know more.

Harold doubted it, though, which led him to think of William's family again. They might have known something, but Harold could not face them; he was just not strong enough.

That left but one other choice he could think of. Harold would need to break into the Greenway Courthouse, to find their reports on both William's death and the incidents since. His heart sank at the thought of what the world had turned him into, but fate had dealt him these cards, and Harold had to play the hand.

Harold would go out and check with *The Times* first thing in the morning. If, as he suspected, that didn't expose William for what he was, Harold would prepare for something that seemed insane – Harold would break into the courthouse.

Chapter 13: A Meeting with Ernest and Neill

As Harold prepared for his first night at Muriel's on the south side of Oakenfall, the cause of his hardships, the Reverend Paul Augustus, was fighting with his demons.

Unlike Harold, whose mind hand began to cement with a purpose, Paul's purpose had begun to falter; his mind was awash with thoughts of his experiment, William, who was lost to him. Worse, the papers were filled with stories of the working girls Paul had experimented on, and now victims that he recognized as the work of the Rakta Ishvara.

Paul had thought that facing his own mortality had been the most haunting thing that would ever face him; he had been wrong. His lack of sleep over the last few weeks was nothing in comparison to the insomnia that plagued him since he'd watched William walk out of Saint Anne's.

Paul had seen the darkness inside William. He recognized it in a memory from the temple that now seemed like a lifetime ago. The guilt ran through him like mold through a blue cheese.

It was not guilt that had prevented him from returning to his home, nor concern of his neighbors overhearing what he was up to – it was fear that William would come back for him. His hovel of a room was not defendable against the Rakta Ishvara.

Paul had turned the catacombs into a fortress designed to weaken William, as all his study had not been for naught.

The catacombs were damp and dark – which would give William strength – but there was only one way in and one way out which could be barred and bulwarked.

With the last of his dwindling strength, Paul had scattered sprigs of the Abrus herb that was volatile to the vampire leech around the stairs making the descent down to the darkness painful for William. It would weaken him, make him manipulatable.

To slow his would-be attacker down even further, Paul had upturned the table he had previously used for his experiments. He pressed it along with two unearthed coffins he had dragged across to the foot of the stairs, the forever sleeping occupants still inside as silent guards.

Paul remained in the catacombs, feeling it was the only safe place for him. His insanity and paranoia had peaked to the point where he now feared the city would learn of his secrets. It had not just been his home that Paul had avoided. He had barely left his sanctuary since William's attack.

He continued to carry out sermons from the church above, so as not to raise suspicion, but as soon as they were over, he scurried back into the dark and clambered over his sleeping watchmen, and sat in silence waiting and watching. So afraid of leaving the walled stone safety of the church had Paul become, he even had to send an altar boy tasked with going to find one of O'Brien's associates.

The young boy found the two brothers about the Greenway Courthouse. They were still busy looking for Harold after he gave them the slip at the hospital while being escorted away by the guards.

When they found out that the man named William that Harold had sent them after was a dead man, they had been infuriated. It meant, in their eyes, that Harold was most definitely guilty.

They would have killed him, and Harold should have been dead long before he made it to Muriel's, but as it had many times for Harold, fate contorted around him, not wanting its plaything to expire.

The morning Harold had been readying to leave for Muriel's, was the day the altar boy had found the O'Brien brothers. They were only a few doors down from Harold's home.

The boy explained to the thugs that Paul wanted to see them, that he had a job for them to do. Remembering the tidy profit they had made from their last interaction with the priest, the brothers concluded that the tailor's son could wait. They sent the boy ahead to tell the priest they would be with him soon.

The boy had rushed back to tell Paul his achievements, feeling sure it would buy him a coin or two. But Oakenfall had become cruel, and Paul had killed him off quickly, bludgeoning the poor young soul to death with a copper candlestick holder.

Paul didn't bother to experiment on the boy's body. Instead, he threw the limp cooling corpse into the hole beneath the sarcophagus that lead down into the labyrinth below the city, and continued ranting to the silence around him.

A skilled physician of the mind might have concluded that the sickness in Paul's four humors had grown so far out of alignment that madness had taken him. Others that had known him might have said he had always had a touch of the demon within him.

"Hush, too much crying boy, too much noise from the darkness," Paul said, talking to the boy he had just killed in cold blood. "Don't blame me. I had to. You'd have told them, they'd have stopped me, and I was so close," Paul continued talking to the shadows in the corners of his mind.

"Ha! Call all you want now, scream, scream to me from the darkness. Scream like the others down there, the women, the pets, and now you, my altar boy," Paul said as he slid the lid back across the opening. "I've built you a temple, given you everything, saved you from the darkness, just like the dark-skinned ones, soon to be blessed by the dark god. The Rakta Ishvara will soon cure me. Make me well, make me a god, and then you'll all stop crying. All hush in the darkness. Now, just leave me in peace."

Paul snapped from his rant, as he heard the creak of steps above, and a shadow blocked the doorway.

"You called for us, Vicar?" Ernest asked nervously.

The sight of the blood splattered across the floor was making him nervous. Ernest wasn't squeamish around bodily fluids usually, but he could sense something wasn't right here, and there was a smell too. It smelled like death. It reminded him of when he found a sack washed up on the canal side and opened it to find the poor helpless corpses of some unwanted kittens. The smell here was the same, but stronger. There were dead things close by; he just knew it.

"I did not think you would have wanted to see us again after our little ..." he paused, taking his time to remove his hat. "... yes, our little chats in your confession box. You know that girl has still not shown up. If this meeting is not of any benefit to us, maybe we can have a chat about that and the money you lost us," Ernest continued, trying to take command of the situation.

Ernest was the more intelligent of the two brothers, although that is like saying a thorn-bush is the most articulate of plants. In reality, it meant he knew which end of the pointy stick should face away from himself.

With his father's death, it would be him that would go on to lead Oakenfall's underworld. There would be a power struggle as families tried to claim what the O'Briens had built up, and Ernest would have to demonstrate he was a capable leader.

"You dare come into the Lord's sanctuary and threaten me? I know you are blasphemers and rogues. I will not permit you to befoul this place," Paul ranted, not believing in the Creator himself anymore, but still knowing the power, his words commanded even in his demented state.

Ernest clambered over the unearthed coffins with the help of his brother.

"What do you call that over there then, Vicar?" he asked. "Looks like you are doing a good job at fouling this place yourself." Ernest paused to help his brother over and noticed the arm hanging out of the coffin closest to his feet.

"What is that goddamn smell? Something died down here?" Ernest flicked his finger back toward the bulwark as he asked the questions.

"It's just a minor precaution," Paul said with a shrug. To his twisted and sleep-deprived mind at that time, having a pile of coffins and leaves on the stairs was just a matter of necessity and made perfect sense.

Ernest nervously flicked a coin between his fingers in his pocket. He was a gambling man and knew it was his tell, but he couldn't help it. He always fiddled with a coin when he was nervous and at that moment, he was very aware he was stuck in a room with two men who were clearly insane.

Ernest seemed to be the only one unsettled by the macabre scene. His brother, Neill, did not even seem fazed by the smell of dead bodies, or that he'd had to clamber over coffins to get into the room. He was busily digging at something stuck between his teeth.

"Let's just get this over with. Why have you called us here?" Ernest shot Paul a look that could have carved through stone, and he half hoped it would. All the way to street level so they could get the hell out of there. They'd taken many jobs from different people in their time and had met people in all sorts of seedy places, hidden rooms, dark alleyways, even in the hull of a sunken boat along the coast once. However, the sense of foreboding and the devastated catacombs were a new low.

"I need you to kill someone," Paul said without flinching. The room fell silent. Neill had never been the sharpest knife in the drawer, but even he realized this was not something a priest should be asking.

"What's in it for us?" Neill asked, to break the silence. With the small chunk of apple finally removed from his tooth, his mind was free to absorb his surroundings.

"We are already short on time looking for the person that killed our old man, we's got to be picky what jobs we's be taking," Ernest added, wishing that he had not postponed his search for the meeting. It didn't look like the priest had much else to give.

"You see, this is where I can help you," Paul interrupted.

142

The fear he had once felt for these thugs had disappeared. He knew his time was running short anyway. Either William or his affliction would kill him, and soon. Smiling, he continued.

"I want you to kill William Bailey. He was the one responsible for the fire at your pub. Yes, William. Dark William. Soulless William, and a mistake he was, but soon you'll clear it up," Paul said.

Ernest's brow wrinkled with obvious confusion.

"He's already dead, Vicar. That maggot, Harold, already had us go looking for him. Took us a few days to realize he was a dead man," Ernest said, confused about why this dead man's name had come up again.

"He is not dead. He should be, but he is not. You must find him, you must kill him," Paul begged as he watched Ernest and Neill exchanging a glance. "Wait, this Harold – who is he?" Paul asked, and with that question, his story was tied to irreversibly to Harold's.

"He was a laborer for our pa. He was there the night it went up in flames. Reckoned he could spin us a yarn about some dead man named William, so we'd not come for him." Ernest said.

"He saw William? Then this Harold should be dealt with too. Though, in any way, no need to stab the chest, as mortal men die easily. Sacellum made us weak. Ashamed of us, the Creator was," Paul rambled.

"Just what is your involvement in all this, Vicar? Why do you want them both dead?" Ernest asked. He was accustomed for people asking him to "remove a problem," but a vicar who wanted two people dead was definitely an unusual situation.

"Does it really matter to the likes of you?" Paul asked bluntly.

Ernest shrugged his huge shoulders. It didn't matter really, they wanted him dead anyway, and it seemed that William was at fault also. How he faked his own death, Ernest had no idea, but if he had, then he would be really eating worms in no time.

"All right, let's say a wunner, and we'll do it," Ernest said, looking toward Neill, who nodded, eager to get back onto the street.

"What do you mean a wunner?" Paul asked bemused. As crazy as he had become, Paul had never been part of Oakenfall's shadier side until very recently.

"Sacellum, you work in a church but can't even speak Oakenfall. I want a hundred, fifty a head," Ernest said, smiling. It was an expensive charge, but he could tell the vicar was crazy and hoped this would mean he was dumb too.

"I don't have that kind of money," Paul spat, furious that the goons would not do it for free. So much rested on his work. Did they not know what they could be part of?

"Then it doesn't get done, simple. Come on, Neill, let's get out of this bloody place. The smell is doing my nose in," Ernest said, turning his back on Paul.

"Wait!" the Reverend exclaimed. "Take the cross," he offered, defeated.

Paul needed someone to take care of William, and if he had to pay, then so be it. The solid gold cross was a symbol of the Sacellum religion. Its four points marked the four ancient powers of the universe that the Creator used to make the world.

It was engraved with seven symbols, each referring to one of the locks put in place to keep the

Spirit Realm separate from the Mortal Realm and should have held value to Paul far more than it's worth in coin, but he had long since lost his faith.

"Take the cross from upstairs. It's gold. That will cover the cost, and I won't even tell the city guard it's missing." It would be days before someone visited the church and noticed the cross was missing, but by the time they did and called the constables, it would be too late.

"Neill, you reckon you know anyone that would be interested in that?" Ernest asked, and Neill nodded. "Well then, Vicar. You better start digging two graves," Ernest said.

Chapter 14: A Final Goodbye to Faith

Unbeknownst to them, Ernest and Neill left Paul alone in the dark to face his worst fears. He knew that his time had run out.

A convulsion rattled through his aged and scrawny chest, forcing him to his knees as if to reinforce his conclusion.

His bones clanged against the cold cobble slabs, and the sharp pain that flared through his arthritis-ridden knee was nothing compared to the burn that engulfed his lungs.

He pressed his hands deep into the stone floor, both for balance and to relieve some of the pressure growing inside him.

Suddenly, Paul began clasping his face as the source of the pain erupted like a volcano charging for his mouth. The hacking cough that escaped sliced at his throat added a third agonizing discomfort.

Frozen in place while he gasped for breath, Paul thought back to a year ago when the doctors told him he had pox on his chest.

They had told him that it was just a chemical imbalance that they could cure. They had tried bloodletting, for which Paul still carried the scars across his wrists and lower arms.

When the knives had not cured it, they turned to leeches, but they were useless and had not worked. The only other choice offered by his low-paid practitioner was to cut the sickness from him.

Though no expert on biology, Paul still had enough savvy to know that cutting his lungs to shreds would kill him. He had begun to pray, spending every free hour at the chapel altar, begging for salvation. When it didn't come, Paul had given up hope, and, in his defeat, he turned to the bishop asking to travel to the colonies, hoping that spreading God's word might be his final salvation.

His wish granted, he boarded a ship for The Dark Gulf. Instead of finding a new lease of life from his God, Paul found only more heartache. During his crusade through the colonies, his sickness began to worsen, at first phlegm had been the main problem but shortness of breath soon followed that.

He was so thankful he had found the secret of the Rakta Ishvara while in the temple and left the village as fast as he could, returning to the city of his birth to work on a cure before this devil's curse took his life.

While Paul sat cradling himself in his arms looking at the blood splattered floor, he knew his time was running out.

The work had been a failure at the start and was still not a total success, with William wreaking havoc on the streets. Paul had wanted to remove the need for feeding on fresh blood before he took the leech to himself, but he no longer had a choice.

He was snapped back to the present by another minor chest murmur, Paul wiped his watering eyes, forced himself to his feet and ignoring the agony that twisted every inch of his body, he made for the upturned table.

Because of his tests, Paul knew that by digesting enough of the Abrus herb, he could take the parasite and have a few days before it took over completely. He just had to hope that would be enough time to find the cure.

It would have to be, as he didn't have enough time for doubts.

Paul grasped the porcelain jar containing the herb, and began to eat, sparing not a morsel. Once the last of the Abrus leaves were forced down his sore throat, Paul took the tongs and removed the little black Rakta, which began to wriggle with excitement at the promise of a new host.

Paul closed his eyes tight and let the leech sink its hooking claws into his skin. The pain was excruciating, and he soon slumped to the floor again, this time falling unconscious.

When he awoke, a new beast would stalk the streets of Oakenfall.

Chapter 15: Papers and Guard Reports

While Paul was becoming the second Rakta Ishvara to plague Oakenfall, Harold awoke early.

He left the house while Muriel was still asleep upstairs. He planned to find a paperboy before the city guards had slept off their hangovers.

The wind outside was the coldest yet. The clouds threatened something worse than the downpours Harold had grown used to in the past couple of weeks.

Their fluffy outer edges and yellow color promised snow. Hoping it would hold off until he was back at Muriel's, Harold walked past the few other early risers and beggars, the tall stone buildings helping to shelter him from the harshest of the winds.

Beggars had lit fires burning whatever rubbish they could find in the streets to stave off the cold and huddled around them like flies to a dung pile.

Above him, Harold could hear the wind testing the tallest structures, nature battling against man.

As Harold walked, he half prayed the wind would send them toppling down onto him, an easy escape from what he imagined he would soon be facing, but the huge stone buildings had survived two wars with the Dragons and the city's occupation, and it would take more than a strong wind to uproot them.

For the first time in days, his mind could wander and be filled with swallows and his family's summer home. It was not long before Harold found a young boy selling papers from within the archway of a closed baker shop.

He did not call out, as usual, no banter and no shouts in his pre-teen voice of what news had befallen the city. It seemed that the bitter cold had managed to curb his vigor for selling the few sheets of print even with the residual heat escaping from the cooling stoves inside.

When Harold dropped the tuppence into the boy's hand, he muttered a frozen thanks and stuck a rolled-up copy of the paper into Harold's free hand.

Harold left him to his statue-like vigil over Meadow Road and walked to a secluded side street close by. Shadowed and sheltered from the bitter cold, his only company a couple of pigeons roosting above him and a grumpy and defiant looking rodent sitting on the spokes of a cartwheel and cleaning its tail, Harold began to flick through the pages taking in the details of William's latest victims.

Another two prostitutes had been found, the body-count now creeping into the dozens. There was nothing else that seemed relevant.

The main story for the day was captured by a poorly printed picture of John Johnson, Lord Mayor of Oakenfall Harbor, and puppet of Malcolm Benedict. The article beside it went on to explain how he had been proud to open Waters Edge Barracks.

Harold knew this would mean that the church would own the council chamber and also hold many of the city guards. Times were indeed changing.

Disheartened, he crumpled the paper under his arm and made to return to Muriel's house.

Still being no closer to finding William, Harold had but one choice left. He would have to read the city guard record of the case, and, for that, he would need Muriel's help.

He'd hoped that the morning papers would have some magic solution to avoid the obvious insanity of what he was going to do next.

Chapter 16: Laying Down the Plans

Harold arrived back at Muriel's home before ten o'clock. To his surprise, she was awake and answered the door quickly.

It was a surprise as neither of them had been sleeping properly. Harold had hoped she would have rested until at least noon to make up for the restless nights and ease the blackening bags that had begun to hang under her eyes like aged leather saddlebags on an ancient donkey.

"Where have you been? I've been worried," she said before sliding aside slightly. Just enough to tease, forcing him to press too close than was proper to get in again.

Harold was sure it was on purpose this time. He felt a small warm caress of breath against his neck as he crab-walked his way past. Once free from the confines of the entrance, Harold turned and waved his paper at her.

"I was just getting this. I thought it might give me some clue as to where William is," Harold explained.

Muriel shook her head and closed the door a little harder than necessary. The aged wood creaked under the sudden pressure before falling silent. If the woodworm lurking inside the damp maple could talk, they would have told Harold that she was not at all happy with his idea of going after William.

"You're still set on that idea, then?" she said, cupping her hands and blowing into them to remove the chill that opening the front door had allowed.

"What choice do I really have?" Harold answered.

If William was left to roam the city and Harold had turned and ran like a coward, he would never forgive himself – and besides, someone had to protect the poor working girls.

Somehow, Harold had gone from being a junior tailor to a prostitute's hero overnight. He wondered if he did vanquish this would-be demon or renegade mage, he'd get his statue in Celebration Square, but it did not take long for the image of the polished marble in his imagination to warp into an old man holding a knitting needle.

The stone face warped to one of sadness and then of pain as images of the city guard cart took over and Harold could taste his own blood. William stood triumphant in front of Harold's cold, lifeless face grinning. Harold shook himself from the daydream before fear paralyzed him.

"Honestly, Muriel, I would rather not have to face down a cold-blooded killer. I would much rather go back to working at my father's shop, but someone has to do something, and it seems I am the only one who knows who is really at fault. If I run, the guard will still be looking for me, and while they waste their time, many more girls will end up dead," Harold voiced the explanation more for his benefit than Muriel's.

Harold guessed that is what really makes a hero. It's not someone who is unduly brave. It's not someone as strong as an ox and fearless, a warrior fighting down hordes of enemies. It isn't someone who travels the world making a name that kings will remember for generations to come. It isn't even someone the bards sing of. No, Harold knew deep down inside, right there and then at that moment, that a hero is someone who, having no choice, does the right thing – regardless of how bloody idiotic it is.

"You have somewhere to go if you were to run, I mean?" Muriel asked, and the question stumped Harold.

The girl was quick; he had to give her that.

"Yes and no, but that's not the point. I have to do this," Harold said, trying to shrug off the question.

He daren't say yes, in case he told her about the summer house, and she wanted to go with him. As scared as Harold was for the people of the city and his family, he knew if she said she wanted to run away with him, he would have gone in an instant.

Muriel's strong demeanor returned, and she began walking toward him. Harold wondered if she was as robust as she looked, or if it was a front, she put on so she could cope with her lifestyle.

Muriel sighed, but beneath the frustration on her face, Harold could see she was glad he had not taken his chance to run away and had instead chosen to help her.

"Come on, take a seat. You're making the place look untidy," she said, pulling out her chair.

Harold joined her keeping his chair back, so things weren't too cozy. Harold wanted nothing more than to cuddle up with her, but he had to be strong, if not for his sake, then for hers.

"Thanks for not running away, Harry. I need you around," Muriel admitted, and the room fell silent.

Before Harold had time to reply, not that he had any words to use, she asked, "So, what have you learned from the paper?" and thereby changed the subject and looked away to stare out the window into the world outside.

Harold knew she had spoken quickly because she was not ready to hear the words, they both know would have followed. Harold needed her too, and she could tell, but instead of telling her how he felt, they spoke of William and the damnable newspaper.

"Nothing much at all really; it was a waste of time, but I had to try," Harold said shrugging his shoulders. "Oh, there was one thing. The Water's Edge Barracks are open," Harold jested. It was the only thing he could remember from the whole paper, purely because of the balding fat-faced lord who had stared out of the paper at him.

"So, you think William's there?" Muriel asked, as serious as a judge in response.

Harold had no choice but to laugh aloud, something he had not done in weeks. It felt great, and when Muriel realized her mistake and joined him with a giggle, the world seemed to slow down and pause.

Another spark for her fluttered through his heart and Harold saws her bite her lip gently. They sat in silence for a few moments – only seconds – but with the tension between them, it may as well have been hours.

"No, no, I don't," Harold said with a smile. "But I have an idea where I might find out," Harold said, forced to re-focus.

He wished things had been different and he had time to investigate the tension further, but he did not.

"Oh?" Muriel's brow wrinkled, and sent a little line down her nose no bigger than the width of a penny's edge.

It was the first time Harold had seen it, and he instantly adored it. He really had become smitten.

Harold understood how silly it would have sounded if he had told anyone that he had fallen for her so quickly. Even crazier was the thought that she mirrored his affections. It was the stress they both were going through, each second felt like days, and they both knew that the end for them was closer than ever.

It made them shake off the normality of thought and let their hearts make the orders for their bodies to follow. It was instinctual, beyond the control of thought or logic.

He knew he should not have spared a thought about lusting for her and should have been shocked and horrified by everything that had happened, but he wasn't.

If he didn't have Muriel to fight for, Harold could not see how he would have kept his sanity. No, it was her allure that keeping him going.

"I need to break into Greenway Courthouse. They'll have the case notes there," Harold explained.

Muriel's face dropped. She blinked a couple of times, and her mouth fell open, like a fish starved of water.

"Are you mad?" she asked, leaning forward in her chair.

If they had had the money for a strong drink, Harold was sure she would have downed the bottle at that point.

"It's the only way, and, well, I need your help," Harold said, hating himself for having to ask, but he had no idea how he could manage it alone.

The same guppy-like expression mixed with one of anxiety occupied Muriel's face for a while before she relaxed into the strong woman Harold had come to know.

The fire that drove her forward blazed, and she spoke with a refreshed determination that still shocked him.

"What do you need?" she asked coolly.

She amazed him with just how quickly she adapted to any situation, and Harold almost felt embarrassed at how weak he seemed in comparison.

"I don't know yet. We need to get inside the courthouse somehow and read the reports," Harold said, feeling a little foolish that he didn't have a plan for how to achieve that.

"For Sacellum's sake, Harry! This is madness!" Muriel exclaimed – and she was right.

Harold had never paid much attention to the courthouse and had no idea of how to break in, or where to go once he succeeded.

"Madness or not, I have to do it. Will you help?" he said, and to his relief, Muriel nodded in reply.

Together they spent the day sat at the table, making plans to get into Greenway Courthouse.

Chapter 17: Thieves and Brigands

Day turned into night, and several pots full of tea later, they had settled on a plan. It was risky, but Harold and Muriel agreed it would – or rather, could – work.

Although their plan relied heavily on the incompetence of the city guard, that seemed a safe bet – at least safer than the alternatives they had thought of.

During their discussions, Harold remembered the tailor's shop where he had taken in an order by a junior constable a couple of days before everything had gone so terribly wrong.

He had been around the same build as Harold, a little fatter, but his uniform would fit Harold with a few quick adjustments.

It was early evening when Harold had left Muriel's to begin work on the alterations. While Harold hid in the back of the tailor's shop busily amending the uniform Muriel was, much to his disgust, out working the streets.

It was risky and Harold hated the idea of it, but at least she was not in it for her normal few pence. She was after a guard officer, well, his badge, to be exact.

The moon rose and fell while the two plied their trades in their own ways, and as dawn rose, they met back at Muriel's.

She was successful in getting the brass shoulder buckles from the officer's uniform; Harold did his best not to think of how she did it.

He had always known what she was but the idea of another man touching her now infuriated him, but he didn't have time to process that now.

Instead, he took his needle to the uniform once more, adding the buckles of office.

Harold dressed quickly, pulling the whole uniform together.

The long blue coat fitted crisp and firm around him, its brass buttons done up to the neck. The shoulder pieces slipped under the lapels on his shoulders. Harold reached for his top hat from his bag of belongings and was ready to go.

The plan was simple – Harold would pretend to be a guard officer, and Muriel would play herself. They would simply walk straight in the front doors and head toward the cells.

Once out of sight of the officer on the front desk, they would begin looking for the files.

The walk to Greenway Courthouse did not take long. They made their way quickly from Muriel's house on the Knoll, past the candle maker's and pawnbroker's out onto Trade Road.

It was still bitterly cold, and Muriel shivered as they walked. How Harold wanted to put his arm around her to keep her warm, but he fought his feelings.

She tried to press into him a few times, but Harold had to remain in character as they approached the courthouse. They could not risk someone seeing through their disguises. His palms began to sweat with nerves. Muriel must have sensed it and turned to him, taking his hand.

"It'll be all right," she whispered, shooting him one of her smiles.

It warmed him slightly and gave him the determination he needed.

He nodded back to her, pulling his shoulders back and muscles tight. Standing tall and determined, they made their way inside.

Inside, the courthouse was bare. The floor and walls shared the same gray coat of plaster matching half the city.

They walked quickly and all was going well. A few more steps and they would make it to the first door.

Harold's hand twitched, eager to grasp the door handle and step inside the corridor that led to the cells. With barely a step remaining, Harold put his hand out, shakily reaching for the small latch when from behind his desk to his left a fat, balding old man who seemed to be bursting from his uniform called out.

"Hey!" was all he said, but Harold's heart sank, and his stomach leaped.

Harold turned as calmly as he could and put a smile across his face. The fat officer sat down behind a shoddy-looking desk. Its top was covered with papers, most of them with teacup stains across their tops.

A sickly plant with huge leaves sat next to the desk, adding only a little color to the mass of gray. The room reminded Harold a little of the hospital ward where he had woken up, but somehow this place was even more depressing – if that was possible.

"What?" Harold asked, trying to sound calm and like he had every right to be there.

"I haven't seen you before. What you are doing here?" the fat man said and got up from behind his desk and began to slide around it.

Harold could see the wooden rattle tucked into his belt ready to call for assistance. He had not bothered reaching for it, though, and Harold noticed the truncheon in his hands. Harold had to think fast if he wanted to keep his teeth.

"I'm just bringing this girl in," Harold said, trying hard to sound like a city guard. "I caught her trying to lift some meat from the butchers." The lie seemed convincing, but Harold did not risk a mental pat on the back just yet.

"You don't work here, what's your game?" the old officer said, sideling up toward him.

Harold saw him flexing his knuckles as he got a good grip on his truncheon.

"What? You mean this serf doesn't even work here?" Muriel suddenly interrupted, a look full of anger flashing across her eyes.

She tried to break free of his grasp with such force Harold had to pull back hard, the sudden jolt marking her wrists. She let out a whimper, and Harold was amazed at how well she acted.

"You better start talking lad," the fat man said, stalking toward him.

Harold knew that if the walrus-looking man brought the truncheon down on him, it would hit him hard, and he would wake up in one of the cells missing a few teeth and with a headache worse than any hangover he had ever experienced.

"All right, I don't work here, but my brother does." Harold said, his brain cheering at its own ingenuity.

It worked. Harold confused the real officer, which brought him time to think and luckily time to remember the name of the young officer whose suit Harold was wearing.

"Frederick Swenson. You must know him." Harold waited, trying his best to look expectant.

"Yeah, I know him," the officer replied. "It doesn't tell me why you're here, though, does it?" He lowered the truncheon, and it looked like Harold's plan was working.

Harold grinned and stepped toward him, his confidence growing.

"If you know him, it should do," Harold said, with a small chuckle.

"He was out last night and is a little unwell today. In fact, he is pig sick. You could smell him halfway down the hall this morning. He didn't want the sergeant giving him another ear-full, so he asked me if I would come in instead. You know, so his beat would still get walked and that, and I thought, what the hell, always good to have your brother owing you a favor, right?" Harold said, releasing his inner thespian.

"Yeah, I saw Fred leave here last night talking about going somewhere. You know, the sergeant is going to kill him if he finds out. He's already on his last warning after getting caught in the alley behind the bell with one of O'Brien's tarts." The old man's face melted, and he actually looked jolly.

Harold could imagine he would have many stories to tell if Harold had the time to listen.

"He won't unless you tell him, right?" Harold said, still in awe that this was working.

"You tell your brother he owes me a brew – actually make that two," the fat man said with a laugh. "If you're anything like your brother, I bet your collar here isn't coming in for stealing a bit of meat. Go on, what did she give you? Bite you when you said you weren't paying?"

"Yeah, something like that, but don't tell him. It will please him no end. Come on you,"

Harold said tugging on Muriel's wrist and leading her away.

Harold did not relax until the door closed behind them and they had walked halfway down the corridor. Harold was glad to let go of Muriel's wrist, still feeling bad that he'd had to manhandle her.

"You were great," she whispered, giving him a quick kiss on the cheek in her excitement and Harold felt instantly proud.

"Thanks for buying me time back there. I couldn't have done it without you," Harold replied, holding his cheek.

"Come on. The files room should be just up here. If we get out of here alive and without cuffs, I will give you another kiss," she said with a giggle, and Harold could tell his face must have turned a bright shade of red.

The filing room was just as Harold expected it to be, dark and filled with cobwebs and dust. A corridor between the bookshelves ran from the main door down to the far wall.

Scattered about the floor were wooden crates containing what he suspected were the older files. There were no candles in the room, and the darkness felt chokingly close and coated everything in a grayscale palette.

While Muriel held the solid door open, just enough to let in what little light there was in the main corridor, Harold pressed forward, his eyes trying their best to scan the small-carved letters under each shelf. His heart leaped, beating against his ribcage when from down the hall, Harold heard a man's voice shout out.

Harold froze watching as the dust fell from the shelves. Breathing deeply, he realized the shout had come from one of the convicts in a cell and not from the guards.

"Any luck?" Muriel whispered from the open doorway and Harold shook his head, a pointless motion in the dark.

"No," he whispered back.

Harold could barely see more than an inch or so in front of his nose, and paranoia began to play with him. He could not help but feel that some unknown shadow, something lurking in the dark, watched him. It was a stupid idea but one that all humans shared.

A sudden squeak as his foot hit something small and fluffy, followed by tiny feet running for cover, exposed his stalker.

A rat scrambled under one of the nearby bookcases. Harold had no idea why he followed the rat's path, out of frustration at the shock it gave him.

Harold wanted to kick the little blighter, so he followed it. Harold stopped once he reached the bookshelf that the rat had escaped under.

Harold could see two shiny orbs glowing back out from under it, watching him. His eyes squinted upon the plaque at eye level. It was either the letters "R to U" or "S to V." Harold really could not tell in the darkness, but either way, this was the rack Harold needed.

Harold couldn't help but feel as if somehow the rat had meant for him to find this shelf. Harold used his finger to run across the bound files brushing the dust until he came to one that felt crisp and new. Harold pulled it free, being careful not to knock any other files to the floor.

They were near the main reception, and any noise could bring that aged, but well built, officer running from behind his desk to investigate. Harold carefully made his way back toward Muriel, doing his best to avoid the litter of crates on the floor and leaving the rat to its solitude.

"You got it?" Muriel asked, obviously eager to get out of the place.

"I think so," Harold said, glancing down at the file in his hands. In the slit of light from the door Harold could make out the word *Spinks*. This was indeed his file! "Yeah this is it," he added. With the file now in his hands, it then occurred to him that in their rush to get in and acquire the file, neither Muriel nor he had actually thought about how they would get out of the courthouse unchallenged.

Chapter 18: Some Strength Never Dies

While Muriel and Harold were trying to think of a way to escape Greenway Courthouse, the O'Brien boys had begun closing the noose around the necks of everyone he held dear.

The two thugs stood on his family's doorstep. They had already knocked, and no one had answered. His mother was upstairs writing in her journal and peeking through the window. She had to be careful not to let the light from her candle escape the curtain's gap as she peered out.

She did not dare open the door with her husband in such a weakened state. It was quite funny that even with the sheltered life Harold's mother led, the harshness of the streets of the common district had seeped its way into her heart and worried her terribly. The daily rendition from the Penny Dreadful added to her concern in more than a small way.

However, on this day, she was right to listen to her fear and not open the door, but goodwill and common-sense save few. If only James had fitted a new lock as he had planned, things may have been so different.

A second knock yielded no answer, so Ernest pulled a river trader's knife, with a curly maple handle and thick blade like a butcher's cleaver, from his pocket and rammed it into the slit between the door and frame.

Years of brutal debt collection and enforcement for his deceased father were evident in his expertise in popping the door open like shucking an oyster.

The old lock gave way within seconds, and the door swung open. Harold's father was asleep in his chair, slippers on, and smoking jacket wrapped around him tightly. He was unaware as the two thugs stampeded into the house.

Ernest was not going to waste his time on a sleeping old man and made straight for the stairs. As he did so, he barked an order for Neill to check downstairs.

Taking the stairs two at a time, Ernest began his search of the upper rooms. It took no more than a few seconds to find Harold's mother. He grabbed her quickly, and again working with a brute's skills, he bound her hands, gagged her, and tied her to the bed.

She couldn't put up much of a fight, as she was well into her fifties and unable to even dent Ernest's assault. She screamed out for help through the poorly tied gag, but with the city's degradation a woman screaming for help during the cold of the night had become all too common, and anyone who heard it allowed her screams to fall on deaf ears.

Ernest went back downstairs to join Neill, leaving Harold's mother tied to the bed panic-stricken. All she could do was to listen as the brutes continued. The house was old and echoed like the acoustics in a theatre, the reverberations playing out on the aged and dampened beams.

James awoke from his wife's scream to see Neill standing in the lounge, with a knife ready in his hand.

"Where is he?" Neill demanded not taking his eyes off the old man in front of him.

There had been a little bit of doubt in his heart if they had the right house when they first arrived, but the old man looked so much like Harold – he had to be Harold's father. James ignored the question, as he had a fair few of his own that he wanted answers for first.

"Who are you? What are you doing in my home?" James challenged, trying to push himself up out of his chair.

Adrenaline surged through his body, making his vision blur and his heart race.

"Look, old man, just tells us where Harold is," Ernest said from the doorway.

Although severely weakened by the flu, Harold's father was a strong and stubborn man – he had fought at the battle with the dragons and was not about to lie down to some Oakenfallian thug.

The mention of his son's name infuriated him even further, and James reached for the iron fire poker, which he kept close to his chair during the colder parts of the year. Grasping it like a Polearm, his father swung it with the strength Harold always imagined he wielded during the battle for Oakenfall some twenty-eight years before.

It struck Neill, who had been standing just in front of what used to be Harold's chair. For a big-set man, Neill's sharp scream sounded more like that of a wounded child at the first successful blow.

The iron poker cut through flesh, sending a spray of blood across the fabric of Harold's chair and up the wall.

It was followed by the sound of metal clattering against the ground as the knife fell away from Neill's fractured wrist to the floor.

As resilient a thug as Neill was, this bone-breaking blow made him recoil in agony, and Harold's father swung again, not missing his chance to get the upper hand in battle.

It had been years since James had disregarded his title as a Pole, but he had not forgotten the art of battle. Rage filled his body as he pushed the brutes back out into the corridor.

"Ernest!" Neill called out, ducking under another swing of the poker.

James swung repeatedly. The table was sent flying with a kick from his aged foot and smashed against Neill's leg, closely followed by James's stripy escaped slipper.

"What the hell?" Ernest exclaimed, finding himself forced back up two or three stairs before he fell onto his back as the deranged old man with the iron weapon swung it madly in his direction.

It sliced at his cheek, digging in deep and sending a spray of blood against the wooden railing that crawled up the stairway.

The power of James's swing sent him stumbling forward and with a push from Ernest, James ended up face-first on the stairs above the injured smuggler.

Ernest took his chance and scrambled on all fours like a dog toward the open front door, and fled into the street leaving a trail of dripping blood from the wound on his cheek.

Neill was left alone to face the aged Pole. It was then that James made his mistake. He turned to the open doorway to face the fleeing Ernest while struggling to stifle a cough as he got up from his knees.

The temptation to chase him would have been strong, but the sickness rapidly drained the surge of adrenaline that had brought James to his feet.

Neill seized his chance and leaped from the lounge, elbowing James hard in the chest with his good arm. James fell, crashing to the floor once more, and he could only watch as Neill escaped in pursuit of Ernest.

It was not like the old days when a blow like that would have taken only moments to recover from. James did not know how long he lay there before he managed to get to his feet, but it seemed like an age.

The sickness had left him fragile, and the blow to his chest would have loosened the phlegm that clogged his lungs.

James got up and closed the door, noticing that the lock was broken. It would remain so until Harold visited again.

Weak and coughing terribly, James struggled up the stairs gasping for air as he went to free his wife. By the top, he was crawling on all fours like a dog. Together they sat on the bed in each other's arms, his wife shaking and sobbing heavily. The trauma of the attack had broken the mask she had worn to hide her sorrow about her husband's sickness.

She cried so hard that she did not even notice when her husband fell asleep. In his weakened state, it had taken everything James had to put up a fight against the intruders.

Chapter 19: Jailbreak

With the realization still ringing in his ears louder than the bells from Saint Anne's, Harold sat in the storeroom's dark confines for too long. He was desperately waiting for inspiration to strike about how both he and Muriel would walk back out.

The officer on the front desk was growing more and more suspicious of his delay in the courthouse, and Harold also knew that the officer he was pretending to be related to could come back at any time. They needed to think of a way out – and quickly.

The way they came in was out of the question. Harold could have easily walked out alone, but that would leave Muriel stuck inside, and if they went out together, the guard would know something was up.

They had to think of another way. There was no back door for them to use, and the few windows on the floor all belonged to holding cells and had large bars across them.

If Harold could get outside on his own somehow, then he could get a cart from somewhere, use chains from the horses to pull the bars from a window the way Harold had read in the storybooks at school – but that was unlikely to work in reality. And the noise would alert every officer in the building, while Harold was still trying to prove his innocence, not confirm his guilt.

That left only one choice. The second-floor windows did not have bars. Harold would have to walk outside, leaving Muriel with the documents and catch her as she jumped out.

"Muriel, I've thought of a way to get you out." Harold whispered in the storeroom darkness, hoping not to horrify her with his suggestion.

"How's that, then?" Muriel asked.

Harold could sense an edge of doubt in her voice. Her resolve was weakening, and Harold hoped she would not break when he told her his idea.

"The windows on the next floor are not barred. You could jump out, and I'll catch you from outside," he said, but he could tell from the look on her face she did not like his idea.

"You hit your head in the bloody dark or something?" she responded despondently.

"No, but I can't think of any other way, can you?" he asked.

However, they were not given time to discuss it, as they heard the voice of the guard from the reception room.

"Hey Fred, you finally got over your hangover, then?" the old guard asked.

"What hangover?" came the reply, and with it, the time to think ended.

Harold did not wait for the other officer to reply. Fear took him, and, in an instant, he grabbed hold of Muriel's arm and made for the stairs.

They heard the officer's wooden rattle from the main entrance, as he called for reinforcements to subdue the would-be infiltrators.

Its click-clack sound was so loud it could be heard over the noise of the pair's shoes clattering on the hard-stone floor.

The sound of their footsteps would give them away, but they did not have time to creep. Harold cleared the steps two at a time dragging Muriel behind him.

He thought afterward that they seemed to have gone full circle. She had saved him when she had dragged him down the side alley and away from danger – and now Harold was returning the favor. The only difference was that he had brought her into danger in the first place. She should not be involved in any of this.

As they reached the top of the stairs, Harold heard a door fly open below them and the sound of footsteps moving swiftly in pursuit. They had to hide and fast.

Harold darted into the first room on the right, shutting the door as quietly as he could.

The room was well-decorated with deep blue wallpaper and a thick carpet covering the floor. There was a well-crafted desk in its center facing the door and a bookshelf built of solid oak close by. It looked aged and must have been a relic from before the war.

Thankfully, the room was void of life.

Harold did not waste the sudden luck they'd been granted and let go of Muriel. He darted for the desk, leaping over it and scattering papers in his wake.

It was heavy, but Harold begun pushing it toward the door. Muriel caught on fast and came around to help him. Her tiny arms, shaking with the effort of sliding it across the deep carpet that began to bundle in waves.

The bookcase came next. Harold could move that alone. He dropped it on top of the desk, scattering guard records across the floor like leaves in autumn.

The doorway was now completely blocked. Muriel had brought across the chair and was jamming it against the handle of the door, arching it across the top of the desk.

It would buy them time, but not long with the gathering number of officers, the rattle had called.

Panting Harold made his way to the window, the glass would not open, and Harold had to break it. He brought his foot up into the corner of the window, and it shattered instantly, sending down an array of sharp fragments to the ground below.

Harold turned, pulling the documents from his pocket. With his back to the window, Harold gave them to Muriel.

"Here, hold these," he said, passing them over, his hands shaking with fright.

"What are you doing?" she asked as she took the documents from him.

"I have to climb down," Harold said. "Once I'm out, then you jump down to me," Harold did not give her time to argue.

It was another occasion where if she had said no to him, Harold would have lost his nerve. He was scared enough, and as he started to climb out of the window, he quickly learned he wasn't a fan of heights either.

He stepped out on to the small seal around the window, slowly lowering himself down until he was hanging by his fingertips, his toes desperately seeking a crevice within the brickwork to balance him.

It took only a few seconds for his fingers to feel tired and start to ache, and Harold began to edge down the wall. As he slid lower the upper ledge of the barred window below became his podium.

Harold could not climb any lower and envied the spider in his father's shop – not for the first time. It would have made the descent look easy.

A crowd had already gathered outside the courthouse, watching the entertainment. Harold did not have time to think as his fingers were growing ever more tired.

No longer able to hold him, they buckled, and after a moment in the air, his legs hit the ground. His knees crumpled, casting him down on his rump.

Harold's backside bruised instantly, but other than that, he was not injured. He pulled himself to his feet, ignoring the chorus of accusations from the crowd and readied himself to catch Muriel.

She was already hanging over the ledge and dropped quickly. Harold held his breath as she sailed through the cold air and did not breathe again until he closed his arms tightly around her.

It is a strange thing that can happen to you, even in the turmoil of the worst of moments. With Muriel pressed tightly against him, time seemed to stand still. Harold could feel her heart beating rapidly. The warmth of her body returned the blood to his chilled fingers, and Harold held her, savoring the moment.

Their eyes met and Harold knew Muriel could read his thoughts. He knew that he had been falling for her, and now she had fallen into his arms, quite literally.

Harold did not want the moment to end, but the world snapped back at the guard calling out from the window above them.

Two tiny heads poked out, glaring down, before disappearing back inside.

The pair knew the guards would be coming down for them, so they began running again, pushing past the crowd and disappearing off into the streets of Oakenfall.

As they ran, Muriel reached for Harold's hand once more.

Interlude 3: Of All the Luck

Dante could not believe his misfortune.

In the last few days, he had escaped a fire with only a few scorched hairs.

Dodged rat-catchers, dogs, cats, and the Creator only know what else, as he made his way back and forth across the city.

He'd scrambled across cobbled streets, in and out of houses, explored sewers and rooftops as he tried to make his way to the harbor.

He'd come close to getting there a few times, even hitching rides on the underside of horses and carts, but somehow something kept getting in his way. It was like fate didn't want him to make it back to the ship.

To top it all off, he sat in a damp cell trapped under a tin bedpan. He'd been happily sitting in the dark, chewing the edges of a rather tasty paper folder when some big-footed moron had stumbled in and kicked him.

Dante really was unable to understand why humans had so much paper neatly pressed into files when they could just as easily tear it up and make a nice comfy bed out of it.

Regardless, Dante had taken off on his toes again and hidden under a bookcase until all hell had let loose, and the noise of the wooden rattle sent him scrambling through a hole in the wall –into his current predicament.

The bedpan had come down so fast that Dante had no time to avoid it, and to make matters worse, it had trapped his tail outside of it.

Dante didn't know it, but the strong smell of ammonia that burned his tiny nose hairs belonged to that of William Boatswain, the once-famous Pirate King and Governor of Oakenfall after the last war.

William had led the city during its golden age and should have retired gracefully back to the White Isle when his governorship failed – and that is what most people thought had happened to him.

The truth was much darker than that and showed just how far Malcolm Benedict would go to ensure he remained in power.

It had been years since William had seen the outside world, and he readied himself, not for the first time in his life, to die in prison.

The reason he trapped the little rat was a simple one. William had torn off a corner of his sheet and, using a fragment of candle wick in the hall, had written a letter.

The rat, Dante, would be his unwilling postman.

William knew it was a one in a billion shot that anyone would see the letter that he tied to the rat's tail – and even more desperately crazy was the idea that it might even end up reaching the person it was meant for. But he had to try.

He had never gotten to tell her. The letter was to his daughter, Erin. The string tied tight, William pulled the bedpan up and just like that Dante was gone, scooting back out the hole he'd entered by and leaving William to his unjustified fate.

Back inside the dark storage room, Dante sniffed at the letter attached to his tail. He decided that he would chew the strings and get it off just as soon as he was somewhere safe, but for now, he had to get back out of that place and into the streets.

Chapter 20: A Safe House

Harold and Muriel had given the crowd the slip. The city guards seemed to have given up the pursuit as the sound of their calls had faded into the distance some time before.

They stopped to have a hushed conversation on the corner of Trade Road amidst the potent smell of candle wax.

"Muriel," Harold gasped, struggling for breath.

"What is it?" Muriel replied, equally struggling.

"Looks like we managed to give them the slip. Do you think anyone recognized us?" Harold asked.

He was worried that in his quest to prove his innocence, he had now broken the law.

"Doubt it. They'd have been too busy laughing about you falling flat on your arse," Muriel said with a wink.

"Sorry, I've not had much practice scaling the side of buildings," Harold said, disgruntled.

"Stick with me, Harold, and you'll be a pro in no time," Muriel added, smiling.

"We should split up; you should head back to yours. Wait for me there until the sun sets," Harold said, ignoring the joke at his expense. "Muriel, give me the files, and I'll take them somewhere safe."

"Where's safer than mine? No one would connect the two of us. No one even knows we've spoken," Muriel said, afraid, if she was honest, to be alone on the way home.

"The guards might have followed us. If they have, they'll be after me. I don't want to lead them back to yours. Please trust me," Harold said.

Reluctantly, Muriel handed over the bundled file.

"Fine. Just watch yourself – don't think you'll get out of the courthouse a second time if they put you back in," Muriel said, smiling again.

Muriel grabbed Harold and pulled him in close, closing her arms around him. Their embrace only lasted a second, and then she was gone heading off into the distance, leaving Harold to watch her walk away.

Harold had to store the documents somewhere safe and have time to read them. He didn't want to take them to Muriel's. Giving himself only a minute or two to gather his breath, Harold began running again, this time toward the shop.

It would be a perfect hideaway and Harold was confident that it would take some time before the guards even realized what was taken and connect it with him.

The run there did not take that long, but the temperature plummeted, and snow had begun to fall, only a flutter for now, but it threatened to get heavier before the day was through.

By the time Harold made it to East Street, his lungs burned with an icy chill, and his legs felt as if someone had coated them in molten bronze that was rapidly solidifying.

To his surprise, the shop was open, and it was only then that Harold remembered Janet's boy was watching it.

Charles had dusted down the shop and evicted the spider. The distinctive smell of bleach filled the air and mixed with that of fresh cotton.

Charles had made a start on the late order of uniforms, and from the potent smells, Harold knew he was in the process of bleaching them.

Harold went toward the back of the shop and through a small-bricked arch into the private working area and found Charles in the back workshop.

The alcove was small, only big enough to house one loom, the bleaching bucket, and the racks of different cloths and spools.

"Good evening, Charles," Harold said, trying to sound as normal as he could.

Charles jumped slightly, dropping the needle he was holding into his lap. He was obviously unaware that Harold had walked in.

That was one aspect of his trade Harold had enjoyed. The time you had to spend working alone and uninterrupted in dull light always gave him plenty of time to daydream.

"All right, boss, I'm about mid-way through this order for you. Won't be done on time, but it'll be done," Charles said.

Harold knew the young lad was hoping to earn a few extra coins and even an apprenticeship with them. His work was of good quality, and he was bloody fast too. Had things been different, Harold might well have offered him the work, but things were far too confused now to involve the poor boy.

"Actually, Charles, I'll take over now, so you can go home. That is some great work, though. If you ever fancy yourself some extra coin, feel free to pop in but not for a few weeks. I have a lot to sort out." Harold hoped he could get Charles away from the shop without needing to explain what was going on.

Charles was a poorly educated boy and Harold doubted he would, or even could read the papers, so Harold was safe from the boy seeking a reward from the city guards.

"Are you sure? I was told I would be working at least a week, and to be honest, Harry, I could use the money." Charles replied, putting down the garment he had been working on.

Feeling sorry for him, Harold rummaged in his pocket and found two small bronze coins. That should cover his week's wages and a little on top.

"Here, take this. Do us a favor, though, on your way home. See if my mother needs any help around the house. My father's not well, as you know," Harold said with a smile.

Some people did not like Charles as he had the kind of eyes that never seemed to blink. and his slurred and slow speech made him seem simple, but he was a good lad, really; it was just that his mother and father knew each other a little too well.

"Yeah, right you are, boss. Should I finish this lot I've started first?" he asked with genuine concern.

"No need, go on now, get." Harold flicked his thumb toward the door, and Charles seemed to take note, nodding his head.

Harold followed him to the front door and slid the bolt, sealing himself from the outside world. With one final glance up the street, Harold made sure he was alone.

No one appeared to have followed him and with the snow now falling in a blizzard, the guard would, Harold hoped, head either to the warmth of the courthouse or a local tavern.

Harold had snuffed the candles in the front of the shop, and in the quickly darkening day, it looked deserted, achieving his aim. He pulled the guard reports open on his lap and started to read:

"On the night of 16th. Thresh, an arson attack upon the Queens Tavern razed it to the ground. A currently untold number of people lost their lives. Officer Bradley was first on the scene and confirmed it was an arson attack and a counterattack to a gang war between the lower classes. Witnesses confirm that a male they now know to be Harold Spinks had been loading something into the cellar moments before the fire started– "

Harold flicked on through the section with the interviews at the hospital as it would not tell him anything he didn't already know. That is something you have to love about the city guard – some drunkard pointed his finger at him lying in the road unconscious, and instantly Harold was the criminal.

"On the evening of 19th., during transit to Greenway Courthouse, suspect Spinks along with, as witnesses confirmed, an accomplice as yet unknown, escaped from custody. The attack upon the guard transit was both brutal and fatal. Early reports from the mortuary confirm that the three officers were killed in a bestial way with bite marks being a primary cause of death– "

The report described the bloody way the officers died, mentioning how the attacker had somehow drained a large amount of their blood. It gave him no clues as to where William might be, but at least Harold knew they were looking for him too. Taking a deep breath to settle his rapidly twisting stomach, Harold continued reading:

"On Dumon 22nd., Harold Spinks remains at large…"

Harold let out a sigh and slid the file onto the table. He was beginning to think the files would not give him any clues, and reading the last extract from Dumon morning confirmed his suspicions. They had broken into the courthouse for nothing.

The guards didn't have any clue he had missed; there was no guiding light to absolve himself. They knew little more than the papers did about the killings of the prostitutes. The report contained little detail on how they died. It only served to confirm the images his mind had already conjured.

There was no mention of anything happening since Dumon, but Harold was sure there would have been more victims.

At that moment, his only choice was to wait for William to strike again and hope he could track him down from there.

Harold was still not sure if he could kill William. He was clearly a mage of some kind, but Harold had never heard of mages with the kind of power William had. The rumors of demons could have had some truth to them, but that prospect did not comfort him.

Harold wondered if he should take heed of the stories and have a stake to use on William, carry garlic or wear a Brilanka cross, all suggested ways to prevent possession.

Harold hoped that he was human enough to die by some means, at least. After all, Harold had been contacted by his widow, so William was a normal father and husband not so long ago.

Harold shook the confusion from his head, snuffed the last candle, and made for the door. It was dark outside, and the snow had already settled to about an inch thick. The walk back to Muriel's would not be pleasant, but at least it should be uninterrupted.

Chapter 21: Winter Wonderland

Harold lay under woolen blankets watching his breath float in white clouds above him as his mind recalled the evening. He had left the documents they had stolen from the courthouse at his father's store. The journey back had been horrid but uneventful with the snow hiding his path; it was lapping at his knees before he arrived back at Muriel's house.

Muriel had still been awake when he arrived and had been waiting for him. She was noticeably glad to see him and did not seem perturbed by the lack of success at finding anything new in the guard reports.

Harold noticed that she seemed to relax a little as if she had been hoping they wouldn't find anything. Harold couldn't be sure, but it would make sense – if they had no leads to go on, they wouldn't have to face William.

It was not the fear of William, nor the insanity of the past few days that kept him from sleep that night, though. It was the butterflies rustling through his stomach, the same way they rustle through a lavender bush in the spring.

He could ignore Muriel's brief touch as they had fled the courthouse – that was fear. But she had hugged Harold again when he returned home. She was clearly overjoyed that he had not been caught, and any doubt Harold had that Muriel was starting to feel for him faded.

Harold still did not know if it was love or friendship. He didn't understand what he was feeling for her. Things were happening far too quickly and not at all like what he had read about.

Harold had to wait. Even the solid stone floor with just a blanket to warm him could not stop him from reminiscing of the closeness they shared.

The night provided a well-needed break after the fatigue of the previous day, and, eventually, Harold fell into the limbo of sleep. However, he did not sleep well.

Visions of William and his victims rolled over his slumbering mind and dragged him back to the waking world several times during the night. When morning finally came, the sight of settled snow filled him with some joy, as Harold knew the guards would delay their search while the weather was this bad.

They would not want to leave the taverns' warmth which meant Harold could relax a little. He was disturbed from his window-gazing by Muriel as she walked down the stairs behind him.

She still wore that same summer dress, and Harold then realized that must be the only clothing she possessed. Even with dwarfen machines able to churn out poorly made garments much quicker than they could be crafted by hand, clothes were still expensive.

Harold made a promise to himself that he would sort her out with some new attire once this was all over. It was not uncommon for the poorest to make do with rags and hand-me-downs, but the weather in Neeska was far too bitter for getting by with just one summer dress.

"Good morning. What are you looking at?" she asked.

Muriel rubbed the sleep from her eyes with a yawn. Her hair all entangled made her look as if she'd been pulled through a hedge backward, but Harold couldn't help but find it endearing.

"The snow's settled," Harold said. "I was thinking of going for a walk," he added. Muriel's eyes lit up and a childish glow ran across her young face that Harold had not seen before.

"I love the snow, can I come with you?" she asked playfully.

Harold liked the thought that it was because he was with her that she could enjoy the turn in the weather rather than having to work the streets in its blistering cold.

She had only had to service one man since he had met her, and that was to obtain a badge, not for a coin.

Even before his feelings for her had flourished, Harold had wanted to keep her from prostitution – and he had done it. So why not enjoy a little time with her and have some playful fun in the gift of winter?

"Of course, you can. We should be safe while the weather is like this, and we have to wait for William to make the news again, anyway. Do you have something a bit warmer to wear?" Harold asked, not wanting her to freeze the moment they opened the door.

The question seemed to pull hard on an emotion strong within Muriel, and her happy expression flickered, just for a second, but Harold was starting to notice the little cracks in her reserve. He wasn't sure if she was opening up more, or if he was now able to see around the edges of her mask.

"I'll be fine in this," she answered, refusing to admit that it was her only dress.

It was another thing that had seemed out of place for a working girl. Most would not have cared in the slightest about admitting something like that, and again it made him wonder what her story was.

Harold was sure she was no ordinary streetwalker. There was more to Muriel than even his longing eyes could see.

"You want to borrow my coat? I have a spare in my case," Harold did not give her time to answer before he reached into his case and pulled it free.

Harold passed it to her, and she put it on. He chuckled.

She looked funny, her long red hair floating down over the collar of his jacket and the jacket itself almost reaching to her knees. Its width was twice that of her own and when she pulled the belt tight, the tanned material bulged.

"Thanks," she said, struggling to get the wooden button through an eyehole with the sleeves trailing down over her hands.

"You look good," Harold jested, pulling his coat from the stand, and fastening it up to the neck.

Together they made their way out into the perfect winter wonderland. The streets outside amazed him. They looked clean. A pure white blanket hid the filth and kept the beggars within the shop doorways.

It made a pleasant change not to be pestered for spare change, and he refused the let the thought of those who had frozen to death ruin his morning.

Children playing in the snow replaced the ordinary streets that always seemed full of sin of some kind.

A snowman smiled at them from the center of the road. It had stones for its eyes and one of the children's scarves around its neck.

Muriel walked close to him, and they wandered aimlessly around. They passed the giggles of happiness, and for a moment, Harold felt human again – not so washed out.

Pigeons roosted up on the windows of the buildings, and every now and again, they sent down another flurry of loose snow.

As they turned a corner, some children had turned a cart onto its side and were using it as a fort for a snowball fight.

A stray ball skimmed his shoulder, and Muriel began giggling next to Harold. He bent down, grabbing a clump of the white powder and tossed it back lightly at the kids, who scurried for cover behind their fortress.

Meanwhile, Muriel had wandered away from him and scooped up a ball herself. She threw it and hit him in the chest. With smiles, they joined in the game.

Harold did not know how long they played but, by the end, his hands were frozen, and he found himself coated in snow, Muriel was a good shot.

The pale sun had risen high in the sky and Harold guessed it was just after midday. It saddened him to know that within a few hours, the streets would be bare again, but he had enjoyed himself enough.

His time playing with Muriel would be something Harold would never forget. They laughed and joked all the way back home. Muriel slipped her hand into his and ran her thumb against the inside of his palm.

"Harold? Isn't it?" a voice inquired, breaking the spell.

Taking his hand from Muriel's, Harold turned, relieved to find it was Janet, his mother's friend.

"Yes, Janet, what can I do for you?" Harold thought she would be mad about him sending her son home and readied himself for a sharp rebuke.

Many a time as a child, Janet had dragged him home by his ears to get a good hiding from his mother.

Instead, she seemed to want the latest of the gossip and started to interrogate him.

"I saw the city guard at your parents' earlier today, what's happening?" she asked bluntly, as her eyes took in Muriel – more gossip for her to spread around the church group next Dumon.

"I don't know," Harold answered truthfully, knowing that he would have to sneak back and check on his parents.

It was a shame to cut short a perfect day, but Harold had to make sure they were alright. He had managed to fool himself for a few hours that things could be better than they were, but the dream had to end. He had to go to them.

Chapter 22: Death and Love

Excusing himself from Janet's company as swiftly as possible, Harold made his way to his father's house alone. As much as he had wanted to ask Muriel to come, there was no time to explain to his parents about her, and although he'd had time to change his opinion of what a working girl could be, his parents had not.

Luckily for Harold, Muriel did not put up much of a fight. The streets were cold, and they had been playing for hours. She was content to return home and get a fire going.

So it was that Harold tracked across the city with his mind fighting hard to try and ignore the foreboding he felt; there were only a few reasons the city guard would have gone to his home. He'd allowed himself to believe again that he could have a morning's peace, but since fate had chosen him, it had been relentless.

Harold's darkened mood mirrored that of the streets, the beauty that had been there mere hours before had started to melt into a black sludge that washed through the gutters.

As Harold approached the house, he noticed the door was open and the doctor's horse-drawn cart was sitting outside. Fear for his family overpowered his caution, and not caring if the city guard was there or not, Harold quickened his step and forced his way past the crowd.

The ground floor was empty, and Harold made his way up the stairs, taking them two at a time. By the time he reached the top step, he could already hear his mother weeping.

Harold's heart sank, and his eyes began to burn, but Harold fought the tears off. He already knew what he was about to face. Harold entered his parents' room for the first time in his life without knocking. As soon as he stepped inside, his mother fell into his arms, squeezing him so tightly that Harold found it hard to breathe.

His mind racing, he looked over her shaking shoulder and could see the lifeless body of his father lying on the bed. The doctor turned and gave him a half-hearted, saddened smile while pulling a sheet over James's emotionless face.

Harold knew he meant well and was trying to tell him that he understood the pain, but it brought him no solace. His father was the last pin that held the family together.

Inside Harold wanted to wail, he wanted to fall to his knees and sob until it brought his father back, until the Creator himself heard his anguish and gave back that which he took – but for his mother's sake, he did not.

Instead, he held her silently, the two of them unmoving in a trance as an industrious throng of people swarmed around the room.

Harold had to hold his mother forcefully within his arms as they took his father's body away. She wanted to go with him. To hell with it, Harold wanted to go with him, too, to whatever lay in the realms outside this world, but Harold knew he could not – and neither could she.

And so, ignoring her screams as she struggled to free herself from his arms, Harold held her tightly. Once the front door clicked shut, her struggle ended, and she sagged in his arms softly sobbing once more.

They sat alone in the lounge for most of the evening, both glazed and distant. Harold had always relied on his father's strength, and now he was alone.

Harold did not know how he would cope. He remembered all the times with his father – the good and the bad – his mind flickering through memories like pages in a fallen book.

The silence was choking, but Harold could not think of any words to comfort his mother. For forty years, this man had been part of her life, and now he was gone. The lump returned to his throat, and Harold had to bite down hard to stop his eyes filling. In the end, his steadfastness abandoned him, and Harold cried too.

"Mother, what happened?" Harold whispered to the ghost of a woman sitting close to him.

There was no reply, no change to her porcelain face. Her tears had dried on her face, and she stared lifelessly at the wall. Harold knew she had turned off and was no longer in her body.

"Janet said that the city guard were here earlier. What happened?" Harold continued.

He had to know who was to blame – was it the O'Briens, or was it just the flu that took him?

"Don't worry about it, dear," his mother said.

She did not look at him as she spoke but kept her eyes fixed on the wall as if she was trying to look through it.

"Mother, what happened?" Harold repeated.

He did not like forcing her, but he could not let it be until he knew.

"It's ok," she repeated.

"Mother!" Harold said, this time louder.

"Someone tried to rob us, but your father saw them off," Elouise said, before letting her head drop to face the floor.

"Who? What did they look like?" Harold asked.

"I don't know, it happened so fast," she said faintly, as her memory replayed the horrid events that had happened. "I was upstairs. They tied me up, but I heard them downstairs. I heard it all."

"What did they sound like?" Harold asked, hating himself as he did.

He could tell his mother didn't want to relive the events, but the anger inside him made him want to find the people responsible. His mother gave him a puzzled look, but she was too tired and too sad to care why he wanted to know. She removed her stare from the bloodstain on the wall for just a second before she answered.

"They were smugglers. Your father took the fire poker to them, and they ran off," Harold knew her heart must have broken.

His anger peaked, as the image of the two bastards from the hospital came to him, but he knew he had to keep calm for his mother's sake.

"You're not safe here, Mother. It would be best if you left," Harold said.

She nodded, and Harold could tell she did not want to be alone and wanted him to stay with her, but Harold could not. He could not give up on William. If he did, even more people would suffer, and it would not be long before the city guard or the O'Brien gang got to them again.

"Why don't you go stay with Aunt Elizabeth?" Harold asked.

He knew his mother had not seen her sister since her wedding day. They had always been close before that, but both married within a short period. They'd been busy raising their families since then.

"Oh no, dear, I couldn't. I wouldn't want to impose on them," Elouise said, and Harold saw the frozen mask fall from her as a small flicker of her returned.

He could still see the redness to her eyes, and she looked exhausted, but it was his mother again, at least for the moment.

Harold did not reply; his look said enough. His mother knew that she had no real choice. It was Aunt Elizabeth or the summerhouse in Port Lust alone, and at least Aunt Elizabeth lived in Oakenfall, so his mother would be close to the funeral.

Chapter 23: Dealing with Grief

Harold left his mother at around 3 am on the 24th. She had finally fallen asleep in his father's chair, and Harold could not handle the horror of sitting and watching her any longer.

His emotions were ready to break free, and Harold had to go before she saw that.

He walked through the streets, alone and in the dark. He knew that it was William's most active time, but Harold did not have the determination to find him.

He couldn't face going back to Muriel's either. No matter how much Harold wanted to hold her, tell her his woes, and have her make them better, it wasn't right.

He wandered down the familiar cobblestones replaying memories of time spent with his father – good times like when they fished at the cottage.

James used to switch the rods, so Harold caught the fish he had baited, and he thought Harold had not noticed. He had often done little things like that, and Harold was never stupid enough not to notice, but he played along to make him feel better.

That image flicked onto the next. They were climbing the trees outside in the orchard. Harold must have been young at the time, as his father had a good head of hair. Harold had been stuck close to the top of a tree after reaching for a juicy red apple. His father sat at its base, telling him how easy it would be to climb down.

When he realized Harold was too scared to move, he climbed up to carry him down, but before he even got halfway, he fell from the tree crashing onto the ground. Oh, how he cursed!

For a second, the sadness subdued, and through tear-sodden eyes, Harold smiled at the image of his father sitting on his backside looking up at him; it was not as easy as he thought.

Harold had not planned his path, but he found himself outside the shop – his shop now, Harold guessed. He unlocked the door and made his way inside, swiftly locking the door behind him.

Alone in the darkness, Harold was sure, just for a moment, that he got a whiff of his father's tobacco in the air, but the smell faded fast, and Harold put it down to imagination.

He had to focus his sorrow. He could not let it consume him, not yet. There would be time for tears later but now was not the time. Harold reached for a bolt of thick cotton and made his way out to the back.

Muriel needed a new dress and Harold knew that would give him the focus he needed. Harold labored through the night, pouring every part of himself into his work, and by daybreak, he had completed it.

It was perfect, the best piece of work he had ever done. Harold had stained it brown, an almost shiny copper-colored brown that glinted in the candlelight like sequins.

It layered over itself in three tiers from waist to ankle. Flowers of pure white grew up it, each connecting to the fold above. There was no slit for cleavage. Instead, a thicker layer enclosed up to the neck where lace netting ran around and then down.

The sleeves would hang to her wrist and flare out like trumpets. This gown was fit for royalty and would have fetched a fortune for the store but, instead, Harold would give it freely to Muriel.

He managed a smile as he folded the dress up and readied himself to go and collect her. Harold decided during the night that they would leave her house and stay at his parent's home. Harold hoped she would be willing, and that way, if O'Brien's boys returned, Harold would be waiting for them.

He would not back down this time. The sickness may have been the thing that finally took his father from him, but O'Brien's bastards had been the ones to cause it, and they would pay.

It was still early when Harold arrived at Muriel's, even though he arrived as late as he could manage. He'd stopped on route at the library to borrow as many books as they had on the occult.

This turned out to be five, and even they looked like they had been rescued from one of the many Benedict book burnings.

The Mages Tower would have had more but they had been distant since the fall of the dragons, with the city fearing they had known the demons would rip through the citizens of Oakenfall too – not to mention it would take a few days to travel by cart, a week or more by foot and that was time Harold just didn't have.

The books were heavy to carry home, and Harold was not sure they would be any use, but they might just help. Surely, they would have some reference to whatever it was that William had become.

Harold sat in the lounge, flicking through the pages of one of the thick books filled with tiny scrawl, but before he could find anything intcresting, the sound of a door opening hinted that Muriel had woken.

She had not bothered to dress but instead stood on the stairs in her undergarments. The long robes were surprisingly woolly and looked to be made of decent stitch craft.

Harold's heart fluttered a beat, and he forced his eyes to remain on hers.

"Sorry, I woke you," Harold said lamely through rapidly drying lips.

"That's okay. Is everything all right? You rushed off so fast yesterday," Muriel said with a yawn. She came and sat close to him at the table.

Harold was glad that there was no hint of anger or annoyance in her voice, but just the normal caring tone she seemed to carry.

Harold wondered how it was that a woman who had lived such a harsh life could have learned to be so caring. He would ask her about her past one day, but as always, right now was not the right time.

"It's father, he was attacked," Harold said, his voice failing to hide the sadness, and he felt that same lump return to his throat that he had been fighting since seeing the cart outside his parents' home.

Harold wondered just how many more bloody times he would have to swallow it down.

"Was it William that done it? Is your father okay?" Muriel's took his shoulder in her hand, her palm closed tighter, and Harold felt his perseverance break.

He could not keep up his defense under her caring embrace. No more could he swallow the lump down. His eyes begun to fill with water, as he looked into her concerned face and that sad little smile on her thin lips that told him she knew what Harold felt.

It was the same look the doctor had given him, but it felt more real with her. She pulled him close, pressing him tightly in the strongest of embraces Harold had ever felt.

It was as if she was trying to squeeze the sadness out of him. Harold had not needed to say the words for Muriel to know his father was no more. Harold sobbed in her arms. He did not ever want to let her go.

"I'm sorry," Harold said finally, pulling back and wiping his eyes when his heartbreak subsided enough to feel embarrassment for his outburst.

"You don't need to be," she said and went to pull him close again.

Harold gently shrugged away, knowing if he felt her warmth again, he would break down once more, and Harold had few tears left inside to shed.

"My father was a great man, and I'm going to miss him, but now isn't the time to mourn for him," Harold said, trying hard to convince himself.

If he stopped his pursuit of William and the truth now, his father would have died for no reason. Harold just wished he had had the time to say one last goodbye and explain why all this had happened.

"I never met him, but he raised you, so he's got to be a true saint," Muriel smiled, her smile helping him more than she could know.

Harold really did like her, and his sadness just added further confirmation to this. With the loss of his father, Harold began to rely on her even more.

"I've got something to ask you, Muriel," Harold said before losing his nerve.

"Go on," she replied expectantly.

"My father's home is to be empty now as my mother is going to stay with family. It has more space than here and seems a shame to let it go to waste. I wondered if you wished to come and stay there with me, just until all this is over. I'd feel much safer with you there," Harold asked.

He had only left the house a few days before for fear of the guard finding him, but the weather should keep them at bay, and Harold just wanted to be close to his father. He needed to go home.

"I don't know what to say. Sure, I guess. I'll just get my things, and we can go," Muriel said, trying unsuccessfully to hide her disappointment that Harold had not asked something else.

Without a doubt, Harold could tell she wanted to be with him. She paused, midway up the stairs to smile at him.

"It'll be okay, you know, Harry. We'll get through this," she said, continuing up the stairs and out of view.

When Muriel finally came back down without a bag and in that same, low cut and soiled dress, Harold smiled, knowing that she would soon have a new gown.

The gift Harold had made himself was waiting already hidden at home and Harold planned to give it to her that night.

"Ready?" Harold asked, trying his best to seem happier than when she left him. Inside, Harold still ached, but he had to be strong. He was his father's son, and Harold knew his father would not have cried, even at the end. Harold would do his best to be like him.

"I'm ready. You sure you want me there?" Muriel asked, wanting more confirmation on how Harold truly felt.

"I wouldn't have asked if I didn't, now, would I?" Harold shot her a smile. "Anyway, it will make me feel safer with you there. Plus, if you haven't noticed, I kind of like having you around,"

Harold offered up, hoping that his feelings were right and that Muriel would not reject him.

"I had noticed. You are an easy man to read, Mr. Spinks – not that I mind your attention. Did you sleep at all? You look exhausted." Muriel moved across the room close to him.

His heart turned into a swarm of butterflies fluttering around inside him.

"A little. I can sleep when all this is over," Harold replied.

The surge of energy from the excitement of the admission of affection between them would undoubtedly lead to another sleepless night.

"You still plan to track down William, even after all this?" Muriel asked.

Harold knew she still disapproved, but he had not picked this path for himself. Harold felt like a goat penned in at the slaughterhouse, just rattling along until the end. He just hoped their ends were different.

"I don't have any choice. The city guard still think I am to blame for all this. The O'Brien boys want to find me, too. If I don't find William, I'm as good as dead," Harold said, giving the same excuse.

Harold didn't know at what point that had become a lie. Now he wanted to find William to kill him. Proving his innocence didn't seem to matter as much as making the city a bit safer for Muriel and taking vengeance for his beloved father's death.

"You don't need to be the hero, you know," Muriel said, running her soft hands down his cheek. "There is no shame in running away. It's not your job to make the streets safe," Muriel said, reading the truth behind what Harold said.

He could tell Muriel realized, the same as Harold did, the chances of taking down William alive were next to none, but he had to try.

"I was there when this all started. Somehow, I feel like I have to try and do something," Harold said, and Muriel looked at him, trying to think of something to talk him out of it, but gave in.

"Fine, you bloody fool. Let's go then," she said, and with that, Harold grabbed his suitcase from its resting place and made for the door.

It would feel good to be home again, and even better to share it with Muriel. They left her house and made their way to his home.

As they walked the streets of Oakenfall, hoping a city guard would not notice them and praying they did not bump into O'Brien's gang or, worse, William, Muriel helped to keep things light-hearted.

"So, have you always been an Oakenfallian then? It's just your accent don't fit?" she asked.

"I've lived up here since I was about five or six. Before that, we were down in Port Lust," Harold said, thinking fondly of the summerhouse.

"Oh, I've always wanted to visit the country! I saw this picture book of a cow when I was younger. I'd love to see one," she said so honestly that Harold laughed. "Hey, be nice." Muriel added, punching him in the arm for laughing at her.

She knew she knew little of the world beyond the Oakenfall Ridge.

"So, why did you move down here anyway?"

"My father came here during the war, I think. He moved down to the coast before William took the throne. That was where he met my mother. She was the daughter of the owner of the tailors he worked in. I don't know how he managed to woo her, but he did," Harold said, smiling at the thought of his father being young and cocksure. "It was my mother's father that paid for our house up here. You see, my father wanted to move back to the city. He always missed it, and her father wouldn't have her moving back in a working-class condition, so he sold half the company to buy our family home," Harold explained.

"So, she came from money?" Muriel asked seeming shocked.

"A little, but not much, it was more from the spoils of the war. When my grandfather died, they moved up here and ended up with his house as a holiday home. My mother was an only child, so she was the only person in my grandfather's will. They used this to open our shop over on East Street. They did not come from money, as such. They just got lucky enough to make ends meet," Harold concluded.

He didn't know for sure if his father had come to the city as an invading Pole, but Harold left that bit out regardless.

"I thought when I saw you that first day heading to the docks, there was something different about you," Muriel said, smiling at him.

"You mean, I didn't treat you like cattle?" Harold asked as Muriel laughed.

Now would have been a perfect time to ask about her life story, but Harold was too shy, and the moment soon passed as they walked on in silence.

"Would you ever move to the country?" Muriel had asked, choosing not to answer his question, but asking one of her own instead.

"Yeah, I would. I've wanted to for a long time, but there is not much call for a tailor down there – at least not one that does the style of work my father taught me," Harold said.

There was also the fear of the demons at Briers Hill. At least within the city wall, the guards kept watching for movement of the Shadow Demons. Harold dodged the contents of a slop bucket, which someone threw from an upper window close by, snapping back from another daydream.

"What is it you make, then?" she asked, actually seeming interested. Most people grew bored at the mere mention of a tailor's work.

"We mainly make suits for businessmen and bankers, some uniforms for the bigger factories too. Sometimes we make evening dresses for the ladies of the city and make the odd repair, but not many," Harold said, trying to make needlework sound less boring than it was.

"You mean them dolled-up scarlets?" Muriel's brow wrinkled, and Harold could not help but chuckle.

That was the reason he had never found the right type of girl. The noble and middle classes were more like dolls than people, and Harold would never have been allowed to date below his standing.

"Yeah, I mean those types. Well, there it is," Harold said, pointing at the house.

Harold was thankful to see that no guard carts were anywhere in sight. Surely only a lunatic would come home when the guard were looking for them.

That was his genius. At least Harold hoped the city guard wouldn't think it was his stupidity.

Chapter 24: A Plan for Love

It had only been a few days since his father had passed, but ever since the war with the Iron Giants, when hundreds of bodies were stockpiled, and brought sicknesses, the priests did not allow much time before bodies were condemned to the soil.

Harold knew it would not be long until the funeral, and the city guards would be there looking for him. He was torn about what to do. His mother would need him, but Muriel and the rest of the city needed him to find and stop William.

It was too much to think of now, though. To keep himself from being swamped by the heartache and sheer magnitude of everything, he kept busy as soon as they entered his parents' home. He showed Muriel his parents' old room.

It was hard for him to walk into the room and be surrounded by the memories of his father, but the lavish blue carpet and thick mattress would seem like a palace to Muriel. Thinking of Muriel enjoying what his father had worked so hard to provide for his mother helped ease his pain.

The house felt chilled and empty, and Harold wanted to inject life and love back into it before it became a mausoleum to the memories of the horrors that had unfolded there.

Harold dumped his bag into his room, taking out the books from the library he had visited the day before and went back to join Muriel, who had no luggage to stash away and no need to unpack.

Leading Muriel downstairs, Harold set a pot of tea on the coffee table in the lounge, placing the heavy books down with a thud.

The table sat next to the chair that had not long before been Harold's father's favorite resting spot. The sunken imprint of his years of sitting still showed in the fabric, and Harold had to fight the sadness to think that even that would fade in time.

It was a hard thought to a man like Harold, but he knew that the memories would always be there. As time went on, they would come up less, being triggered only by the odd smell or thought, but, for now, they burned into his brain like a farmer's branding iron on the hide of a cow.

As the two spent the afternoon and into the evening studying, the neat pile of books from the library scattered around the ornate top like playing cards in some strange game until after a few hours of silent reading, Muriel spoke.

"Harold," Muriel said, looking from behind one of the books. "This seems to be describing the way that William has been acting."

It had surprised Harold that Muriel could read. He had not had many dealings with working girls other than seeing them go in and out of the Queens, but he doubted the ability to read the written language was needed for their line of work.

Some of them could barely speak Oakenfallian let alone read it. It felt like another missed opportunity to find out more about her, but he had other things to focus on.

Muriel slid the book across the table to him and pointed to a faded article inside.

"There, that page." Muriel said, pointing to a sun-stained page that had been read by countless eyes over the centuries.

Harold took the book from Muriel and began to read. The author explained how in eastern parts of the Green Stone Isles during the early parts of the fourteenth century of the old calendar, there were reports of men and women who seemed to move in packs, much like those of wolves.

These humans slaughtered countless victims and consumed their blood in a hideous cannibalistic way. This led to stories that these people had been consumed by the spirits of wolves in the local area.

The wolf people of the jungles would later spark stories of vampires in the traders and sailors that encountered them during the early exploration of the known world.

The wolf people shared a single intelligence, a pack mentality that allowed their blood lust to drive them on to pillage and ravage the small villages of the Isles, but they seemed almost protective of each other.

When Maria Theresa of Northholm, the leading power in the world, ordered their complete annihilation, the general office kept several specimens found inside the temples for observation.

Defiling the temples and slaughtering many of the so-called wolf people dispelled the false belief that they were cohorts of demons or wolf spirits, but not before the myth of vampires and werewolves spread throughout the taverns of the world.

In truth, the specimens kept for testing within Northholm led to other theories that an unknown substance secreted by the leech-like creatures that filled the spawning pits at the hearts of the temples changed people.

These vampire-like or blood-sucking people possessed extreme strength and a reaction to sunlight. As hard to believe as it was, the sun weakened them.

The reports from the brave knights who valiantly battled the wolf people reported that the only way to kill them was to sever the head from the body or to drive something deep into the chest cavity where a large crab-like structure was always present.

However, no reports were found in the ransacked libraries after the invasion of Northholm to confirm they even existed. The wolf people of the isles subsequently vanished into myth with no temples remaining since the great crusades.

Harold let the book close. At least they had some idea what they were after now. It wasn't some magic abomination or raised zombie. It was a creature of a kind that had somehow existed since olden times.

"This certainly seems like William," Harold said, wondering how the strange species being described in the book suddenly reappeared after being absent for so long from the chronicles of the world.

"Maybe he's a survivor of that war," Muriel said, sliding the book back away from Harold, so she could read more.

"No, he can't be. He had family here, remember? The city guard found his body some time ago," Harold said as he wondered just how William could have come into contact with one of these leeches or spawning pits. "I guess William isn't acting alone; someone must have done this to him."

That thought was horrifying. Ever since the fire at the Queens, Harold had thought he might be facing a rogue mage, or necromancer, a creature, an undead, but if it was this Rakta Ishvara, then someone had done it to him. Suddenly Harold's chest pocket filled with hypothetical lead, as his mind remembered the letter from William's wife within it. He had promised to tell her what happened.

"You mean there might be more of them?" Muriel asked, letting the book slip from her hands back to the table.

"There could be, but I don't think so, else we would have heard about them, so it's probably a human doing it. But that's not to say there won't be if we don't do something soon. William was a success; he could be making more as we speak," Harold said.

"This just gets better by the day, doesn't it! If only you never gave me those coins!" Muriel joked. "At least it says how to kill him," Muriel said, relaxing slightly.

Harold nodded doubtfully. Inside, he was filled with uncertainty. After finding out how to kill the Rakta Ishvara, he should have been filled with hope. It was what they had been seeking for days, but now he had the answer, he did not know if he had the resolve to slice a man's head off.

"Are you okay, you look pale?" Muriel asked looking at him with her deep and beautiful eyes.

"I'm all right, just in a little bit of shock. How are you taking this so calmly?" Harold asked.

The shock and horror had faded from Muriel, so fast Harold was worried she was bottling it all up and would pop like an overheated cask of wine.

"I've learned not to let much bring me down. I'm a whore remember," Muriel said, and the words hit Harold like a sledgehammer.

He had stopped seeing her as the working girl she had been. He had started seeing her as his equal without realizing his perception had changed.

"I've seen the evil side of humanity. I know there is a hell, and I know that there are demons.

Most of them walk the streets of the harbor at night. There's little that can scare or shock me anymore, Harry. I've serviced mages; I've lain with thugs. William is nothing compared to some of the sick and strange things I have seen …" she paused. "That I have had to do," Muriel said, with a heavy heart.

Harold had no words that could follow a statement like that, and noticed Muriel was uncomfortable with the silence, so he broke it, the only way he could think of.

"It is getting late. I have a favor to ask of you, but first, if you want a bath, feel free. The bathroom is next to your room. Shall I start heating the water for you?" he asked.

"A bath? In hot water?" Muriel said, instantly recovering from the tension that had filled the room. In all her years, she had never had a hot bath. In her hostel, she had occasionally filled a tub with water from one of the canals to bathe in.

"Dwarven engineering at its finest," Harold said with a half-hearted smile. He had not recovered quite so quickly.

"How can I pass that up, sure – if that's all right," Muriel replied. It would make a change to bathe in warm water.

It would be a luxury to take her mind away from the memories trying to force their way to the surface.

"Yes, of course. I'll start the fire now," Harold paused. The next question was one he'd wanted to ask since he had found out how quickly it was going to happen, but as with everything Harold often tried saying, he couldn't find the words. "Say, Muriel. I received word from Janet's boy that my father is to be buried tomorrow. Will you come with me?" he asked, not wanting to face it alone.

"Harold, I'm so sorry, but I don't think it would be proper," Muriel replied.

Funerals in Oakenfall had become a procession, a way to mark the many the city had lost and were often an expensive and extravagant affair. Harold guessed it was because the only dress Muriel had would not be proper for mourning.

"Who dictates what is proper?" Harold replied.

"Can I sleep on it and give you my answer in the dawn?" she asked – after seeing the look on his disappointed face, Harold guessed.

"Enjoy your bath," Harold said.

The truth was he needed the support of her being there. The funeral would not usually be this soon, but with his father's sickness, they wanted to get him in the ground quickly to stop the chance of any infection.

Harold waited until he heard the last bucket of water poured and then made his way upstairs. He took the dress he had made for Muriel from under his mother's chair and cradled it in his arms.

Muriel's soiled dress lay crumpled on the bed. Harold moved it into the wicker basket that sat on the floor and laid her gift in pride of place in its place, waiting for her return.

Smiling to himself, Harold made his way downstairs to finish cooking the turnip soup; the excitement of Muriel's surprise pushed the sadness from his mind if only for a few moments.

With perfect timing, Harold heard Muriel come out of the bathroom just as he was dishing the soup out into little bowls on the table.

The last of the candles lay between in brass holders, giving a dim light to the room. The fire flickered slowly on the damp logs to keep them warm.

Hearing steps on the stairs, Harold held his breath and turned, expecting to see Muriel in her new dress, but Harold was mistaken. Instead, she stopped on the stairs, wrapped in a towel with her still wet hair hanging in clumpy red locks around her shoulders.

There was no makeup or powder on her young face, yet she was beautiful to him. She held the dress Harold had made in her arms loosely as if she might break it.

"Harold, this dress– " was all that she said, as she stood there holding it in the dim light from the flickering candles.

Muriel had never held such a wonderfully made dress, and no one in her life had ever given her something so beautiful without expecting something in return. Harold really was different to anyone else, she decided.

"It's for you. I made it for you. Don't you like it?" Harold asked, worried he had made a mistake in her taste or got the sizes wrong.

Harold had only gone from his memory of her figure to make it. As it turned out, his eyes had traced her figure so often, his measurements were exact.

"It's beautiful, but I can't take it. It's too fine for me," she replied.

Harold could see in the reflection of the dim light that her eyes had glazed. Her hard exterior breached, she was so close to tears. Now was his chance and, as scared as Harold was, he had to take it.

"Nothing is too beautiful or fine for you," Harold said, standing up from the table.

"Please, stop," Muriel said, but the look in her eyes told him she did not mean it.

"Muriel. I must tell you. I might not get another chance. Ever since I first saw you, my feelings for you have been growing. I have never felt this way about anyone," Harold said through dry lips. His throat was so parched, but he could not stop. He could not waste this chance. For once, he would find the words he needed. He could not let the only woman he had ever loved, get away. So, Harold pressed on. "Your past is your past. What you have done for me – you are the most perfect woman I've ever met," Harold said, feeling his hands shake.

"Harold, I don't know what to say," she said, with a small silver tear staining her cheek.

The smile she gave him then would stay with him to the end of his days.

"Then, don't say anything. Go and get dressed. Our soup will soon go cold," Harold said, smiling at her and sitting back down.

"Harold …" Muriel said. "Well, thank you."

Discreetly as she could, she slipped back up the stairs. She never actually said anything, but from that moment on, Harold knew he was not alone in the world.

It was true what Harold had told her – of all the women he had known in his life, Harold had loved none as much as he had grown to love her.

It could have been because everything else had been stripped away, and she shone out like a beacon of something good in the night. He did not know or care for the reasons. All Harold knew was how much he loved her.

Muriel did come back down in the dress Harold had made and an angel could not have looked any more beautiful.

As they sat down to eat the plain soup, the meal seemed to taste better than any before in his life. His taste was empowered with a new zest for life, even with the loss of his father, never far from his thoughts.

Seeing her in the candlelight, Harold felt his father would approve.

Chapter 25: Goodbye Father

Harold found it so hard to rest that night, knowing his love was asleep in the next room and knowing that he had finally told her how he felt. He eventually slept and awoke with a warm feeling in his belly and his heart feeling fuller than ever before. This should have been a perfect day to start the rest of his life, but as fate would have it, it was not. It was the day Harold had to bury his father, but at least he would have Muriel by his side. That would give him the strength he needed to make it through the day.

She had told him as they washed the pots the previous night that she would come with him and had held his hand later that evening while they sat in the lounge watching the fire. They had not spoken much. They did not seem to need to. They sat watching the flames dance until Muriel grew tired and started to nod off in the chair next to him. Harold woke her by gently shaking her shoulder, and she awoke with a smile staring back up at him with tired eyes.

Harold helped her up to her room before saying goodnight. Muriel lent in and kissed him on the cheek before closing the door to her chamber, and Harold retired to his holding his cheek to feel the warmth coming from its reddening.

Those moments seemed like an almost distant dream as the morning of Duwek started. Harold couldn't believe how quickly the month of Wastelar had come around. The early snow hinted that it would be yet another hard winter. Harold took out his suit from the wardrobe and put it on. Black silk and a white shirt both pressed to perfection, a nice change to living out of a bag, as he had recently become used to. Harold pulled his top hat on, so it pressed down tightly, completing his sober look, and made his way across the corridor to see if Muriel had awoken.

The funeral was not for a while yet, but Harold did not wish to be late – his father could not abide lateness. Harold dared not give himself the time to mourn. With the lack of time to prepare since his father's passing, neither Muriel nor Harold had the funeral clothing they should. This would have saddened Harold if he did not know his father would not have wanted that anyway. Harold knocked on Muriel's bedroom door and waited for her to answer. She opened the door dressed in the frock Harold had made for her and she looked wonderful. Although Harold had guessed her size, the dress fitted her well and confirmed how much his eyes must have traced her form.

"What time will the carriage be here?" Muriel inquired in her soft and caring voice.

"Around an hour, maybe just before," Harold said as he reached for a packet of cigars his father had left at the chair's side. He never smoked them as they were "to be saved for a special occasion." Harold could not think of a more appropriate time, so he opened the dusty packet to find just one cigar and a match. It was as if his father had known, had known the sickness would take him. If he had, then it would not have surprised Harold that his father kept it to himself; it was his way of staying strong. Lighting the cigar Harold, took a deep breath to fight the urge to cough. His lungs hadn't hurt as much since the fire. Eleven days since the fire at the Queens! Harold could barely believe it.

"Are you okay, Harold?" Muriel asked, from the other side of the lounge. He looked tired or worn down, or it could have just been the green color filling his face.

Harold had not smoked in a long time, but for some reason felt obliged to that day. Looking back, Harold guessed it was his way of grieving.

Its foul smell reminded him of his father, and all he wanted was to feel him in his arms once more, to say goodbye to the man who had raised him.

"You should have your family around you now," Muriel continued, and Harold nodded. It was true. If this had been a regular funeral, then the family would have been here all morning. They would have gathered and sent off his father in style, but Harold had not been prepared for this.

"Yes, I'm okay. I'm just glad you're here with me. I don't think I could do this alone," Harold said.

Muriel crossed the lounge and wrapped her arms around him tightly. It happened so fast Harold almost caught her with the hot tip of the cigar, and only a swift flick of his wrist saved the dress that he had worked so hard on.

Harold did cry again, but this time he did not care. He trusted Muriel enough to show her the pain inside, and she was right, his family should have been there.

It was usual to have a feast at the home of the deceased before the funeral. The body of his father should have been present, but it was not there. Instead, he waited in the hospital morgue.

Harold's heart sank and as much as he didn't want to, he was forced to think about what they would have had if they'd had the time to prepare the goodbye as they should have. There would have been ham, cider, ale, pies, and cakes freshly baked by neighbors or aunts. Not only would the immediate family have been present, but all their distant relatives too.

Harold wondered how his family would take to Muriel, but he did not care. She was his, and that was how it would stay. Harold managed to get control again but did not pull away.

Although his father did not have the send-off, he should have had, Harold guessed his father knew he was doing the best he could. The morning was a little blurry for him, but Harold stayed clasped between Muriel's arms until the knock at the door marked the arrival of the hearse. It was time for one last goodbye.

Chapter 26: The Funeral

A funeral procession is always a sight to behold, and the one for Harold's father was no exception. They made their way through Oakenfall led by various foot attendants.

A pallbearer carrying batons at the forefront was followed closely behind by the feather man and scattered behind them walked the pages and mutes dressed in gowns and carrying wands wrapped in blackened bows.

Harold did not know why things were done this way, but whatever the reason, it was a beautiful sight and well worth the six pounds his mother had paid.

The weather was cold, but at least the snow had melted, and it was not raining. The cold weather made Harold think of the only bit of trivia he knew about the mutes, and that was because these men often had to stand out in the cold, they were given lots of gin to drink.

Harold whispered a silent prayer that they would behave today and not ruin his father's last walk.

The first coach in the procession was the hearse pulled by six black horses with ostrich feather plumes on their heads.

The hearse was also black, with glass sides and lots of silver and gold decoration. Inside lay the coffin, an inscribed plate running along its side carrying his father's name.

A purple cloth showing their family's crest covered it, and Harold recognized it as the same cloth used at his Uncle Alfred's funeral. That explained how things had been put together in just a couple of days.

Flowers were in abundance. His mother had picked the waterlilies that shone in a brilliant white compared to the darkness.

Harold looked out through the slim slit behind the curtain of his carriage.

His mother, Muriel, and he were in the first of the coaches to follow the hearse. His mother was still in shock and had withdrawn into herself, unaware of Muriel's presence.

The two coaches behind theirs each contained more mourners, no doubt distant family members. The procession made its way from his father's house along the main roads to Saint Anne's cemetery at a walking pace.

The Spinks family had been buried in a tomb bought in its depths since it was built. Not only did his father share the same hearse and plate as his uncle, but he would rest alongside him too.

Even with a heavy heart, Harold acknowledged that it was nice to see the busy streets stop and give respect to his father.

Most of them would not have even known of him, yet still, as the coach passed, men dropped their top hats, and women looked down at the ground.

A kind of silence followed them through the city. After a while, everyone on foot climbed on to the coaches, and the procession was led at a brisk trot.

It would not be long until they got to Saint Anne's. Harold could feel the sadness growing in him, making it real – there was no way his father was coming back.

Muriel must have sensed his sudden sorrow and slipped her hand into his. Harold looked into her beautiful hazel eyes and could see they were moist.

This was saddening for her, yet she still found the power from somewhere to support him. On arrival at the cemetery gates, the foot attendants climbed down from the coaches, and the procession continued at a walking pace.

This was the first time Harold had been to Saint Anne's in a long time, but it was not to be the last. The procession stopped at the chapel. The mourners, many faces Harold did not know, remained dignified and calm as they entered the chapel.

The coffin was carried in and laid on a bier, and Harold was thankful to put it down. There were four of them carrying it, but it still felt heavy.

All those sad faces turned to look at him as they carried it onto the bier. The sad little whispers and covered sobs from the women were hard to bear.

Once his father rested at the front of the church, Harold returned to Muriel's side and the pair sat down next to his mother.

The church was filled with hushed sobs while waiting for the priest to start. Harold glanced around at his family.

The men wore full mourning suits with crepe bands around their top hats. The women wore black gowns also made of crepe, with black veils and black gloves.

They held black-edged handkerchiefs to their eyes and carried mourning fans made of dark ostrich feathers by their tortoiseshell handles. He and Muriel were the only two without them, but Harold did not care.

Muriel looked beautiful in her new dress, and Harold was smart in his suit, but neither was black, and Harold knew it would set the tongues of the city gossips a-wagging.

Harold smiled at the thought of his father watching and chuckling to himself at the odd sight his son and companion made at his funeral. Harold's attention snapped back to the front as the priest started the reading.

"Dearly beloved, we are gathered here today to celebrate the life of James Spinks and mourn his loss as he passed to Sacellum."

Harold could not help but notice the priest's eyes shifting across the crowd so swiftly, from one side to the other, never seeming to stop.

There was a strange hollow and labored sound to his voice, which seemed out of place, but Harold didn't know why. It sounded like he was out of breath as if his chest was weighted.

At the time, Harold thought he had been crying himself, as surely a man of the cloth would feel sorrow before every funeral he had to conduct.

All the while the priest rattled on, Harold drifted aimlessly for what felt like forever. His mind once again flashed back to past times spent with his father. While the priest spoke, Harold remembered the first day his father took him to work with him.

Harold could have only been eleven or twelve. He had rattled on for hours about different types of cloth and ways to cut or stain them.

The smell from the bleaches had made Harold's head spin even more than listening to what he had to say. Then he had given Harold a needle and taught him how to stitch.

That first pricked-thumb-filled day had led Harold to the life he had known. It was his father's patience with his unskilled hands that had allowed Harold to make Muriel the dress she now wore so proudly.

The world would be a sadder place without James.

Time continued to pass as obituaries were spoken, a press against his arm awoke Harold to what was happening around him.

Muriel got his attention and passed him an open hymn book. His aunt had picked the song. Although she was from the lower classes, she liked to think she was better than the rest of the family, so she had always kept a step ahead of the rest of them in the arts.

It was a sign of her determination to avoid her true place in life. Harold focused and sang with all his heart, hoping that his father could hear him from his golden seat in Sacellum. As a chorus of one, the church was full of voices.

> "Oh Father, that dwellest in the high and glorious place, when shall I regain thy presence, and again behold thy face?" Your reply thus came, "Not until thy holy habitation, thy spirit once resides, but now will I be nurtured near thy side."

The organ changed key, and the crowd continued.

> "For a wise and glorious purpose, thou hast placed him there and withheld the recollection of his former friends and birth. Yet, oft times, a secret something whispered, a breeze of thought, a memory shared, but alas for a time, you are a stranger there, and now he wanders a more exalted sphere in Sacellum."

The organ sang deeper, still echoing the sadness of the singers.

> "Alone my father walks in heaven, this falsehood, is called out for what it is, for we ask the skies are parents single? No, the thought makes reason stare. Truth is reason and truth eternal tells me, I have a mother there. When I leave this frail existence, when I lay this mortal by, Father, Mother, may I meet you in your royal courts on high? Then, at length, when I have completed all you sent me forth to do, with your mutual approbation, let me come and dwell with you in the golden kingdom. I will see you again one day in Sacellum."

The hymn finished, and as one, they all put the prayer book down.

Hushed sniffling filled the room and whispered voices of condolence. Harold returned to his memories. He knew he was crying, but all his strength to hide it was gone.

Harold could see his father's face and smell his tobacco pipe, and all he wanted to do was reach out and hold him.

Harold felt Muriel's arm around his shoulder in a comforting embrace but barely had the energy to lean into it. Reverend Paul rattled on again, but Harold's ears were deaf to the words he said from the pounding inside his skull.

The organ burst into life again, startling him from his daydream and Harold saw the coffin being lowered into the catacombs by the mutes, each holding one of the heavy ropes.

The trapdoor pulled shut, and people prepared to leave the church. Harold had not been to many funerals, but he was sure this was customarily done at the pace of the mourners, but the priest seemed so eager for them all to leave, and something about his stance seemed odd.

It may have been because of his heightened paranoia from the last few days, but Harold couldn't ignore the priest's strange behavior. He linked his arm through Muriel's and dragged her toward Paul as he tried to retire behind the dark red silken curtains hanging at the rear of the church.

"Father, please wait. Can I have a moment?" Harold asked, his throat still filled with sorrow that made his voice weak. Harold didn't know what made him call out, nor did he know why he felt the need to speak with the priest at all, but when Paul didn't stop, Harold became more determined. Harold called out again, quickening his step. "Father, please wait. I need to speak to you."

"Harold, what are you doing?" Muriel whispered, next to him, her bemusement clear on her face.

Reluctantly, the priest stopped and turned to look at Harold. His stone-cold eyes glazed, staring past Harold, and Harold could sense his frustration at being interrupted during his escape.

"What is it, my child?" Paul said, but Harold could tell it was not what he wanted to say. Paul wanted to tell them to get lost and leave his church. The words might not have been said, but it was clear from how he looked toward them.

"I just wanted to say thank you for the service. My father would have loved it." Harold lied, not that his father would not have been satisfied with his send-off, as he would have been.

"Why, thank you, my child," Paul said, but again his words didn't match his attitude, and his eyes fell hungrily on Muriel.

She noticed it too and stepped behind Harold for comfort.

"Harold, I think we should get going," Muriel said, turning away from the priest's ravenous stare. "The coach is waiting," she added and began pulling away from Harold but not letting go of his hand, so he would be forced to go with her.

"Harold?" the Reverend Paul questioned, remembering his discussions with the O'Briens.

Harold nodded, before being forced to turn around by Muriel's quickening retreat toward the open door.

Her hand still in his was clasped tighter, giving him no choice but to follow behind her.

They quickly made their way outside. Whatever it was that had been so urgent to the Reverend behind that curtain seemed to have slipped his mind. He stood staring at them as they left.

Chapter 27: Good Little Sacellum Boys

It is strange how things turn out, and Harold sometimes wondered if everything was pre-ordained.

After they left the intrusive stare of Paul behind, they slowed down to a more normal walking pace hoping not to draw any more attention to themselves than their attire already had.

The priest's interest was not the most unforeseen event of the day – that had been the absence of the city guards. Harold's escape was less important than other crimes in the city.

Whatever the reason, they had been allowed the day to mourn and with the main chapel behind them, they walked through the solemn crowds with unease refusing to leave them.

As they approached the edge of the holy grounds, the coaches had begun filling fast.

Harold glanced around for his mother, but she was nowhere to be seen. It was more likely than not that she had been led away by some well-meaning relative.

The burial over, the family all made their way back to Harold's house. Once there, they would drink far too much and eat the food brought in by distant relatives whose faces Harold had long ago forgotten.

It was the night to begin the mourning of his late father but, also for Harold, it would turn out to be one graced by hidden blessings.

Harold and his family would spend the night sitting, drinking, and reminiscing, while his father's body still cooled in Saint Anne's catacombs.

Meanwhile, Ernest and Neill closed in on them. Word had got back to them about the old man's funeral passing through the streets earlier that day, and they could only hope that Harold would be at the wake.

Although the city guard had halted their pursuit, Ernest and Neill had been searching for Harold since they had retreated from Harold's father's surprising turn of strength.

Since Harold had eluded them by escaping at the hospital, the thugs' interest in seeing Harold dead had doubled. This was compounded by the embarrassment of defeat by an old man.

The O'Brien gang had been losing face ever since the Queens burned down. It was a symbol of their power, and without it, their family's iron grip on the city's underworld had crumbled. If word got out that a tailor's son was eluding them, that would just add to their problems.

The families of Oakenfall harbor had already started battling for control over depravity, and several would-be gang lords had begun muscling in on O'Brien operations.

The harbor had never really recovered from the damage sustained during the last war with the Poles, and fights had been a constant even in Lord Boatswain's rule.

However, brawls had become even more common in the sea salt coated streets and far more deadly. If the O'Brien's clung to any chance of holding onto the dominance their father had built up, they had to show they still had might enough to be reckoned with.

Reverend Augustus had provided the fuel to drive their hunt for Harold, and in doing so, it was only a matter of time until they came back to his father's home, the site of their defeat.

This time they wanted to finish the job they started, but whatever god was toying with Harold got in the way.

Ernest was ecstatic about his plan. It would make a statement, and, somehow, it seemed like karma.

The plan was simple – barricade the front door, the only way in or out of the Spinks household.

Then take a fistful of fire sticks they bought from a black-market mage, combine them with a pound and a half of gunpowder, and turn the inside into an inferno.

Ernest stomped in front of Neill, who kept rubbing his arm that had swollen in size and looked like he was smuggling stone eggs under his skin, the bones obviously broken.

Ernest swigged down the last of some unknown alcohol before he pushed the dirty brown bottle back into its resting place inside his jacket.

Life seemed a little easier after a tipple. The city streets were dark because of the heavy rain dowsing the candlelit streetlamps and making it hard to see.

The wet cobbles were slippery and already half-drunk, the two muddled on through the wettest night of the year with difficulty.

A sharp crash and clatter followed by a loud outburst from behind made Ernest stop.

"Sacellum-n-dam!" Neill called out, kicking the small tin soldier figure he had tripped over into the road.

"Bloody brats 'ere are rich enough to leave their toys out to rust in the rain then. Kids, I bloody hate kids." Neill continued rubbing his sore shin that had been stabbed by the tiny tin warrior's sword.

"You hate everyone, you báltaí," Ernest chuckled as they turned another blind corner.

An empty road greeted them, and the lights had been snuffed there too.

Only the faint glow from house windows shone off the surface water along the road marking the edge of the footpath that ran either side of the gutter that ran through the middle of the street.

"Téigh trasna ort féin," Neill replied in his native tongue. His ankle was still throbbing as he hobbled close behind. "You even know where we're going?"

"Of course, I know where we are going. You think I'm daft or something?" Ernest stopped abruptly.

He couldn't help but feel unnerved by the lack of people on the streets around them. Ernest was a predator, top of the food chain, but he felt like a deer in the sights of a poacher's bow for some reason.

The pair had made their way lurking in shadows in the foulest of nights. They had thought they were utterly alone, but something had been following the odor of tobacco and spirits trailing behind them.

That something was William.

They had paved a clear and colorful path through the night, and now William watched from the darkness like a mountain lion waiting for the moment to pounce.

"Come on, halfwit. Try to keep up and leave the kid's toy alone," Ernest said, fighting the nagging feeling he was being watched.

He turned his back on Neill and made his way onward. It was only two roads to Harold's father's house.

William had tracked the two since they left the pub. The cold and rain did not bother him, but it kept the working girls inside, and his hunger never seemed to fade.

Male flesh was not his preference, but beggars could not be choosers, and it was better than rat or dog.

Any trace of William the husband and father had been consumed by the Rakta Ishvara. He was the Blood God from the beautiful Green Stone Isles.

The knowledge and history he'd had thrust upon him was amazing. He knew everything about the Rakta, from the first days when the tribe of man encountered the Rakta larvae, the leech.

His memories glowered with the glory years when the Rakta had hunted in packs ripping through weak humans, and taking some to increase their numbers.

William knew how those golden years had ended with the fall of the Titans. The tribes of men fell on the encampments killing every Rakta Ishvara and burning their bodies.

William felt their pain just as every single host had. The Rakta had gone into hiding until only one survived. It had learned of humankind's foolish need for a god and used that to control them.

William felt the burn of the spearhead that had pressed into the chest of the chieftain as if it was his own.

Then there was a period of darkness until the face of Reverend Paul burned into his mind like a jack-o-lantern.

The priest had brought the Rakta Ishvara to this place. His experiments had saved the fallen god, but now the shared consciousness knew that the weak priest had soiled the mighty bloodline with a frail body.

The Rakta Ishvara could not allow this, and, in time, William would strike, but for now, he needed to feed.

All this information sloshed around William's mind as he skulked in the shadows. The two thugs walked past Cheapside School only moments away from Harold's home.

As they turned into the Greenway, the hard rain crashing against the windows hid their footsteps.

They were close now, and William could sense this, fearing he would lose his prey. He had to take his chance and strike now. He wasted no time.

His turn of speed would have left a stallion standing as he pounced onto them.

He went for Ernest first. The smell of testosterone oozing from his pores signaled that he would be the harder prey to bring down.

Ernest spun on his heels as he heard footsteps splashing through the puddles lining the footpath. He pressed his hand down into his jacket, trying to grab his knife, but his reaction was too slow.

William closed in like a bull and knocked him to the floor. The impact hurt, but Ernest was tough, and he would not go down without a fight.

With William on top of him, Ernest threw a punch at his attacker, but his hand was stopped in mid-air and clamped by William's own.

Ernest yelped as his bones shattered like a stale crusty bun being mashed by a disgruntled baker. William's unmatched strength demolished Ernest's hand, leaving it as a flat sack of skin and sinews.

Ernest was sure he would die right there and then, but Neill moved quickly and sunk his blade into William's lower back, puncturing a kidney.

This would not kill William, not now, not much could. The only truly living part of him was the parasite deep within his ribcage, but he still felt the pain.

William's concentration lapsed for just a second, but that was long enough for Ernest, who seized his chance and kicked out with both legs.

This sent William staggering back a few paces before he regained his balance. He glared at Ernest and watched as the little smuggler gasped for breath and scrambled backward from his attacker.

With his right hand hanging lifelessly from his wrist, Ernest watched William pull the knife from his back with a roar of agony.

Neill had managed to push it in so deep that removing it sent a spray of blood into the rain from the torn artery.

As William stood holding the blade, Ernest noticed his eyes. Those pure black pits made him feel as if he was looking into a gateway to hell.

William grew bored with his prey and was more interested in what was going on behind him. He dropped the blade to the floor inches in front of Ernest before spinning, his injury not disabling him in the slightest, and closed the same crushing strength that had ruined Ernest's hand around Neill's throat.

What happened next scared and sickened Ernest more than anything he had seen before in his life. William opened his mouth with his jaw parting wide like a snake swallowing a rat and bit down into Neill's neck.

Neill opened his mouth to scream, but nothing came out. He tried fighting off William helplessly.

Soon his body began shaking violently with uncontrollable spasms as William drank from him.

A steady trickle of blood escaped William's mouth and ran down his chin mixing with the rain that dripped onto the ground.

The color drained from Neill, and his eyes rolled back, leaving him looking like a waxwork.

By the time William dropped Neil to the ground, he was dead. William turned his attention to Ernest who had not moved, paralyzed with shock watching his brother's last moments being sucked into nothingness.

A mix of pain and panic blended inside Ernest's stomach as he sobbed, trying to roll himself onto his knees.

As the shock faded into realization, Ernest tried to crawl away, but he could not stand. His legs had turned to jelly.

William laughed and slowly walked around until he blocked Ernest's escape.

"No, please, please don't," Ernest begged.

William ignored the plea and pressed his foot onto Ernest's back, kicking him to the floor hard enough to sever Ernest's spine from his pelvis with a crack.

William reached down and grasped Ernest's short cut hair and wrenched his neck back until he heard a snap and saw the skin pulled taut over bone.

William felt it free from the rest of the body. The fight over, William knelt to finish his meal.

Once sated, William stood and walked away without looking back. The night was growing late, and dawn was not far away. William knew he would feel weak then. It was time to return to the sewers, time to rest.

There was no way William would know, but he had saved Harold that night. However, the gods of fate are fickle. By saving one tailor's son, William had doomed the harbor to a bloody war that would rage for decades as rival criminal families carved up and fought over the docks that had once been held by the mighty O'Brien family.

The remaining family would have to fight hard if they wanted to keep their place in the city. There was many an Iron Giant and White Flag who would happily kill to take the money to be made, now that the last O'Brien would no longer collect – but that bloody story is one for another time.

Chapter 28: Realization

On Midwek morning, Harold was still unaware of how lucky he was to be alive. The first of his family left just before daybreak to head home.

Once the sun had risen, the day was not much brighter with the rain still pelting down outside. Only Harold's mother, aunt, and a cousin whose name Harold could not recall remained.

He was so glad to see his mother when he had arrived home. Part of him had worried needlessly that she might have done something stupid after they left the church, but Harold would not have admitted that to her.

Shaking himself from his latest daydream, Harold couldn't help but notice how uncomfortably silent the room was. Harold tried to warm the atmosphere with small talk.

"Will you be going to church today, Auntie?" Harold asked.

She was renowned for her talking, and Harold hoped that getting her going would lighten the mood. His father used to say she never shut up, and that was what had sent Uncle Peter to his grave – so that he could rest.

"No, not today. Are you still fine with your mother coming to stay with me?" she asked.

Harold watched as his aunt stuffed another pastry into her mouth. She was a larger woman; her sister's distress and the loss of her brother-in-law did little to dampen her appetite.

"Yes, I think it will do her good," Harold said.

He was thankful for his mother being away from the house and out of the city.

"What about you?" His aunt asked, meaning no doubt for him to go with his mother and stay with her.

Offering up her home allowed his aunt to feel important in the family, but Harold had no interest in going. He had to finish what he had started with William.

"I have Muriel – I'll be alright here," Harold said, hoping she would not ask any more questions.

He could tell she wanted to pry by the glint that flashed across her eyes as she looked over at Muriel, who was warming her hands by the fire, but Harold was thankful his aunt's reserve managed to restrain her from asking.

"We better get going soon. I want to get us home before the city wakes," she said, reaching for the dregs of wine in her glass.

The liquor cupboard had been drunk bare overnight. It had been well stocked and Harold couldn't help but feel that people hadn't just used the wines and spirits to soften the pain. They had taken the liberty to use the excuse to drink to excess.

"Let me grab your coats," Harold replied, keen to see the last of his guests leave, so he could head up to bed. He had been awake all night, and now with the day dawning, he wanted to rest.

The goodbye was swift. His mother, still in shock, said nothing to him as Harold kissed her on the cheek. He waited and watched as they climbed into the black carriage and waved them off before stepping back inside and closing the door.

Harold rested his back against it and closed his eyes, far too tired to even make the trek upstairs. Harold sat down on the floor and listened as his aunt's coach rattled off, southwards out of Greenway.

Harold would later be so glad that they left that way instead of heading north. Moments after the last clip-clop sound of their departure, his eyes were snapped open as the sound of a woman screaming somewhere just north of his door rang out, startling the birds from their morning chorus.

Harold's body found energy from somewhere, and he stood and threw the door open. With no shoes on, he ran through the puddles, striding as wide as he could and covered the few hundred yards to where the scream had come from in seconds.

Instinct had driven him, and he had no plans of what he would do when he got there.

The scream had come from a young girl who now sat huddled up against a neighbor's front door, sobbing.

She did not look up as Harold approached, and Harold soon saw why.

Ernest and Neill lay dead in the street. The footpath was stained red, and a morbid trail led into the center of the road, making it look as if it had rusted.

Harold did not know who to go to first, the crying child or the thugs.

Self-preservation drove him to examine them first.

He had not forgotten their faces from his hospital bed, and it didn't take much to realize they had been there for him, but someone had dispatched them. And Harold had seen this brutality before, the day the guard coach was assaulted.

Harold went to Neill, slumped against the Switzler's front wall, an elderly couple who had lived down the street for a few years.

Neill's neck had been ripped open, and Harold did not need to check his pulse to know that he was dead.

Stepping over him trying not to think too hard about what happened, Harold checked on Ernest and noticed the same gaping neck wound and that his neck had been snapped in two.

Ernest's hand was a mess, bone poking through the skin and blood congealed over it making it looks like sliced bacon left too long in a stewing pan.

Again, Harold did not need to check his pulse, but he went closer for some reason. His tiredness having drained any emotions he may have had left, he pulled Ernest onto his side and began to search him.

Harold almost cut himself as his hand pressed into his chest pocket where a broken bottle of absinthe rested. There was something made of paper in there, and Harold pulled it free quickly, putting it in his pocket.

Harold would read it later when the neighbors' eyes weren't all over him.

Harold's hand was about to move lower to check the rest of Ernest's pockets when a door opened and Mr. Switzler came out holding an old worn rapier, his weapon of choice in his younger days. He looked at Harold, expecting some kind of explanation.

"They are dead," Harold said lamely, as he hovered only inches over Ernest.

Yet again, Harold was the first on the scene of a crime, but thankfully he had the best of alibis this time, and they would not be able to pin this on him, even if they were still looking for him for the other murders.

"I can damn well see that. Do you know what happened?" Mr. Switzler demanded, as his wife led the young girl inside. Harold never did find out why such a young girl was on the streets so early in the morning. That was a secret between her and the woman she called Granny.

"I don't know," Harold lied. He didn't know for sure, but he had a good idea, who was to blame – William. Harold began to walk away, only now realizing his bare feet were soaked and frozen.

"Hey, wait!" Harold heard Mr. Switzler shout from behind him, but Harold did not stop until he was home.

He went straight to the kitchen, washed the blood from his hands before settling by the fire to warm his feet. Harold chose to sit in his father's old chair. Muriel was sitting in his chair, concern clear on her face.

"What's going on out there?" she asked him.

Harold had been surprised she didn't follow him into the kitchen when he first came back in. Surely the sight of his blood-soaked hands should have raised some questions, but then again, maybe a man coming in covered in blood was not as much of a shock to a woman of Muriel's profession as it would have been to him.

"There's been another murder, two, in fact. I doubt it'll be long before the guard are called. It's early, so many of them will still be sleeping their hangovers off, but there's the odd one who still remembers what being a city guard is all about, and they'll come to investigate," Harold said, closing his eyes.

He had known he would not have long to mourn his father. He had been in the church catacombs a mere twelve hours ago, and once again, fate had thrown Harold into the scene of another gruesome act of the horror that was becoming his everyday life.

"So, are we going to have to run? We can always go back to mine again," Muriel offered.

Harold didn't say anything in reply; he didn't know what to do. They had only just moved out from Muriel's back to his father's home in the hopes that they would get a chance to take revenge on the O'Briens, and now they lay dead outside in the street. The house became a mausoleum for his father once again.

Harold pulled the piece of paper from his pocket that he had found in the dead thug's pocket. It was damp and stunk of alcohol, but it was still readable.

To the O'Brien family, I have tasked my altar boy with finding you in the hopes that you can do me a service, a service that will benefit us both. Reverend Paul Augustus.

Harold read and almost dropped the paper in shock. He read the name repeatedly. Reverend Paul Augustus! The man who had buried his father! The priest that Harold had been standing next to yesterday with the acid in his stomach churning like sour milk, telling him something was wrong.

It would take a leap of faith, and it was a conclusion only a sleep-deprived and paranoid mind could ever connect – but Harold was sure. It all fell into place for him at that moment.

All the little things that Harold had missed seemed to be linked like the eyes of a shoe tailored in his father's shop; alone all separate, but with the lace, they became one.

The priest had dealings with the O'Briens –
the same family that had been attacked by William
once before.

William had been buried at Saint Anne's,
and his body must have been dug up there.

The brutal attack was identical, which meant
William had been close.

The only link – the only lace – was the
priest.

Harold had felt that the way Paul had looked
at Muriel, with the blackness in his eyes, was
unsettling.

The letter connecting the O'Briens to Paul
made irrefutable evidence that Paul had dealings
with the underworld.

A priest should not need to contact criminals
unless he was doing something that people did not
need to see, like digging up bodies and turning them
into demons.

Harold had to go back to the church – he
could rest later.

"Muriel. I have to go somewhere. Wait here
for me. If the guard come, light a candle in the front
bedroom upstairs, and I'll know not to come back. I
won't be long," Harold said, trying to hide the fear
from his voice.

"What's on that bit of paper? Tell me what's
going on?" she begged, not missing the change in his
demeanor after he read the note.

"I think the priest has something to do with
all this. The two murders outside were the thugs that
attacked my father. With them dead, I only have to
watch out for the guard, but they'll be here soon, no
doubt. So, I must go to Saint Anne's now. I have to
find out what the priest knows – if he knows about
William or what's behind all this. It might help prove

my innocence or, if nothing else, help me find out who started this," Harold said, determined.

"Just come back safe, Harold," Muriel said, before turning away from him and walking toward the stairs.

Harold slipped on his shoes with his feet still damp, but he did not care.

Harold headed out, leaving Muriel to try and sleep. It was too risky to take her with him, for all Harold knew William could be at Saint Anne's waiting for him.

Harold left in such a hurry he forgot his coat and was soaked through before he got to the end of the road. He briefly thought of going back to change, but the chance of the guard being on their way was too great. Harold couldn't get caught now they finally had a lead that might start answering some questions.

Harold battled onward, twitching as ice-cold droplets dripped from his sodden hair down his spine. As Harold turned out of Greenway heading toward Saint Anne's, a guard cart rolled past him, steam rising from the lead horse's nose in the biting cold.

Harold hoped they did not see him. They did not stop, and as soon as the coach rattled past, Harold quickened his step, almost breaking into a run.

The cobblestones slid past underfoot like waves on the ocean. The city was just starting to wake up, and Harold jogged past families dressed in their best as they headed off to morning mass.

It did not dawn on him until Harold was halfway to Saint Anne's with his legs ready to buckle under him that a sermon would be on when he got there.

Harold would not be able to rush in and confront Paul. He would have to wait at the back, or he would risk being lynched by devout Sacellumians.

The cold was starting to sting, and Harold felt goose-bumps spreading up and down his arms. He quickened his pace to a sprint.

His legs complained even more, and his chest started to wheeze, but it kept him warm, or at least, less cold.

A strong wind blew across Celebration Square as Harold turned the corner into Common Road. The granite statues that had been put back up during William's lordship looked black, and the pigeons that normally defaced them hid below their legs, trying to keep out of the worst of the weather.

Harold recognized one of the faces of the statues, that of a Darcy Dean. A noble who had died bringing the Dragon's Heart back to Oakenfall. A plump pigeon seemed very at home nested on the statue's shoe.

The rain was starting to ease, but it was so damnably cold, Harold was worried his shirt would freeze to his back.

He did not want to go the same way as his father and hoped that with all the bad luck he had been having, he was due some good and would avoid the flu.

By the time Harold got to the fence surrounding Saint Anne's, he was exhausted. The alcohol he had consumed had burned from his system, but his legs were still wobbly, and he leaned against a metal fence to hold himself upright while he caught his breath.

Harold could hear singing from inside and could tell the service was underway. He had not had the chance to take in the beauty of the church on his last visit. His had been preoccupied by the weight of his father's casket resting on his shoulder.

Panting for breath, Harold spared himself a moment to take in the splendor. Three distinct sections made up the church itself. The left section was a tall pointed building with a large square base; it contained a grand, stained glass window showing pictures of religious idols.

Below the window, a pure white plastered arch masked the doorway inside. The central section was a smaller version of the last with a white arch and two small stained windows.

It looked like a child standing next to its father, and Harold wondered if the architect had planned it like that.

The huge spire on the right climbed skywards and Harold could just make out the cross on its top. The church was huge and had taken years to complete. They had started building Saint Anne's in the year 107AB, and construction was still periodically ongoing as the numbers of faithful Sacellumians seemed to grow in the city. It was a massive structure and had taken hundreds of people to construct the huge stone towers, even with the strange machines borrowed from the Dwarves.

It was the biggest building erected since the Dragon overlords were pushed from the city and rivaled the Hanson castle.

Until recently, it would have taken centuries to build. It made Harold wonder just what splendor the Dwarves had hidden on the deep roads in the dark away from the eyes of humans if their machines could create such amazing structures.

Sliding open the gate, which creaked with the effort, Harold made his way to the large arch and slipped through the door, scuttling like a scared crab as he made his way across the chequered floor to the back pew.

It was empty, as were many other seats in the nave of the church.

Harold guessed the foul weather had kept all but the most devout at home. Reverend Paul Augustus led the sermon from the front of the church, backed by another collection of four stained glass windows.

The light shining behind him gave him a glowing halo, even in the grim weather.

Harold sat and listened through the sermon, listening to how wonderful this Creator God was. It annoyed him. It wasn't that Harold didn't believe in the Golden City in the sky or disagree with the monks. If anyone did, it was them who would push the demons back from the world.

What annoyed Harold was how could this Creator God, who steered their fates, be so wonderful after everything that had been happening to him?

As angry with the Creator as Harold was at the end of the sermon when it was time to pray, he found himself down on one knee.

Harold prayed that he would make it through the day. He prayed that his mother would find the strength to deal with her loss, and, mostly, Harold prayed for Muriel.

"Atone thee, Creator," Harold said in chorus with everyone else to end the prayer and hoped that if there really was an all-powerful being, he heard his wishes.

Harold watched as Reverend Paul made his escape behind the curtain that led down into the catacombs with the same haste he had used after his father's funeral.

Harold waited as the crowds left slowly one by one, keeping his head bent as if he was still praying and not wanting to draw attention. For someone who, only a week before, had been a tailor's son that no one would have recognized, Harold was learning fast about what it took to survive in the new world of infamy that had opened up to him.

When the last straggler was gone, and the door was shut behind them, Harold began tiptoeing toward the curtain, pressing his feet down as softly as he could against the stone floor.

He tried to stay on the deep red carpet to deaden the sound. He wanted to catch Paul unaware, so he could see what he was doing down there.

Pushing past the curtains, Harold was thankful to see that the wooden door at the head of the stairs was ajar, and Harold knelt beside it, gazing down into the darkness.

At the foot of the stairs, Harold could see two coffins against which a table was propped.

Harold wondered how the old man was able to hop over them each time he came down there. Surely his old bones should have disintegrated under the effort.

Then Harold saw something which sickened him. Sitting deep in the shadows was Paul Augustus and one of the catacomb residents.

It was his father's body, and that bastard was biting it!

Harold had seen William do the same to the guard officers the night he had escaped. Harold gave up his hiding place and tossed the door aside, making a rapid descent and almost losing his footing more than once on the herbs that scattered on the steps.

Reverend Paul dropped Harold's father to the floor, and turned to face him.

"Harold! How wonderful of you to join us. We were just having lunch," Paul said, smiling with blood-soaked teeth.

"Screw you, Priest!" Harold bellowed as he clambered over the coffins, kicking the table aside.

It was out of character for him, but his anger turned to fury, and Harold wanted to kill Paul there and then.

Harold forgot that he came for answers to find out what William was. None of that mattered in the light of his father being desecrated like that.

Harold slammed his foot down on the leg of the table, breaking it free from the frame. He was tired, and it took a lot of effort, but with his blood boiling, his muscles pulled tight with the surge of power felt only in the moments of purest rage.

The broken leg in his hand, Harold made his way toward Paul. His mouth was dry as and his heart beat faster than it ever had before in his life.

"Now, my child, let's not do anything hasty," Paul said.

Harold was too enraged to argue back.

He could not shake the image of his father's lifeless corpse being sullied like that. When they had lowered his father's body down the day before, it was to rest forever with his lost kin, not to feed some crazed old priest.

"Harold. I think I owe you some answers," Paul continued, wiping his mouth on a handkerchief he pulled from his robes.

"Too right you do, old man, and once I have them, I intend to kill you," Harold said, tightening his grip on the table leg.

The whole time he and Muriel had been planning to kill William, Harold had had no idea if he could kill someone. But now, standing there in front of Paul, Harold had no doubt about his ability to end the priest's life.

"I've come to know a lot about you, Harold. I know about the Queens. I know how you got blamed."

"You did this to me?"

"No, course not, I didn't even know about you until they came here. I called them here to kill William. You see, he was a mistake of mine. The O'Briens made me aware of your involvement, and I could not risk you ruining all of this. So, I ordered them to kill you too," Paul answered, quickly and calmly.

The priest's honesty shocked Harold, and he found himself looking around the room while trying to think of what he wanted to say back.

The knowledge gained from the library flashed through his mind. He knew what Paul was, but Harold noticed an opening in the wall where a coffin would once have rested.

Hidden inside were a pillow and a huge amount of the same herb that coated the stairs.

Harold guessed that Paul had been sleeping there to protect himself. That meant he had not always been a demon; he had changed – and recently.

"He was a mistake?! What do you mean a mistake?" Harold asked, holding the table leg out in front of him more for protection than in anger.

"It's a long story. I mean, are you sure you and your lady friend have the time? I mean, while you're here, she is all alone," Paul said trying to anger him. He wanted Harold to make a move, to lunge at him.

"Don't you dare threaten Muriel, Priest," Harold replied.

"I'm not, but William is still out there. He knows about you too. You see, we share the same memories. All of us do. We are more than you could imagine," Paul said.

"What are you on about, old man?" Harold said, taking another look around the cold, damp room.

The brickwork changed halfway down the wall, and even with his limited knowledge of the lore of Oakenfall, Harold could tell the catacombs had broken into the old labyrinth below the city.

"You're really not the brightest of young men, are you?" Paul said. "You look at me as if I'm evil. I can see that in your eyes, but you are wrong. You do not realize the power the Rakta Ishvara, the Blood God, can give you. I've learned how to control it. The leaves you see around here stop it taking total control," Paul said.

Paul turned to point around the catacombs. At that moment, Harold took his chance, swinging the table leg as hard as he could at Paul's head.

It never connected.

Paul's movement was lightning fast, and he splintered the leg with a sideward swipe.

"You fool of a boy. Don't let my looks deceive you. You cannot win. It is only by my restraint that you still breathe," Paul spat at Harold, venomously.

The lunge had taken Harold past Paul, and Paul was now blocking his escape back up the stairs.

Harold could see the mass on Paul's chest, starting to pulsate.

It was almost instinctive, like the jackrabbit darting into its burrow at the sight of a hawk's shadow. Harold dropped the shattered stick to the floor and darted into the wall opening. Harold hoped that if Paul really had been using it to sleep safely without fear of William, then the herbs would keep Paul at bay too.

It worked as Paul skulked back and forth, keeping off the mass of leaves. Harold was lucky.

"It seems you are not as stupid as you look. You understand the old magics, it seems. It matters little though for you sadly, Harold. I might not be able to risk touching so many Abrus leaves, but I am not going anywhere," Paul said as he bent down, looking into the dark with eyes that glinted like cat's eyes. "Let us see how long you can stay in there, shall we? Maybe me and your father could get back to dinner while you watch?" Paul disappeared from Harold's line of sight.

He was right, though. Harold could not stay in there forever. Harold closed his eyes and pressed his hands over his ears, trying to block out the sucking sound as Paul returned to feeding on his father's corpse.

The mention of the old magics made Harold wonder if these beasts were the demons that Sacellum warned the people of. Had the time of the last Seal finally come?

Chapter 29: Blood Lust and Protection

Harold hid in the rocky crevice for an hour listening to the priest pottering around as if Harold was not there. He couldn't see what he was doing, but that was for the best.

Thankfully, he left his father's body alone after a time.

Harold was more worried about Muriel than himself, though. She would have woken by now, and Harold had left so quickly. He hoped she wouldn't come for him. If she did, then Harold did not think he could save her from the demon creature that Paul had become.

Harold had little to do but sit and worry as he grew colder and damper.

It was then that Harold noticed Paul's journal. which must have been knocked into the crevice when he upturned Paul's table.

Harold had the time, stuck with the shadows and spiders to read through it and learn what he could from it.

It was hard to see it in the dim light given off by the wall-mounted candles outside of his hideaway, but Harold had to do something to keep his mind off what he had just seen and heard.

Even while reading, the image of his father's body slumped against the wall flashed in front of his eyes, sometimes followed by one of Muriel laid out the same.

Harold had to keep reading. There had to be something in the diary that would help him – he just knew it.

It turned out there was. The pages were written by a mad man but between the insane rants, there was a wealth of knowledge.

It explained everything Paul knew about the Rakta Ishvara. How the race of the Rakta Ishvara was around since long before man, and how they survived in the muddy swamps of The Dark Gulf.

Harold did not know much about the colonies, but Harold knew they had their religions that dated back to the time of the Titans. How many people worshipped the Rakta Ishvara there? How many were treated like cattle because of it?

Harold wondered how many followed these false gods. For how long had people had their loved ones slaughtered to feed these beasts?

It was then that Harold realized that if he was killed and failed to stop Paul and his creation, William, that would happen to the city.

The creatures could gain a strong foothold before people realized, and they would all fall to them. The city was so afraid of the demons in the fields by Briers Hill that they would not notice the darkness spreading in the streets around them. It would be worse than being under the ruthless rule of the Dragons again.

His mind was prized away from its gruesome daydream by the sound of creaking upstairs. The large wooden door at the entrance to Saint Anne's had opened, and Harold could hear the clatter of shoes against the stonework.

They stopped somewhere above on the ground floor. There was a click as the latch sprung open on the door to the catacombs. Whoever it was had started descending the stairs. Harold's heart skipped a beat.

"No, not Muriel! Please, not Muriel!" Harold prayed to himself and waited to hear the priest move.

Harold's muscles had gone to sleep in the cold dampness, but he forced them to tense in readiness determined that if Paul made one move at her, he would leap from his hiding place. Harold would be dead before he even wounded the demon priest, but that would give Muriel time to escape.

"William?" Paul called out, and Harold's heart jumped with happiness before realization dawned.

William being there, did not bode well for him.

"Why do you use that name for me, Priest? You know nothing of that host remains," William said, as he continued to creep down the stairs.

Harold risked sliding forward and peeking around the edge of the shaped, igneous rock.

William had stopped only a few feet in front of Paul, and Harold waited, watching as events unfolded much to his surprise.

"I will call you by your spawn name then, Brother, השני את אחד. I hadn't thought I would see you again," Paul said.

Even with Paul's death rattle, Harold could sense his nerves. William remained silent. Harold wondered if he had spoken in another way.

Paul had said they shared a single memory. It seemed only reasonable that they could communicate the same way without the need for words.

"Stay still एक कमजोर, and I will make this painless," William hissed, after whatever silent conversation may have taken place beyond his hearing.

Harold risked leaning out further as William had not noticed him, and Harold studied him. His clothes were torn and grubby, and he looked like a beggar, with his mottled brown trousers ripped and threaded.

Even from a distance, Harold could see the dried blood matted within his hair. With his bestial appearance, Harold could see why they had once been called wolfmen.

"But השני את אחד, I am one of you now, soon to be your brother, your kin," Paul pleaded, interrupting Harold's study of William.

"No, old man, you are not. You may have one of my brothers living inside you, but you are too weak. Your sickness and weak mind make you a risk to us. Your foolish antics have already disgraced us, and we will not let your pride risk ending our kind. You studied our ways, but you are not of them; you have shamed us. For three million years, we have existed behind men's eyes, and you risk it all."

The moment the last word slid out from between William's tight lips, he attacked.

The fight between them both shook the very foundations of the church. The first hit William sent crashing against Paul's chest should have killed the frail old man, but it did not.

Harold watched from his hiding place, assessing just how strong the Rakta Ishvara made each of them.

Harold had seen William kill the guard, but that was back outside the hospital just after the Queens fire, and they were just ordinary people.

Paul would give him a true match of strength and Harold wanted to see just what he was up against.

A hit sent Paul flailing backward, crashing into the catacombs' rear wall and bringing down an array of rubble and loose mortar.

The coffins within the wall rattled as if their occupants were banging on the wall, annoyed by their neighbors' ruckus.

William did not give Paul any time to recover and lunged at him again.

He covered the distance between them in no more than three bounds. He sideswiped Paul with his iron-like hands across the face, sending him to the ground.

Even from his relatively-safe safe haven, Harold could hear as the bones in Paul's face crumbled.

To his sheer amazement, the priest rolled as he hit the floor and was back on his feet, facing William.

The blood on his face seemed old like what you would get from a pheasant that had hung for some time before you slit its throat.

It was Paul's turn to attack, and he did so quickly, swiping one of the small brass candelabras from the sidewall and ripping the bricks away with it.

He made for William with the burning candle held out at arm's reach like a sword's point.

It collided with William's neck sending wax flying until the cold hard metal connected, tearing through the flesh.

Harold closed his eyes, not wanting to see the fountain of life fluid squirt free. After not hearing the splatter that Harold had been waiting for, he slowly opened his eyes just in time to see William go back at Paul, the wound not affecting him as it was barely bleeding at all.

Harold realized then that the body did not matter much to the Rakta Ishvara – it was just a shell. Like the hermit crabs Harold had played with at the beach as a boy – if the shell broke, the crab would find another. Only the parasite had to survive.

As if to back up his presumptions, William sank his teeth into Paul's neck, tearing at it. Chunks of flesh fell to the ground before Paul managed to push William back.

The final blow came shortly after – William pressed his fist into Paul's chest. Harold heard his ribs crack, and Harold watched as Paul's black eyes faded to white.

Paul fell forwards into William's grasp, his legs falling out from under him. Harold knew he was dead.

William pulled a small black sphere from Paul, and Harold guessed it was the parasite itself.

William moved toward a jar that rested in an alcove not too far from him and placed the little ball inside.

Harold saw the creature inside squirm and uncoil. It was still alive.

Chapter 30: Peace for Saint Paul

Harold waited for what seemed like forever until he heard the door at the top of the stairs click shut signaling that William had left. William had finished feeding on Paul, and then wrapped the rags that he had ripped from Paul's clothing around his wounds, yelping as he pulled them tight. Although his wounds would not kill him, they still hurt.

Even in his weakened state, Harold did not want to face William now. Harold knew he would not stand a chance.

He would be killed before he could get close enough to kill the creature in William's chest.

Harold would have to leave it for someone else. He would have to rely on the city building an army to face William. Harold now had the letter from Paul to the O'Briens and Paul's diary. He could prove his innocence.

Harold made his way out of the catacombs into the main church, which thankfully, William had left.

There were no clues as to where he went or how long ago. With no sun to tell the time, it looked the same as when Harold had arrived, the only difference being the morning rain had moved off, and the afternoon downpour was washing in from the front arch.

Harold was not sure of the time, but it could not be any later than three or four o'clock. He had spent most of the day squashed into a small corner of damp stone, and his tired body yelled at him with aches and pains.

Harold stood flicking through the church records and finally found what he was looking for, Paul Augustus's address. Harold left the church of

Saint Anne's and made his way back across the city, heading to Paul's home in the hope he could find something more to prove his innocence.

Paul's journal would go a long way to proving it, but Harold had to be sure the city guards couldn't dispute his innocence.

The alley outside Paul's residence was busy, bustling with traders and patrons making their way to market. Harold knew he would have to be quick, Muriel would be worried sick, and Harold was beginning to feel nauseous from fatigue.

He was thankful Paul lived in such a slum area where people would be used to the sound of the collection of unpaid dues. Harold called on all the strength he had and kicked the lock just below the handle. The old wood gave way much more easily than Harold had expected.

A ragged old mutt who had been sniffing through a pile of rubbish close by raised his head and barked, warning him against disturbing him again before returning to his foraging, but that was the only creature that took notice of Harold's break and entry.

Inside Paul's hovel, it was black. Harold kept the door ajar while he fumbled across a shadow, he presumed to be a table. Finally, his fingers rested against the matches he had been looking for, and Harold slid them into his hand, careful not to drop any. Lighting them gave off a gentle glow across the room.

In the center, Harold could make out a coffee table and what looked like a candle, so he made his way toward it, almost falling over a pile of books left in his path.

With the candle lit, the room slowly started to light up, but Harold did not have to look far for what he was after. A diary, that predated the one Harold had read was the only book not piled on the floor or hidden away in the spider-infested bookshelf. It sat proudly on the table.

Harold was tempted to sit there and read it, but he knew that although no one looked up at him when he entered, someone may well have alerted the city guard.

The sound of a rattle from outside told Harold that he was right, and he bolted for the door, crashing out into the street with the diary held under his arm more protectively than most would hold a baby, and Harold ran – he ran with all the decorum of a shot fox, but he ran, all the same.

He took the side roads most of the way home, never stopping. The streets were busy, so it was not easy, and his chest burned with ice in the cold air. It had begun raining again, not surprisingly, the short break in the clouds fading back to darkness.

Harold knew that if he stopped, he would not have the energy to start again, and he had no idea if the guard were tracking him down or not. The last thing he wanted was get thrown into a cell for breaking an entry now that he was so close to clearing his name.

After what seemed like forever, Harold fell against his front door. He panted, waiting for his breath to return before knocking. His legs as weak as a rotten beam, Harold waited until he felt safe before slipping the book into his left hand and rapping against the woodwork with his right. The door slid open slightly.

"Harold, is that you? I was worried sick. The guard were here earlier," Muriel said, and his stomach churned over like a mason's drill.

"Are you okay, did they hurt you?" Harold asked, taking Muriel's face in his hand and looking deep into her eyes.

She pressed into his palm, and Harold felt his fear melt away. If only his exhaustion had gone with it.

"I'm fine. They only came about the men down the street. Someone said they saw you there."

"What did you tell them?" Harold asked, looking out through the sodden windows to see if anyone was watching the house.

"Nothing much. I told them I was watching the place for your mother, and as far as I knew, you had gone with her down to Port Lust," Muriel said.

"My mother hasn't gone to Port Lust," Harold replied, puzzled.

"I know that. Didn't think you'd want them snooping where she is, though," Muriel said, smiling at him again.

She always smiled, no matter what, and Harold loved that about her. Muriel's street life had given her a wisdom Harold was trying to learn fast. Her simple lie was believed, and why wouldn't they believe it?

The guard were looking for a murderer and a prostitute, not a woman who could afford the kind of dress Muriel was wearing.

Harold knew they would not return. The house was safe at last. He would still have to watch out on the streets, but he could sleep safely in his bed for the time being.

The city guard would send word to Port Lust, and the village constables could look for him there until he had time to organize his defense.

Harold sat to rest in his father's chair and began telling Muriel what had happened. He was so exhausted that he drifted off to sleep before reaching the end of his story.

It was still dark when Harold awoke covered in a blanket Muriel must have laid over him as he slept.

He could hear the bell towers in the distance ring out five times. Muriel must have left him in the night and gone to her room upstairs.

Harold crept up, making sure the old stairs did not creak under his feet. He remembered the times he had snuck out when he was younger and knew exactly where to put his feet, so the old beams remained silent.

Harold listened at Muriel's door, her gentle breathing letting him know she was safely asleep, before making his way downstairs again where Harold returned to his father's chair with Paul's diary in his hands once more.

He flicked through the pages reading as quickly as he could. Paul had written everything right up to the moment he hid himself away in the catacombs. Harold now had the two books he needed. One filled with the mad scribbling of a dying man, the other containing the full story of what he had done since his return from The Dark Gulf.

Harold closed the book and laid it to rest above the fireplace. Harold had been reading for hours. The sound of the bells chiming ten must have woken Muriel as Harold heard the bedsprings shift, and the door creak open shortly after.

Today was the first day of the rest of his life – or so Harold thought at the time.

Muriel came downstairs, her hair still entangled from her sleep and already dressed in her new gown. She now had two dresses, though Harold was not sure that she would ever want to wear the old one again – he would have to find the time to make her more. She sat down beside him, and Harold began to talk, trying to find some answers from the night before, his memory still blank.

After a breakfast of oats and tea, with the pots cleared away Muriel had her questions.

"So, what happens now, Harold?" she asked, fiddling with the embroidering at the edge of her sleeves. "Harold?" she repeated with such urgency, Harold felt confused.

"We try to enjoy ourselves a bit." Harold said, throwing her a smile, hoping to lighten the mood.

She returned it but only half-heartedly. Harold could tell Muriel was unsure if things would last between them, now that normality was on the brink of returning.

"What do you mean?" she asked nervously, rubbing the sleep from her eyes.

"How about we go visit the palace, go watch the guards change with the rest of the toffs?" Harold hated to admit it, but he enjoyed walking through the noble parts of town with their cobbled roads and statues.

The nobles' houses themselves had been restored under William's wise leadership. The irony of the best and worst person to enter the city sharing the same name was not lost on him, and although just about all his savings were gone, he was sure he could reopen the shop soon.

"I don't think it's wise to. We should get your evidence before a noble, so they can represent you in a court hearing. Just showing it to a guard won't necessarily mean you'll be free," Muriel said.

She was happy it might all be ending but she could tell Harold had no idea what to do with the books he had gathered or how to use them to prove he wasn't behind it. She could see him handing them over to some guard who would lose them and cash in on the bounty, now on Harold's head, no doubt.

"I know a noble. I used to do work for him; he's something to do with the newspaper presses. I'll get a courier to take word to him later today I promise," Harold said, not questioning how Muriel knew so much about the noble houses' legal workings.

So, it's finally over for us?" Muriel asked.

"Yes, the city guard will have to find and stop William now. We know what he is and how to kill him, and once the court pardons me, I can reopen the shop, and we can plan what we'll do next."

"So, you still plan for it to be 'us' then?" Muriel asked bluntly.

"Of course, Muriel. You mean more to me than I think you know. Tell me how you came to be on that street the day this all started? I want to know it all."

"If I tell you, Harry, will you still want to be with me?" Muriel asked, and Harold nodded.

He called her over with a gesture of his arms, and they sat together in the armchair. For so long, he had wanted to know everything about Muriel, and that morning might be his last chance.

"There's no one in this world or the next I would want more."

"If you're sure," Muriel said, unsure.

She had never told anyone her story, but after sharing such an adventure with Harold, she felt he might be able to hear her story without judging her too harshly. She had grown to care for him and

266

needed to know if he could still love her if he truly knew her.

Harold listened intently as the strong woman he had fallen in love with melted as she started her story and told him everything.

Her mother had run away from her drunkard of a father back in Bracetire Harbor when Muriel was just five years old.

They had taken a ship straight to Oakenfall docks. Her mother changed her name shortly after arriving, wanting a new start in a new kingdom. She took her first name from the current lord at that time – William's wife – and her surname from one that seemed common within the city, thus becoming Adelaide Smith and her daughter Muriel Smith.

Neither of them could speak Oakenfallian when they first arrived, and the first few weeks were hard until Adelaide managed to get a job as a dancer at the Plucked Eagle. Things were going well until Adelaide was viciously attacked one night, coming back to the boarding lodge they had been staying at.

She was raped and severely beaten. Her legs were so badly damaged by the three men who soiled her, she was unable to walk properly again, let alone dance.

Once her wounds healed enough to walk the harbor, Adelaide took to being a sailor's woman, having three or four "husbands," who helped pay the rent and returned to visit her while they were on land. Instead of dancing for coin, she turned to the only other trade that seemed plentiful for a woman of poor birth.

When Muriel turned around ten, she remembered finally moving out of the boarding lodges and having a permanent home in the public harbor where pleasure ships and foreign traders could dock. There were a lot of other working girls in that street, and they became like sisters to Muriel.

While her mother was entertaining her "husbands", Muriel would go out, sometimes until late at night and spend time with them.

This lasted until around Muriel's twelfth birthday when one of her mother's sailors brought an unfortunate gift for her mother. Not a fine necklace or spices, but cholera, from another of his wives in The Dark Gulf. Muriel took to looking after her mother as her symptoms worsened.

At first, it was just internal disturbances, nausea, and dizziness that led to violent vomiting and diarrhea. Muriel cried as she told him how at such a young age, it worried her so, but when her mother's stools started turning to a gray liquid and with the muscular cramps that followed, she could not cope alone anymore.

Muriel's street sisters started caring for her mother, sparing what money and time they could for the little girl they knew. It took a full year for Adelaide to die.

Muriel told Harold how the image of her mother's puckered blue lips in a cadaverous face stayed with her forever. When she had seen what William could do, that was why she was not scared – she had seen something worse and saw it every time she closed her eyes.

Alone and scared, Muriel relied more on her street sisters who took to showing her their trade. Muriel's first client had been when she was just thirteen. She would never be able to forget that time, the feelings as the man's hands probed her.

The rawness she felt and his sharp thrusts as he ignored her yelps of pain. She told Harold that sometimes before she met him, she would wake up screaming at night, still able to smell the foulness of spirits on his breath and feel the blood staining her legs after he finished.

Muriel had worked as a bunter, a helper for the older girls, for the next few years, just trying to make enough money to pay the rent on the house and for food. She had learned the language well, and you would never have known she had not been born to this life.

Things had been hard for her, and she had seen and done things no child should have to, but she had been lucky, in some respects, to work for herself.

That was until one night she took on a smuggler client. He was over from Portsea on work – or so he said. It turned out that he had been staying for a long time. Her "still tight cunny," as he put it, would be worth more than she was getting, and he offered her a home in return for a share of the money each week.

That was how she came by her current home and had been working for O'Brien's gang down by the docks that night.

O'Brien had been good for her when he was sober – even helping her to learn to read in return for a little action now and again.

Muriel had planned to learn to read and get away from the docks. She wanted to get a job as a scribe for a noble, or even as a housemaid, but it hadn't worked out that way.

When O'Brien was drunk, the night she had met Harold, he had beaten Muriel for not getting a client, demanding double the money by the end of the evening. Muriel's voice trailed off, and with her story over, Harold did not know what to say to her.

He longed to make her happy to take her away from all this, but the horrors she had been through came as such a shock to him that all words failed in its wake. It was no wonder Muriel had been so strong for him. She had always had to be. She didn't know any other life than one of pain and fear.

"Muriel, I don't know what to say. I wish I could take all that away. Give you the life you deserve. Stop all those things happening." Harold paused in thought.

"Nothing will ever take it away; it is what it is," Muriel said with her same confident tone as always.

"I can't take it away, but I can make the future better, I want you to have the keys to Thistlebrook Cottage. It was our summer home when I was a boy. It's the place I told you of in Port Lust. It needs work, but you will be safe there. I want you to have it," Harold said.

"I couldn't. It's too much," she replied. The gesture Harold had made when he first gave her a few coins had been too much. Handing her the keys – quite literally – to his kingdom was more than she could bear.

"I insist," Harold said.

Muriel cradled his face and smiled before shifting, so she sat in his lap. His heart began racing, and she kissed him. Harold knew she felt it, as his excitement rose beneath her. With the same caring look that Harold had loved since Harold first saw it, Muriel smiled at him.

"But only if you come with me," she said, kissing him again.

Muriel had never told anyone the story of her life. It was too shocking for her to cope with most of the time, and she expected people to run away after hearing it.

People tended not to be able to see past what she'd done. They saw her as soiled, but Harold was not like that. Not anymore.

Her hands reached down to his fastening, and gently she took him and caressed him as he grew hard. They began to move as one. Their beings entwined as their bodies combined, and their lips met repeatedly.

Panting and glowing deep red, she laid abreast of him. She moaned, and Harold's body replied. He could see the sadness in her eyes still, but it was being replaced with warmth.

Chapter 31: Green Mile

Harold didn't know how they got from the saddest story he had ever heard to lying with Muriel. It had all happened so fast.

He guessed they had been feeling that way for days, and the prospect of finally being free spurred it to happen. They crawled from bed around four in the evening. It was still calm and mostly dry outside, with only a few clouds threatening to change that and bring the rain back.

They both dressed and prepared to make their way to find a courier to take a letter to *The Times* noble. It was strange how pleasant the walk was.

The long lie-in had fully re-energized them and any doubt they had of being together had been erased in the moment of ecstasy.

Harold thought to hell with what was proper for a middle-class-gentleman and held Muriel close to him, their steps exactly in time.

The sun's golden rays cascading down over the water reflected a beautiful contrast to the city, even with the water as dirty as it was. The moment in time was perfect.

They stopped at the jetty just outside the Fishmonger's Guild, and there below the setting sun, Harold kissed Muriel.

As Harold pulled away, still feeling her warmth on his lips, he watched as Muriel's eyes grew wide. Harold moved too slowly as he saw her gaze turn to fear. The impact hit his ribs like a war hammer, and Harold fell into the water.

The world spun out of control as Harold sank deep into the icy waters. With barely a moment to think, he struggled and thrashed back into the open-air gasping for breath. His eyes found Muriel grasped tightly in William's embrace.

"You did not think we had forgotten about you did you, Harold? You know where to find me if you're brave enough. You might even be in time to save your little sweetheart if you're quick," William said and then forcefully kissed Muriel and began to drag her away.

She struggled and tried to scream, but his hand was clasped tightly over her mouth. Harold began swimming frantically for the jetty, but by the time he pulled himself to the shore, she was gone.

The crowd of people that had stopped and gathered in the street did nothing but stare at him. It angered him that the typical city-dweller would not raise a hand to help a woman being dragged off like that. A sad fact of the time, it had become all too common.

Not one of them had moved to save her. Harold knew they would not have stood a chance, but it might have given Harold the time he needed to have gotten to her. Harold had no choice now but to go and face William. It seemed that what the priest said had been true. The Rakta Ishvara would not leave anyone alive that knew about it. Harold left the canals and headed home to prepare.

He figured William would be at Saint Anne's, and as much as Harold wanted to rush straight there to save Muriel, he knew he would need to even the odds if he was to have any chance of saving her. He would risk death for a chance to save Muriel.

Heading home he made his way up into the attic, fully expecting the spectacle at the docks to alert the city guard that he was still in the city.

The guard had come more than once to search the lower floors, but they hadn't come up into the small hatch all but hidden above the wardrobe in what had been Muriel's room.

Day turned to night as Harold desperately hunted for any clue in Paul's books, anything he had missed that could let him save Muriel. Alone in the dark with a few candles burning, Harold began to realize he would have to trade his life for Muriel's, so he reached for his diary. He would document everything he knew; he would make sure word got out.

The silence drove him to insanity, and by the time the bells called out midnight, Harold was scared of shadows flickering from his candles, he was scared of the beast that is the Rakta Ishvara.

When morning came, Harold finished writing in his diary and slammed it shut, sealing it with twine along with the books he had kept from Paul.

He planned to send it to his mother. Harold knew it was unlikely he would return, and proving his innocence was now second to explaining to his mother why she would lose both men in her life so closely together.

Harold hoped she would understand. He had lived in fear for weeks, but he realized he could not run anymore. He attached a note to the books in which he instructed his mother to sell the shop. He was not coming back, and Harold was no longer a tailor. He could see no way of returning to that life now.

There was only one way he could see him beating William. Even if he could save Muriel, his life would be changed forever. He ended the letter by telling his mother how he loved her but that he could never come back. Harold planned to go back to Saint Anne's. He would arm himself with the herbs the priest had so stupidly told him were toxic to the Rakta Ishvara. Grabbing the iron fire poker his father had used so well as a weapon, Harold slipped it under his trench coat and made for the door.

The morning outside was still as dark as night, and the wind howled through the valleys between buildings.

Harold was on edge as he made his way to Saint Anne's, expecting William to appear from every shadow.

He found the door to Saint Anne's locked. The fire poker wedged into the side of the frame, made light work of the latch, and the door flew open after the second or third tug.

Inside, the smell of flash powder from detectives confirmed Harold's suspicion. They had found Paul's body.

The church was all but empty, only the bats fluttering above in the roof's wooden arches, and the odd moth that followed Harold inside kept him company.

Thick clouds of mist from the river blocked any light from entering the chapel's windows. Harold strained his eyes in the darkness, looking for the prayer candles he'd seen on his last visit. He found them atop a table close to the font and lit one of the small wicks. The gentle glow it gave off was practically useless but better than nothing.

He cradled its tiny flame from the breeze created as he walked and made for the catacombs. Creeping as quietly as he could, Harold made his way down into the darkness. A swift darkening shadow below almost made him drop the candle as the breeze caught the flame.

275

A second dark shadow raced across the wall much closer. There was a crash from below and the sound of something soft hitting the floor before scurrying off. Harold sucked in his breath, ready to face William.

"Muriel?" he called out.

The scratching stopped, but no one answered. "Muriel, are you there?" Suddenly a shadow caught the corner of his eye.

Harold dropped the candle and swinging the poker with all his might, he struck something soft. He heard a squeak and watched as the mouse's beaten body fell behind the candle toward the foot of the stairs. His heart pounding, he gazed into the room below.

William was not there, and neither was Muriel. Harold was glad to see that the bodies of Paul and his father had been removed.

At least they had not been left to be feasted on by rats. It was just a shame the smell of rotting flesh hadn't left with them.

Harold gasped for breath as he held onto the handrail leading down into the depths. The coffins had been slid aside and most of the leaves gathered up into piles.

The rest of the priest's experiments had not been touched, the leeches remained in their jars, and Harold wondered just how many Rakta Ishvara would have been unleashed if William had not ended Paul's life.

Harold would save Muriel. He knew the leaves weakened the creature and had read enough of the priest's diary to have a plan.

He scooped up a good handful of them. He couldn't believe what he was going to do next; there was no coming back from what it would take to save Muriel. Harold just prayed the priest was right.

If William had not meant Saint Anne's, then where could he mean? There was only one other place Harold could think of – the place his misery had started.

The Queens – that was where it had all started, the first time he had seen William.

Using three of his last five shillings, Harold took a cart to the building site that had already formed around the old tavern's ashes.

Just as he hoped, the hatch was still accessible. As Harold waved the cart off and paid his dues, he approached it.

Even better, the lock had recently been broken. Harold scattered a few Abrus leaves around the hatch's entrance his skin burning as he did so.

He hoped it would persuade William to stay in the darkness below. He crushed the rest of the leaves against the iron fire poker, the oil coating the bladed edge. Harold gripped the handle and remembered the description of the spears in the temple from Paul's diary.

Now was not the time to daydream though; he needed to focus.

Keeping an image of Muriel in his mind, he made his way down, dropping into the darkness below.

The cellar light was dull, but the holes in the roof where the tavern supports used to be, let a little light slither through.

The dusty beam of light seemed afraid to enter the cellar fully. No cockroaches were scuttling around down there, and Harold knew it was because William was there, somewhere out of sight.

It was too quiet, far too calm. Even the noise from the busy dockyard above did not breach the walls and cascade down. There was no sound of loose rubble falling, no sound as stones heated up again after the freezing night.

Even the noise of continual dripping sounded wrong. It was as though the droplets fell reluctantly. Standing there mesmerized, Harold gazed around, trying to take in every shadow that might be a threat.

To his immediate left, a pile of rubble had fallen from the ceiling. A scorched oak beam had collapsed with it and jutted out like a tree growing in a forest.

The western wall that was once filled with kegs from floor to ceiling was now empty, the brickwork battered and flaking. The plaster was crisp and hanging off in weak strands. If the wind could find its way in from above, the wall would fall easily, bringing in the moist soil that lay just beyond it. The sound of rushing water hinted that an underground river passed close by or flooded a part of the labyrinth below the cellar, at least.

To Harold's right lay a small doorway leading to the cellar's second room. It was the larder's entrance. Harold remembered how it used to smell of fine herbs, strong meats, and fresh vegetables.

As he approached the doorway, the door itself blown through and burned, all he could smell was smoke and ashes. Pausing with his back against the lime bricks making up the arch, Harold listened through into the next room. Somewhere inside was a faint breathing sound carried on the breeze.

"Muriel!" he called out, unable to help himself.

The sound of a muffled voice was heard in response.

"You surprise me, Harold. I really wasn't sure if you would be foolish enough to come," William said from the small room's darkness.

Harold needed to get him talking, to pinpoint where he was, before leaping through into the pitch black.

"You better not have hurt her," Harold shouted.

Harold listened so hard for a reply his eardrums ached with the effort.

"Not yet. You are lucky. I found a steady supply of whores to feed on while I waited. I wanted you to watch this one die," William said.

William took a step, the ash below his feet, parting softly, but not silently.

This let Harold know he was to the right of the doorway, somewhere close too. Harold felt a light dusting fall down the back of his neck and knew that William was directly on the other side of the wall, with less than a foot of brickwork separating them.

"Let her go, and I will be yours without a fight," Harold said, trying to buy some time.

"What would I have to gain from that? You won't win against me, and I would lose a snack," William's confidence annoyed Harold but he knew he must not get angry. He needed to keep a clear head – that was the reality.

"This is your last warning, השני את אחד," Harold said, keeping William behind him on the other side of the wall.

William laughed, giving Harold the chance to move along slightly, until his fingertips were tracing the edge of the doorway.

"Well, you surprise me with the lengths you will go to. I hope you are ready to deal with the consequences," William said.

Harold gripped the wall's edge with his free hand and spun himself around the wall, swinging the iron poker in front of him as he went.

It clashed against William faster than even he could dodge and pinned William against the wall. William growled and pushed back hard, gripping Harold's neck like a vice.

Harold choked on his own blood, but he would not give up that easily. Harold, with his hand still stinging from the impact against the brickwork, wasted no time in lunging again in William's direction.

The poker pierced flesh and Harold kept pushing, William's resistance, at first strong as an ox, seemed to be failing as Harold used all his might to press into the unseen.

The Abrus oil seemed to be working as William's grip weakened. Harold had no idea where he had punctured William, but he didn't care.

Charging forward, the two interlocked and crashed into the central wall, bringing down a landslide from the roof falling in as they broke through.

Daylight flooded in and for the first time Harold saw William clearly. His dark black eyes stared, fixed squarely on him. Both William's hands clasped the sharp end of the poker which was rammed into his gut.

Harold so much wanted to spare a glance toward Muriel, just to make sure she was safe. To check that the roof hadn't hurt her as it had fallen, but with William waiting for his chance and the room rapidly filling with freezing water from the adjacent tunnel escaping in through the newly broken masonry, Harold knew he couldn't afford the luxury and had to be fast.

He let go of the poker just long enough to cup his hands together into a fist, and he smacked down onto the poker handle, forcing the poker to pivot and rise upwards. Harold's hands were sliced open like soft cheese, but he hit it again.

A spray of congealed blood followed the sound of breaking bone and a screech from William as the poker wedged itself between William's ribs and the Rakta Ishvara callus.

William's body fell limply to the floor. Harold hit the handle repeatedly wanting to be sure that William really was dead. Eventually the poker ripped free and sank to the bottom of the water.

William's ribs had been cracked open, exposing the weak larva inside for what it was. Clasped around William's heart, the small creature pulsated for a few seconds, and then finally stopped.

Harold could not believe he had won, it had seemed too easy, after everything he has seen and knew.

The leech-like creature let go of the heart and started to swim away, but Harold bent down and picked it up. In his lacerated hands, it was no bigger than a halfpenny.

Harold dropped it to the floor and, with his heel, put an end to it, only then to look for Muriel.

She lay close by coated in filth, her mouth barely above water level, but alive. She'd been lucky and avoided the heaviest of the cave-in. Harold fell to his knees and quickly pulled the rag from her mouth.

"Is he dead?" she asked glancing over at the body that had fallen to the ground behind Harold.

"Yes, it's over. It's finally over," Harold said as he kissed her.

Her lips were still as soft as he remembered, her smile afterward still as sweet, and the feeling still as perfect. "I can't wait to show you the coast," Harold said, helping Muriel to her feet.

Epilogue: The Sun Sets on the 16th

The sun set over the canals that night and Oakenfall continued under its deep red rays. The evening newspapers filled with the story of the killer priest denting the faith people had in Sacellum. Still, it would not be hamstrung for long, as soon farmers would come in from the fields with more stories of the Shadow Demon, and Rinwid, and people would flock back into the pews of Saint Anne's.

The catacombs would be sealed shut to bury this mad man's sins forever in Saint Anne's bowels. Flooding below the Queens would wash William's body into the canals and eventually out to sea. It would not be long before people forgot about the poor dead prostitutes as more flocked to take their place. A city is a fickle beast, and Oakenfall had always seen more than its share of death and pain.

Oakenfall Ridge fell behind Harold and Muriel a mile at a time as they headed west. The cart rolled onward with its windows pulled shut to the setting sun shining through the lush blue material.

Apart from the clatter of horseshoes on the uneven road and the gentle sound of Muriel's snoring, there was silence as she slept in Harold's arms.

Harold would propose once they reached the beaches. He didn't know what would become of him. If Paul was right, he would be able to control his hunger. If not, then the lands of the north would have another monster to fight.

Somehow though, Harold felt that with Muriel on his arm he'd battle his demons and win. The horrors of the last few weeks fell into oblivion in his dreams as he wondered if the beaches would look as beautiful as he remembered.

Harold slid his eyes open slightly, just enough so that he could see her. She was still sleeping. Harold pulled her closer, a slight murmur signaling Muriel's ease in his embrace. He knew he would one day have to face the choice he made, but he would be with her until then.

Dante's journeys led him to the *Cassandra* and climbing up the anchor's wet chain marked a new journey for him.

One that would take him all the way to the Green Stone Isles. Oddly this little creature's journey would play a part in the events of Neeska long after his death that would one day be legendary.

The letter from William still tied to his tail was also a story for another time, much like that of the Rose and Granny, for we have not seen the last of the haggard old woman of the north.

In the abandoned tailor shop on East Street, a couple of mice played happily around a dusty ball of string. A strange odor filled the air. A memory of fresh tobacco smoke sailed through and went as quickly as it came. It was gone. Spinks and Son had shut for the last time.

For more Oakenfall Chronicles head over to
https://www.facebook.com/OakenfallChronicles/

Printed in Great Britain
by Amazon